MURDER WITH
A THEME SONG

Virginia Rath

MURDER WITH A THEME SONG

VIRGINIA RATH

COACHWHIP PUBLICATIONS

Greenville, Ohio

Murder with a Theme Song, by Virginia Rath
© 2019 Coachwhip Publications

Published 1939
No claims made on public domain material.
Cover image: Musical theme © Sveta Aho

CoachwhipBooks.com

ISBN 1-61646-479-8
ISBN-13 978-1-61646-479-0

MURDER WITH A THEME SONG

CHAPTER 1

The woman in the leopard coat was not drunk yet but the waiter, looking at her with experienced eyes, estimated that with three more drinks she would be. A fight with her boy friend, he thought. Middle-aged dames like her took it hard. She wasn't one of the regulars: he couldn't remember ever having seen her before. She'd come in at eight, sat down in the booth farthest from the door and ordered a Bronx.

It was past eleven now and she was still there. Whenever he approached the booth she looked up and ordered another drink. As long as she did that and paid there was nothing he could do about it—except whisper to the bartender to go light on the gin.

She wasn't making any trouble or noise. She just sat there with her coat slipping off her plump shoulders, her peaked hat crooked on her forehead, and stared into her glass or at the opposite wall of the booth.

Sometimes—since she'd had that last drink—her lips moved like she was talking to herself. You couldn't hear anything she said; there was too much noise with all the other booths besides every stool at the bar taken.

Seeing that, the couple who had just come in stopped at the door. The man said:

"Will you stand up or do you want to go somewhere else?"

"I can't stand," the girl said pathetically. "My feet want to get out of these shoes."

"And who could blame them?" Her husband glanced disapprovingly at the narrow alligator pumps. "I wondered when you would weaken, my darling Clementine."

"Oh, I do not wear nines! Only sevens. And it was you who told me this outfit required reptile shoes. Let's go home—"

But the waiter, recognizing them, came forward quickly. Neither were they what he termed regulars but they had been here before and he hadn't forgotten the gentleman was one who didn't bother to scoop up change from a dollar.

"There's a place back here. Plenty of room if you don't mind sitting with someone. . . . You don't care if this lady and gentleman sit here?" he finished perfunctorily.

The woman in the leopard coat started nervously at his question and gave the intruders a hostile look that surprisingly turned almost at once to one of welcome.

"Not a bit," she said with labored distinctness. "We're old friends, only I can tell you don't recognize me. I'm Edith Parnell. And you're Valerie Sheridan."

"I was. This is my husband, Mr. Dundas," Valerie said, slipping into the booth.

"So-o pleased. My, but you have grown up. Well, it's been about four years—"

"May I order something for you, Miss Parnell?"

Mr. Dundas' inquiry was commendably polite, for his eyes took on a glazed look whenever he regarded the leopard coat. Any self-respecting leopard would have considered it a blot on the family scutcheon and Miss Parnell's perfume assailed one's nostrils with a vigor that suggested it came from a plebeian but long-lived stock.

Miss Parnell would have another Bronx and Mr. Dundas scotch and soda. Mrs. Dundas, blissfully wriggling her toes under the table, expressed a wish for strawberry soda but supposed she could make plain ginger ale do.

"And I still can't place you," she admitted. "Unless you were the nurse we had for my stepfather?"

"That's it. I certainly felt bad when we couldn't save him. Well, I guess you never saw me except in uniform. It makes quite a difference when a person's dressed up."

"Doesn't it?" Valerie said feebly, not wanting to point out that Miss Parnell had certainly not been a blonde four years ago. She remembered her as cheerfully and chattily efficient; a large starched person who smelled of antiseptics. Not at all the sort you expected to find in a cocktail lounge engaged in a little serious drinking.

"Such a co-cinc'dence meeting you here," Miss Parnell went on. "It's a small world after all."

"Oh, we live on Green Street, not far from here. You're still nursing?"

"Oh yes. Didn't you read about— Well, of course it's not important and you mightn't remember anyway." Miss Parnell swallowed half the cocktail the waiter put before her and hiccoughed. "'Scuse me being so hasty. And don't think I do this often. A person in my position can't. But I'm not on a case right now and I—I get lonely."

"'Alone, alone—all, all alone; Alone on a wide, wide sea,'" Mr. Dundas suggested blandly. Miss Parnell looked at him unsuspiciously.

"That's it: alone in a crowd." She finished her drink. "Now it's my treat. Waiter! Oh, you're not through yet. Well, bring me another of the same.

And put some gin in it this time. You aren't fooling me."

The waiter shrugged resignedly and moved away. "It's funny," said Miss Parnell with sudden lucidity, "how a person like me goes on year after year and never realizes she hasn't any real friends. Sometimes she thinks she's found someone who— But then you usually find out different. If I died tomorrow there wouldn't be anyone to care. Nobody would know— That is, if I killed myself nobody would know why I did it."

Her eyes watered. Michael finished his whisky with unusual haste, pushed the popcorn bowl away from Valerie and nodded toward her tall glass of ginger ale.

"I'm done—when you are," he said significantly.

What he meant was that if Miss Parnell was heading toward a crying jag he didn't want any part of it. Valerie grinned at him and picked up her glass but not before the waiter returned with what proved to be Miss Parnell's last cocktail. She disposed of it with a speed that made Michael's lashes flicker.

"Six will get you ten that one does it," he murmured and got up. "It's been nice, meeting you, but we must go."

"Oh, don't! If you—if you knew how glad I was to look up after sitting here all evening and see someone I actually knew. I'm—I'm not just lonely. I'm scared. Scared to go home and think. That's why I've done this for two nights. If I drink enough I don't care. And it's all right when I'm with you. So please don't go! I can't stand it if you do."

She put her head down on the table. Michael said under his breath: "Válgame Dios!" and to Valerie: "Remember this the next time you start to comment upon the number of peculiar people I know." He patted the spotted shoulder.

"You can't stay here all night. Let us take you home."

"No, can't stay here all night," Miss Parnell agreed. "C-cert'nly can't stay here all night."

She heaved herself up and wavered toward the door. With some difficulty they got her into the front seat of the car and themselves into the space that remained. She roused to give an address on Hyde as Michael turned off Polk and began to sing; a lilting, interminable refrain for which she seemed to have no words except: "Ta da da *da*. Ta da da da *da* da."

Valerie, divided between amusement and exasperation, broke in with the first question that occurred to her. "You aren't really frightened, are you?"

Miss Parnell continued to sing until she came to what she considered a stopping point, though to Valerie it appeared that the song had none.

"Ever hear that before? I can't get it out of my head; it runs in it all the time ever since I re-membered it again. And I am scared sometimes, though I know that's foolish. Though maybe it isn't. I can't always tell. Sometimes it seems I've been foolish when I didn't know I was—"

Michael stopped the car in front of a large, shabby wooden house that shared with a similar building an iron arch and the name El Portal as well as the walk that ran between them. Miss Par-nell got out, rather unsteadily but unassisted.

"This is it. And it was nice, running into you. You must remember me to your mother."

"She's in Florida but I'll tell her I saw you when I write to her."

"And I—I hope you'll come to see me some-times and —and forget my acting so unladylike. Good night. Oh, you mustn't bother to come in with me, Mr. Dundas. So nice of you to bring me home." Miss Parnell smiled at him, suddenly coy. "I'm sure Valerie's a very lucky girl and . . . Well, good night."

"Well!" Valerie said when Miss Parnell had dis-appeared along the walk. "What do you think?

And no remarks about my past coming back to haunt me."

"I think," said Michael, still irritated by the grins that had accompanied their exit from the cocktail lounge, "that you'd better leave that window down and let the car air. You may break, you may shatter the vase if you will, but the scent of the roses hangs round it still."

Miss Amy Bond had one bottle of beer opened and was attacking a second when she first heard the man's voice. Instantly she bent forward and laid her ear against the wall above her midget sink. The kitchenette had originally been a large closet, and as Miss Bond knew quite well, Miss Parnell's bed-sitting room was just on the other side of it.

This, she thought, is rich. That dame entertaining a man at midnight after telling the landlady I oughtn't to let my boy friend stay here so late. As if we wasn't going to get married soon's we get enough money. I'll bet this one isn't going to marry her. He sounds too young. . . .

"I'm sorry about that," the masculine voice was saying. "But you should have told in the first place. It wouldn't have hurt you any—then."

It was disappointing to catch no more of Miss Parnell's reply than the word "police" but the man's answer was distinct—and impatient.

"Where will that get you? Try it if you like. You ought to know what you'll let yourself in for. What danger could you be in? If I thought there was any I wouldn't . . ."

He seemed to move away to the other side of the room and his final words were lost to Miss Bond. But she heard Miss Parnell say: "There's matches on that table," and she sounded like she was crying.

So that was it, Miss Bond thought. Imagine, at her age, and a nurse too. The fellow was whistling now; a funny kind of tune Miss Bond hadn't heard before. Miss Parnell said: "Don't! I can't get it out of my head. You know I wouldn't have listened if I hadn't thought everything was all right." And then, but not as if she was going to argue about it: "If you've made up your mind to go . . ."

Miss Bond lost interest; besides, Joe was yelling from the other room: "What about that beer?" She opened the other bottle and with one in each hand went back to him.

"Listen, Joe," she began, "this will slay you. What do you think that dame next door— Listen: he's leaving now. But you remember how Sunday night you thought you heard a man talking in her room and I said, "Oh no? Well, I guess you were right. What do you think she—"

CHAPTER 2

"It is a terrible thing," Mrs. Dundas said sadly, "to be married to a man who's always in a bad humor until he's had his coffee and doesn't want that before ten."

"Arr-rh!" said Mr. Dundas forbiddingly, burrowing deeper into his pillow.

"Why, it was only by a superhuman effort of will that you didn't snarl at me on our honeymoon. I knew then that it was hopeless; that I'd never dare talk to you before breakfast."

"Then don't." Michael turned over on his back with an arm across his eyes. "'Stir not up, nor awake my love, till he please.' In other words, let me sleep."

"But I want to talk to you about our vacation."

"Again?"

"Still. I do want to go someplace where they have summer in July. You certainly never need summer storage for a fur coat in San Francisco. . . . Are you listening to me?"

"Unwillingly."

"Well, you promised we'd leave Saturday—"

"If all early birds made as much noise as you the worms would be safely hidden long before the bird arrived. I haven't forgotten and certainly we'll leave Saturday and yes, you're right. I need a vacation. I'm getting to the point where I wish all women were nudists."

Valerie giggled. "If you'd been with Eve in the garden it wouldn't have been long before you were designing superior fig leaves for her. Once a couturier, always a—"

"Dressmaker."

"I know better than to call you that even with my sweetest smile. But where shall we go?"

"Haven't you made up our minds?"

"No. I don't want to go to the trouble of changing mine as soon as you've made up yours."

"Just a dutiful, downtrodden wife, aren't you?"

"I'm dutiful. But you try treading on me sometime! I think you might consider Tahiti or Siam but since you won't, why don't we accept Eleanor Allan's invitation?"

"And why didn't we settle this when we got home last night? I don't object to being talked to in bed—at night."

"I've a single-track mind and my attention was otherwise occupied. Or had you forgotten?"

"My dear," Michael said with a reminiscent grin, "you do me—and yourself—a grave injustice. Blushing again? Who began this vulgar conversation?"

"If I did you can be depended on to finish it. I know you don't care for the mountains but Brookdale is supposed to be a pretty town and easy to get to now that the Feather River Highway's finished. People say that's worth seeing too."

"Mr. Allan being Brookdale's principal claim for fame."

"Is he? Madge Orton— You know she's a nurse and so was Eleanor once and I met her through the Ortons. But Madge always speaks as if Eleanor had thrown herself away on a railroader who's a sheriff now—"

"She threw herself away on a county sheriff who's damn well known for his competence," Michael said dryly. "But I liked Mrs. Allan." He laughed. "Did I ever tell you that she explained to me that she had a three-months-old son and that a woman's first thought after producing a child is to buy new clothes and paint the town red? Only, she said sadly, one usually has to put that off until she's lost some weight. That was a good ten months ago, wasn't it? I remember she sent us that waffle iron that was almost our only useful wedding gift."

"And she's asked us at least half a dozen times to visit them. We wouldn't have to stay long in Brookdale. Then we could go on to Reno and do a little gambling and perhaps come back through Tahoe—"

"Allowing ourselves several days at home to recover from our vacation before going back to work."

"If you stayed here you wouldn't stop working. So I'll write to Eleanor before you change your mind."

Valerie got up and closed the window; a long side window from which you saw not only the bay and red span of the Golden Gate Bridge but as far south as the brown humps of Twin Peaks. On clear days you could give names to the green patches that were parks and cemeteries—Laurel Hill, Calvary, Alta Plaza, Lafayette Square—and single out the little beehive that was the Palace of Fine Arts near Yacht Harbor. But today peaks and hills were already bonneted with fog.

Valerie said resignedly: "What sun there is won't last," and sat down to brush her hair. She began to whistle without realizing it until Michael said:

"You too?"

"Me too what? Oh: Miss Parnell's tune. It does get in your head."

"You haven't that last strain quite right or she didn't have. I remember the tune now. I was too anxious to get rid of her last night to pay much attention. It's a French-Canadian song called 'Alouette.' 'Alouette, gentille Alouette, Alouette, je te plumerai.' I picked it up in Montreal one summer."

"What does it mean?"

"Roughly: my pretty skylark, I will pluck you."

"There's no sense to that. 'I will pluck you'! I suppose you might say someone was blackmailing her or she was blackmailing someone, but that's very farfetched."

"How well did you know her?"

"Why—she was a good nurse and very obliging. Terribly coy with men and subservient toward doctors, who, I suppose, were more than mere men to her. She's bleached her hair since then, but perhaps that's her way of keeping herself up."

"That would also be the kindest way to account for her festive raiment," Michael said, yawning and closing his eyes. "Call me when breakfast's ready, Lady Macbeth. You've murdered my morning nap so your coffee had better be superlative. . . ."

Valerie had breakfast on the table before she remembered the morning paper, got it from the hall and without unfolding it put it beside Michael's plate. He looked at it pessimistically as he sat down.

"Don't tell me that's another anti-New Deal editorial. If it is, the coffee will have to be good to wash it down."

"Why do you read editorials when you disagree with them violently? Anyway, the President's going to be here tomorrow so everyone will rally round the flag, boys. Give me the second section?"

Michael unfolded the paper. "Your beloved comic strip? Why do you— María santísima!"

"What is it?" Valerie slid her chair around to his. "Is the editorial that bad or— Oh! Oh, she wasn't just drunk."

At three o'clock that morning a gentleman who was taking home a load with manly pride passed Edith Parnell's room, saw the door swinging open and glanced in. What he saw sent him running to the communal telephone in the lower hall to notify the police that someone had strangled a woman in a room on the second floor.

As the newspaper was a 6 A.M. edition even much padding did not disguise a scarcity of facts. The police surgeon's opinion, subject to change, was that Edith Parnell had been killed not later than two o'clock. A Miss Amy Bond, restaurant cashier, had heard Miss Parnell talking to a man around midnight. Miss Bond had thought, however, that she heard him leave the house a few minutes after that.

She had certainly heard no outcry of any kind but she had been asleep by a quarter of one. Miss Bond's story was verified by Joseph Scatena, grocery clerk, who had left her at twelve-twenty and seen no one in the halls on his way out. There followed a surprisingly detailed account of Miss Parnell's life and an excellent picture of her in uniform.

"But how did they find out all that about her in such a short time and at three o'clock in the morning?" Valerie said.

"Use your eyes, child. And your brains. They already had her biography in the morgue."

"But why— Oh! 'It will be remembered that Miss Parnell was employed as a nurse in the Dumont home at the time nine-year-old Frederick Armstrong, Jr, was kidnaped.'"

"That," Michael said grimly, "was what she thought we must have read about."

"I didn't when the case first broke. You remember it helped erase me from the newspapers. I've heard it talked of a lot since then, but people usually referred to her as 'the nurse.' Besides, she wasn't seriously under suspicion, was she?"

"Not so far as I know. But perhaps she did know something and, being half swacked, might have told it to us if we'd encouraged her. You might have if you hadn't known she irritated me. I'm afraid Sullivan isn't going to understand the demoralizing effect that God-awful leopard coat and the vigor and abundance of her perfume had on me. Certainly I should have known who she was—"

"But I'd never realized the nurse I knew was the same one Ariadne Holaday had when the boy was kidnaped. And people have even stopped talking about the case lately. Well, I'm glad Inspector Sullivan's in charge of this one and not someone we don't know."

"Yes, but even he is going to have a great deal to say to us and all of it uncomplimentary," Michael said.

He got up and went to the telephone in the bedroom, leaving Valerie to consider what she knew of the Armstrong kidnaping. It was a case still unsolved though it had been more than a year ago—in June of 1937—that Basil Dumont announced his stepson had been kidnaped.

In many of its details the case followed a familiar pattern. There was a ransom note, carefully suppressed, the payment of fifty thousand dollars in unmarked bills, the fruitless period of waiting following that payment and finally the taking over of the case by local police and federal agents.

It was not such customary facts that intrigued the public as much as the circumstance that Frederick Armstrong was not only heir to a more than million-dollar estate but also an orphan.

In 1927 Gloria Holaday had married Frederick Armstrong, Sr. Gloria was nineteen and Armstrong in his fifties, but he seemed not to have repented of his bargain when he died four years later. He created no trust for his three-year-old son, and except for a small annuity to a cousin, Jonathan, left his entire estate to Gloria with no strings attached.

A year later Gloria married Basil Dumont. He was not more than thirty-five but he had a four-teen-year-old son, Philip, by a former marriage. The boy had been looked after by Dumont's aunt, Miss Hortense Dumont, and she moved into the vast Armstrong house on California Street along with Philip and his father.

Not, a woman slightly acquainted with Dumont had said to Valerie, that one or two more made any difference. Gloria's family had settled down on her when she married Armstrong. He hadn't seemed to mind that any more than he minded Jonathan's being always underfoot. And Gloria, Valerie's informant added grudgingly, had always been very good to her father and sister.

The father, Daniel Holaday, was an old vaude-villian but his career had pre-deceased vaudeville itself by a good many years. Gloria had left school at fifteen and was dancing in one of the Fan-chon-Marco choruses when she met Armstrong. Her sister, Ariadne, was only nine when Gloria married him, and his money paid for Ariadne's very expensive education. It had been halted by

pneumonia in the early spring of '37. She was
convalescent but still under Edith Parnell's care
when her nephew was kidnaped.

Gloria Dumont died two years after her second
marriage and her will was immediately pronounced
dangerous. She left her son to the guardianship of
his stepfather and a lawyer who had been a friend
of the boy's father. Unfortunately Blake was nearly
eighty, very feeble and, surprisingly, very much
attached to Basil Dumont.

Gloria had left her father five thousand dollars outright and a small annuity. Ariadne was
to receive a substantial allowance until she was
twenty-one and then the same flat sum as her father. Basil Dumont and Jonathan Armstrong got
ten thousand each and the rest was to be held in
trust for Frederick until he was twenty-one. But
if he died before then it was to be split equally
among the Holadays, Dumont and Jonathan Armstrong.

That was why it was constantly implied if never
stated that the kidnaping was an inside job. Everyone in that household gained by the child's death,
even Philip and Hortense Dumont, through Basil.
"Why," Valerie had heard more than one ask,
"wasn't the ransom at least a hundred grand? They
could have paid it—unless fifty was all Dumont
would pay someone to do the job for him."

There had been a young man serving as Frederick Armstrong's bodyguard besides the usual servants. So Dumont had escaped the charge of being criminally careless, and however suspiciously the investigators might have regarded the Dumonts and Holadays, they must never have discovered any evidence that incriminated them. The case was dead—and the boy, apparently. That is, the case had been dead. . . .

"I couldn't get in touch with Sullivan," Michael said, coming back. "I left my name but I didn't explain because they would send someone else around if I had. I suppose there's nothing to do but wait for him to turn up."

CHAPTER 3

"I've told you before, Inspector: I never had any complaints against Miss Parnell. I didn't think she knew any men—not what you'd call socially—and I still don't think so. I don't care what that little Bond hussy says. She's no better than she should be."

"I see you're a good judge of people, Mrs. Knibbs," Sullivan said diplomatically. "Still, she's positive she heard a man talking to Miss Parnell and you admit you saw one—"

"Admit's not the word," the manager said belligerently. "I said I saw this man in front of her door early yesterday evening. I was on the third floor looking down and his back was to me, so I never saw his face. He was humming a tune and he reached over and tried the door. I yelled: 'What do you want?' and he was gone like a flash. He was medium height and I think he wore dark clothes, but that's all I can tell you.

"But naturally I didn't forget it," Mrs. Knibbs went on. "And I happened to mention it to Miss Elston here and that reminded her of something."

"I've got insomnia so bad I can't sleep," Miss Elston said mournfully. "My room's a ground-floor front so my window opens on the walk and I hear people come along it. I was awake last night and heard someone come along, quiet and kind of— kind of furtive, you know. But he was humming a funny tune. He came in here all right; I can hear the front door open and close. I don't know what time it was, only it was after eleven."

"That's very interesting," Sullivan said perfunctorily, but Miss Elston, who resembled a rag doll that had faded badly in the wash, was not finished.

"I'd heard that tune before. Let's see: this is Wednesday, isn't it? Well, the first time was Sunday night, only he was whistling that time. It wasn't long after that I heard the Bond girl come home with her gentleman friend. And I understand she says when they passed Miss Parnell's room that night they thought she was talking to some man in it?"

Sullivan smiled noncommittally and turned back to Mrs. Knibbs. "The front door's never locked— Oh, I'm not blaming you," he said hastily as she drew herself up like an offended pouter pigeon. "They don't lock up in lots of these places. But she must have opened her own door to him. Miss Bond swears she heard the man who was with Miss Parnell around midnight leave—"

"She'd be too busy saying good night to her own young man to know for certain," Mrs. Knibbs remarked. "Anyway, he could come back, and if she'd let him in once she would again."

"Maybe. But . . . Well, you say Miss Parnell's had a room on and off here for five years. Do you remember when the little Armstrong boy was kidnaped last spring?"

"Oh yes. She wouldn't talk about it except she was indignant at the idea maybe someone in the family hired him kidnaped. She didn't keep her room then, so I never saw her till Miss Holaday was well again. She always said they treated her so well. That flattered her and made her like them. She was kindhearted as they come, but you know how it is? Sometimes people like that aren't—aren't interesting," Mrs. Knibbs said shrewdly, "and other people don't bother with 'em."

"And she was grateful when they did? Well, when she came back here did any of them ever come to see her?"

"I don't know. I keep pretty busy, Inspector. She'd had other cases since then and came back here just to rest when she was on duty. Once in a while I'd see her all dressed up and she'd say she was going out to lunch, but the last time I know of that she said that was several months ago."

"And you hadn't seen her since Sunday night?"

"Not really. Just passed her in the hall Monday afternoon and said hello. She was out Monday evening because I put some towels in her room kind of late. Yesterday I didn't see her at all. You can ask the others in the house if they did, but most of them work in the daytime, while Miss Parnell was on night duty a lot."

"I've talked to nearly everyone and they couldn't tell me anything," Sullivan admitted. "Well, leave her room like it is, Mrs. Knibbs, and we'll get through there as soon as we can."

Her father, Ariadne saw as soon as she entered the breakfast room, had managed to get his hands on the newspaper before Phil did this morning. He lowered it, folded over to the theatrical section, to say benignly:

"Good morning, my dear. I hope you slept well?"

"Yes, thank you, Father," Ariadne said because it saved trouble to give him the answer he wanted.

He didn't really care who slept well so long as he did. He hadn't when she and Gloria called him Pop and he breakfasted and spent the morning in a gray bathrobe whose seat finally had to be patched with darker gray. He didn't care to be called Pop now and he did his morning lounging in an expensive jacket designed for that purpose but he was the same old Pop.

Silly women—like Miss Parnell—thought his smooth cap of white hair and round pink face "distinguished." Ariadne had long ago decided he resembled a pedigreed lap dog. His slightly protruding eyes could beg so pathetically to be shielded from a frightening world or to be comforted with soft cushions and the best bones.

"He isn't any more fitted to look after himself than a pet Pomeranian is," Gloria had said once. But Pop had always looked after himself very well and he'd continue to do so. And to play little games like this one with the newspaper.

He hadn't ever bothered to be up early enough to get it before anyone else until he discovered Phil felt he had prior rights to it. Phil had a foul temper but still Ariadne could see why, if you wanted to read the newspaper yourself, Daniel Holaday's deliberate perusal of it, the virtuous care with which he handled its pages and the small tutting noises he made over its contents were enough to make you want to throw something at him. It wasn't at all impossible that some morning Phil would.

"If you're asleep, go back to bed," he said now. "Or do you want all the sugar for yourself?"

He sweetened his coffee generously when Ariadne silently pushed the cream-and-sugar tray
down to him. Basil hadn't heard him; there was so
much Basil seemed not to hear nowadays. There
was still no gray in his dark brown hair: it was the
deepening of lines about his mouth and the slight
thickening of waist and shoulders that made him
look so much older. He'd lost his tan, too, giving
up golf because—though he hadn't said so—some
of the men he'd always played with were either too
friendly or not friendly at all.

If Gloria only hadn't died, Ariadne thought for
the thousandth time. It was odd that her child
should have been such a thoroughly unpleasant
brat. He might not have been if Gloria had lived
long enough. But he had been a sneak and tattletale
and perfectly aware they were all poor relations.

Mr. Blake had meant well, telling Freddie he
must study hard and "not be lazy because someday
you will have a great deal of money. And money
is power, but you want to use that power for good
so you must train yourself now so that you can."

Then Freddie had asked questions and Mr. Blake
had answered them truthfully. After that Freddie's
favorite threat was: "I'll tell Uncle Blake you're
mean to me when he isn't here," or: "You just wait
till I'm grown up and then you'll all see!"

Because of Phil, Hortense would have resented Freddie even if he had been a lovable child, just as she'd always disliked Gloria simply because she married Basil. Ariadne looked at her now, not surprised to see that she was staring venomously at the newspaper shielding Daniel's face. Or to hear her whisper to Phil:

"Never mind, lover: I'll order another paper tomorrow and pay for it myself."

"Two papers?" Daniel looked up from his. "Isn't that a needless extravagance? Why didn't you say you wanted the paper, my boy? You shall have it—when I've finished it."

"I like to hear you talk about extravagance," Hortense snapped. "You're an expert at spending other people's money."

"My dear Hortense, remember what is due your own dignity even if you have no respect for my feelings," Daniel said forgivingly, turned to the sporting section and folded the paper so that what Phil could see of it was upside down. Phil's knobby fingers with their long nails tightened on his spoon. A vein swelled in his forehead and his sallow face flushed darkly. He had often looked like that after an encounter with Freddie. He was the one who had really hated Freddie. It wasn't that he was fond enough of Basil honestly to resent anyone else's having a claim on him, but it had made a good talking point. . . .

"You aren't by any chance thinking of our dear departed, are you?" Phil said softly. "I'll tell you something that should thrill you. I thought I saw Ted Smith on Market Street yesterday."

"He's free to come and go, isn't he?"

"I understood he went. The last Dad heard, he'd given them the slip. They were keeping an eye on him. They should have: that guy knows more than he ever told."

"I agree with you," Ariadne said. "He didn't tell anyone that he was drugged the night Freddie was kidnaped!"

Phil laughed. "Is that what he told you? Convenient, him being drugged that particular night. And so obliging of him to keep still about it."

"It was just as obliging of him not to tell about the time you knocked Freddie down. He knew, even if the servants didn't, just how fond we all were of Freddie," Ariadne said. "But he kept still and then we didn't stand by him."

"Pardon me while I laugh. Ha-ha! He's probably had his cut by now and is figuring on getting away to some place where he can spend it. So you might as well stop mooning over him, pretending you're thinking about Freddie—"

"Phil!" Basil's voice was quiet enough but Phil stopped instantly, his feet shuffling nervously under the table. He took full advantage of Basil's usually even temper but he knew he could be roused to action. He had used a riding whip on Phil after he had turned on Freddie, and Phil hadn't forgotten.

"I wish," Basil went on, "that you'd told me what Ted said, Ariadne. Or that he had."

"Of course he wouldn't tell you, Basil," Hortense broke in. "Because of course it wasn't true. It's just the kind of story he'd tell Ariadne to play on her sympathies."

"Whether or not it was true, he said nothing to me until the last time I saw him. That was four months ago," Ariadne said. "When Freddie had already been missing more than eight months."

"I didn't know you'd seen him that recently," Basil said.

"I didn't tell anyone. He telephoned and I met him in a little restaurant on Polk Street."

"What," Phil asked with a wary eye on his father, "was the big idea? A last fond farewell?"

"It wasn't fond and he didn't say it was farewell. He was very—surly," Ariadne said. "He blamed us because the authorities put him through a third degree and took so long to release him. After that

no one would give him work. I asked him to come
to see you, Basil—"

"I wanted to see him again. I did talk to him in
February. That was the same month that you saw
him? He was living at a rooming house on Howard
Street then. But though I wanted to help him he
didn't come to see me here. I tried in April to see
him again but he'd moved. I don't blame him for
being resentful: we persuaded him not to talk and
then didn't help him."

"It's like you to blame yourself," Hortense said.
"But we weren't responsible if the authorities suspected him. I always thought there was something
hangdog about him. And he was hired to guard
Freddie and he didn't."

"He certainly was a little careless, but boys will
be boys," Daniel said. "And Freddie was full of
boyish little tricks. He'd left pillows covered over
in his bed before to make Ted think he was safely
in it."

"Another thing Ted didn't tell," Ariadne said.

"I wonder why? And just what was this story
he told you, daughter? Just how did he say he was
drugged?"

"There were plenty of drugs in the house then,"
Ariadne said, resenting this bland condescension.
"Miss Parnell didn't guard them very carefully.
There was a decanter of whisky in Ted's room and

he always had a nightcap from it. It could have been done very easily."

"And does my little girl realize what she's implying?"

"Oh, I realize that. And I won't tell anyone. It's too late to save Freddie now and probably too late to save the rest of us."

"Dear me, how dramatic we are," Hortense said. "When you are older you'll learn that trials like this must be borne—"

"I don't know which is the most complete hypocrite, you or Pop," Ariadne said deliberately. "Of course Pop has a talent for it, while you slip sometimes and let people see how glad you really are to have Freddie out of the way."

"Basil, are you going to let that little chit talk to me that way? I've put up with these people because you asked me to and you know I'd do anything to please you. But when they become absolutely insulting—"

"You've forgotten you would never have seen the inside of this house if it hadn't been for my daughter Gloria," Daniel drawled. "And that I was her father. You forget you're only Gloria's second husband's aunt. But I apologize for Ariadne's rudeness and forgive her for her disrespect—"

Ariadne laughed hysterically. "You've always been good at forgiving people whether they want forgiveness or not and regardless of whether they've done anything to be forgiven for."

"Because I realize that she is not well," Daniel continued smoothly. "She has never recovered from her illness, and considering the events that interrupted her convalescence, there is bound to be a certain lack of mental balance—"

"Will you stop this senseless wrangling!" Basil brought one clenched hand down on the table. All the cups danced in their saucers. "Do you think I don't notice it? And I'm tired of it. You frequently remind me that I'm head of this household. Very well: from now on, if you can't speak to each other pleasantly, don't speak at all.

"And don't bother to protest, Daniel," he added as that gentleman opened aggrieved lips. "I know you always speak pleasantly, no matter what you say. As to Ariadne, she's the sanest of us all. She realizes what has happened to us. And we'll have no more of this childish business about the morning paper. As head of the household, I'll read it first. Don't order another, Hortense, even if you are willing to pay for it yourself."

He reached across her and pounded the bell in front of her plate. "Tell Mr. Armstrong I'd like to see him in here," he said to the maid when she appeared. "Please see that he comes: don't let him begin working again."

CHAPTER 4

Daniel folded the newspaper very slowly and carefully. The rustle of its sheets as he smoothed them out was a sigh of patient martyrdom. After an instant Hortense said timidly: "Will you have more coffee, Basil?" and Phil, clearing his throat ostentatiously, turned to Ariadne.

"Isn't it kind of early to be diked out in diamonds, Spider?"

The use of her nickname was an extended olive branch that Ariadne accepted. Phil could be agreeable enough when he chose and he wasn't to blame if a silly aunt had always babied him and it was difficult for Basil to be severe with anyone.

"It's pretty ostentatious at breakfast," she agreed, looking at the wide diamond-and-sapphire bracelet above her wrist. It was so thin now that she had to push the bracelet up on her arm to keep it on. "But somehow I feel even diamonds should be worn sometimes to keep their sparkle. And since I don't go out evenings any more—"

"It should be in a safe-deposit box," Hortense said, though she managed to speak pleasantly enough. "It's too valuable to keep in your room and you lost it once—"

"I only mislaid it for a few days. That's easy to do when your bureau drawers are as messy as mine. I always hide it very carefully now. Gloria didn't give it to me to be tucked away into a safe-deposit box."

Ariadne did not add that however much Frederick Armstrong had paid for the bracelet when he and Gloria were honeymooning in New York, its only value for her was that Gloria had given it to her. She did not care for jewelry and the bracelet was too showy. Just the sort of thing Frederick had loved to buy. But Hortense could never pass a jeweler's window without stopping to look in it. She had a rather good string of pearls that were a fixture on her stringy neck. When she was younger Ariadne had tried to find out, without ever being able to, whether or not Hortense wore the pearls at night and in the bathtub.

"Of course you don't consider the monetary value of anything our dear Gloria gave you," Daniel said. "But you should not tempt the servants by being careless with valuable property. However, women are clever at finding little hiding places for their valuables. I remember your dear mother was forever finding new ones for the housekeeping money."

"You wouldn't have been the reason she had to, would you?" Phil remarked so that only Ariadne could hear him.

She wanted to say: "Right the first time," but a certain loyalty, badly worn as it was, kept her from it. Phil squirmed uneasily under Basil's frigid gaze but Jonathan came in just then, eagerly apologetic.

"I forgot about breakfast. I was up early and thought I would work for a while but somehow I seem to have lost myself."

No one smiled; they were all so used to Jonathan's losing himself. Frederick Armstrong, whose knowledge of the American Revolution did not extend further than the fact that "Washington won it," had always had a great admiration for his cousin's familiarity with little-known Revolutionary names and incidents. It had pleased him to provide Jonathan with a comfortable sanctuary in which to carry on his research and write books that either were never quite finished or so dryly authoritative that few people cared to read them when they were.

"I would like some coffee now I'm down to earth again," Jonathan went on with the shy smile that admitted his own weakness. "Don't order fresh, Hortense. What's in the pot will do very well."

He tucked himself in before his unused cup and plate and looked at Basil questioningly over his enormous glasses. The other features in Jonathan's egg-shaped face were small and neat but his nose seemed to have made a special effort to develop itself into a suitable site for those glasses.

"Is something wrong, Basil?" Divorce Jonathan from his desk and keep him from opening a book and he was not at all absent-minded. "Is it something concerning Freddie?"

"Indirectly, I suppose it does. We didn't go to the mountains last summer because of the—situation here. But after thinking it over I see no reason why we shouldn't go this year as we always used to."

"Do you think people will—will talk if we do?" Hortense said. "Think we're not showing proper feeling—"

Basil smiled wearily. "We've been in seclusion so long now it isn't impossible they're saying we're afraid to come out of it. What do you think, Jonathan?"

"You know I'd like very much to go. I wasted several hours looking through my fishing tackle the other day. The fishing's reported still generally good along the Feather River because the water was high until so late this year. I'd like to go down to Bancross for a day too."

"I hope you're not suggesting we stay there?" Hortense said. "That hotel isn't fit to stay in."

"We'll have the usual chalet at the Pluma Blanca Inn," Basil said. "I think we should get away for a while."

"Quite right, my boy. We must show the world we are not afraid to face it. Life must go on and . . . and . . ." Daniel paused, searching for a suitable cliché in a mind well stocked with them.

"Then we'll plan to leave sometime this week—Yes, Gertrude?"

"There's a Mr. Sullivan wants to see you," the maid said, glancing furtively at the folded newspaper on the table. "I think he's a policeman, sir. He's waiting—"

Basil got up and left the room without saying anything. Hortense, twirling her coffee cup nervously between smooth, tapering fingers, muttered:

"That girl won't do: too curious by far."

"She hasn't been here long enough to be used to ushering in all sorts and conditions of police," Ariadne said. "Do we know Sullivan?"

"He was among those present," Jonathan said. "A very nice fellow too. I wonder if he might be a descendant of General John Sullivan? I must ask him sometime."

"He's always well spoken of," Daniel said patronizingly. "He'd been in charge when they had those murders over on Gough Street last year just before Freddie was kidnaped."

"The one where the Sheridan girl's fiancé killed her stepsister?" Hortense said. "I wonder what ever became of her? . . . Oh, good morning, Mr. Sullivan. We—we were just talking about you."

"Nothing bad, I hope? Mr. Dumont tells me none of you has read the news section of the newspaper yet so you don't know Edith Parnell was killed sometime early this morning. Of course you remember her?"

"Oh, yes indeed. Her nursing saved my little girl's life. Well, if I'd guessed there was such news in the paper I would have read the front page first instead of saving it for the last," Daniel said. "Well, poor soul. In life we are in death. But surely, Inspector, her relatives—"

"She didn't have any, Father." He knows that, Ariadne thought: she told him more than once, when they used to talk together, that she was lonely. "No relatives here, at least. And I don't think she had any really intimate friends either."

"That's right," Sullivan said. "We already know all there was to know about her life up to last June. It was—"

"An open book?" Daniel suggested. "With no pages that needed to be skipped?"

"That's it," Sullivan said soberly, though his eyes twinkled a little. "And nothing's happened since last June to account for her being killed—so far as we know now. Well, you remember that when the boy was kidnaped last year her story was that she slept with one eye open in the room adjoining yours, Miss Holaday, and that she never heard or saw a thing all night long. We always believed her. Did you?"

"I had no reason not to. But I was still being given a sedative at night so I was no good as a witness."

Actually she had been restless that night. But afterward she couldn't be certain what she had really heard and what she had dreamed. Except that someone certainly had come along the hall and softly closed the door that Miss Parnell had left a little ajar. And later she had thought she heard Miss Parnell talking to someone in the hall. But when she spoke of it to her afterward Miss Parnell had said, "Oh, you were just dreaming, dearie."

"I suppose I should tell you I saw her in April," Ariadne went on. "We had lunch together downtown. Because I suppose it was really her nursing that pulled me through—"

"She was considered pretty good in pneumonia cases. Did you think she had anything on her mind in April?"

"No. Of course we talked about Freddie. But that was natural enough, wasn't it?"

"Oh, sure. And we don't know her death was connected with the kidnaping," Sullivan said quickly. "But you can see why we have to consider the possibility that it might be, because that's about the only lead we have."

"I went to see her last month," Basil said. "She'd left her address with us. I thought that perhaps if we talked things over quietly she might remember—"

"What?"

"Oh, I don't know! Something—anything. But she didn't."

"Didn't know anything or just wouldn't tell it?"

"I thought she didn't know anything. And I wouldn't have thought she was—was actress enough to convince me of that if it wasn't true."

"Neither would I from what I saw of her. Well, that was last month and it may have been just the last few days that things began to come to a head."

"I believe you said she was killed after midnight? I think," Basil said, "you had better talk to the servants."

"Well, if you think so," Sullivan said carelessly. "None of the rest of you saw Miss Parnell after she left here? In that case I hope I won't have to bother you again. Now if I can have just a word with the servants, Mr. Dumont . . ."

It was more than an hour later, when Sullivan had been gone some time, that Ariadne passed through the lower hall on her way upstairs. The door of a small room that Jonathan used as a study was open and he was saying to someone:

"I was right by the telephone and got it on its first ring. I don't think anyone else heard it. She gave her name and I identified myself. She was a trifle incoherent but at last she asked who was here. I told her everyone but you; that you were dining with Blake. She hesitated for some time and finally she said—sounding as if she didn't quite know what she wanted—that I wasn't to bother anyone and that she'd call again.

"That was about seven-thirty last night. I was on my way in here and I came on in and never thought of it again," Jonathan said contritely. "Until Sullivan turned up, that is. But she didn't tell me anything, and how do we know that call had anything to do with her death? We've suppressed other telephone calls the authorities might conceivably have been interested in—"

"That's different. We should tell the police Edith Parnell tried to get in touch with us," Basil said. "But I'm not going to insist we do so. What she knew died with her—"

"Exactly. If they discover she knew something, let them do it from the other end and not drag us through another investigation. If they can't connect her with us in any way during this past year they'll let us alone. I want to be let alone, Basil. I've the scholar's temperament and it doesn't fit me to cope with affairs like this."

"You aren't the only one who has defects of temperament. But it's too late now—"

"I don't suppose there's one chance in a thousand Freddie is still alive," Jonathan said impersonally. "It isn't safe for a kidnaper to return a child as old as Freddie was. Of course one always hopes the bargain will be fulfilled."

"The general opinion seems to be that we made a good bargain. That fifty thousand was little enough to pay for the privilege of splitting the Armstrong estate among us."

Ariadne did not wait for Jonathan's answer. She tiptoed past the door and on up the stairs. Presently, lying across her bed, she found herself shivering though the room was well heated. For she was remembering what Ted Smith had said to her in the little chophouse on Polk Street.

"Maybe it wasn't kidnaping at all. Unless it's kidnaping to carry away a dead body . . ."

CHAPTER 5

On the whole Inspector Sullivan restrained himself admirably, though several times during Michael's story he was heard to mutter: "Holy Mother of God!" and when it was finished he said bitterly: "I don't expect women to read the news in newspapers—my wife doesn't—but don't tell me her name didn't mean anything to *you*."

"There is more than one Parnell in the world." Michael might blame himself for not inclining a sympathetic ear toward Miss Parnell but he had no intention of allowing Sullivan to do so. "And if I had connected her with the Armstrong kidnaping, what business of mine were her troubles?"

"You ought to be a good Samaritan. Oh well, I might have done the same thing. Women can be an awful nuisance when they're tight. Well, let's hear that tune she was singing. What did you call it?"

"'Alouette.' Do you think it might be important?"

"Well, you told me what she said about it."

"Not good enough. What have you been doing all day, Inspector? It's nearly eight and I've waited for you since morning. Very confining."

"And very trying to the temper," Valerie said, looking at the overloaded ash trays.

"If I'd known what you wanted I'd have been here sooner. I suppose there's no harm in telling you all I've found out so far. . . . So that song she was singing might be important," Sullivan concluded. "Let's hear it. . . . Kind of catchy, isn't it? Does it go on and on like that forever?"

"Nearly. You pluck the skylark from beak to toes."

"Well, let's you teach it to me." The inspector cleared his throat loudly. "My voice isn't much but I guess I can learn that."

Midway of the singing lesson Valerie remarked pensively: "And this place was just beginning to seem like home. It's too bad we should be asked to move after only six months."

"It's one of those voices that started out with good intentions," said Michael. "It should be bass but isn't quite convinced it may not still manage to be tenor."

"Lay off, will you?" Sullivan wiped his hot forehead. "Listen: I think I've got it now. . . . How's that?"

"There's at least a faint resemblance to the original."

"Well, I'll try it on those women. Not that I hope to find that someone among that bunch out on California Street has a habit of humming it all the time."

"The woman who suffers from insomnia said that the man she heard Sunday night was whistling. So was the one Miss Bond heard."

"Whistling or humming: what's the difference?"

"Then why don't you try whistling?" Valerie suggested.

"I whistle flat. You said this 'Alouette' is a French-Canadian tune and Dumont's a French name, but Basil Dumont was born here."

"What did he do before he married Gloria Armstrong?"

"Oh, he joined up in '18 but didn't get overseas. He married young. A bad marriage for him, though her father was a well-to-do jeweler and gave Dumont a job. But the girl turned into one of these secret drinkers. She was in a sanitarium but they didn't watch her well enough. She got hold of a razor and cut her throat. Dumont finally left Burris and he and the boy lived with the aunt. She's got a little income: not much. Dumont developed into a pretty fair golfer. He's been runner-up in some local tournaments and had a job

with a sporting-goods house when he married
Gloria Armstrong.

"You can't help liking him," Sullivan said.
"Blake, the other guardian, won't hear a word
against him. Everything along the financial line
was all straight and Dumont seems to have looked
after the kid the best he could. He hired a guard
for him, and so far as his delay in notifying the
authorities goes—"

"I've forgotten how long he did delay," Michael
said.

"Oh, not an unusually long time. They found
the kid gone the first of June and a note on the bed
saying to keep still and wait for a message about
delivering the ransom. They played safe. Dumont
got the money that day. They didn't hear anything
until the next morning, when they had this phone
call. Told him to chuck the money in a clump of
bushes at a certain spot in Golden Gate Park. He
did, waited till the next morning and, when the
kid wasn't returned then, called us in.

"We could howl about the delay—and the Feds
did—but it didn't do any good. Dumont swears
they locked the boy's room up at once and handled the ransom note carefully. It was made out
of words cut out of newspapers, you know. The
family insists someone used a ladder to enter the

boy's room through an open window. That's very improbable—"

"Didn't the guard sleep in a room adjoining the boy's?"

"Yes, and we put him through it. But he didn't break down and we hadn't any evidence against him. He'd been a ringer; played football for three colleges and quit Washington State just ahead of an investigation. Tried prize fighting, worked as a life guard and at a riding academy. We kept an eye on him but about a month ago he dropped out of sight. He kept moving into cheaper places. The Trilby Hotel—you know it, don't you?—was the last place he stayed.

"He did admit he was careless not to go in and take a close look at the boy that night. He didn't go farther than the door and the pillows had been arranged under the bedcovers to make it look like the boy was there."

"I suppose you've been in touch with the federal agents?" Michael said.

"Yes, but so far we haven't connected the Parnell woman's death with the kidnaping. Dumont admitted he saw her last month but that's no help. They have two new maids, and the gardener-chauffeur and the cook stayed on. They're married. But the servants' quarters are by themselves at the back of the house. If anyone was out last night the servants don't know it.

"But one of the maids was out Monday night herself and got home late. She tells a story about seeing a veiled lady— Oh sure: it sounds screwy," Sullivan said as Michael groaned. "But her story is that she saw someone enter the house by a side door that opens into the garden. If she did see someone it wasn't Edith Parnell. She spent Monday night in a different cocktail bar but

just sitting and drinking like she did last night, from about eight until midnight. Of course the gang at the Armstrong house just laughed at that story of the maid's. Though I didn't ask Ariadne Holaday about it. If any one of them cracks up it's going to be her. She looks bad: all eyes and thin as a rail."

"And that reminds me that we'd decided to take a vacation the last of this week," Valerie said. "It took me long enough to make Michael admit he needs a rest, so please don't tell me we have to put off going for more than a day or two."

"I don't think you will. She didn't really tell you anythin—"

"You mean, don't you, that you don't intend to make our testimony public unless you have to?" Michael said.

"We-ell. We do intend to emphasize the Bond girl's testimony because it's ambiguous. She thought she heard an interview between a woman and a man who was going to run out on her. So it looks like the best thing to do is to make out we think some guy who was tired of her killed her and then keep on investigating on the q.t. You just answer the questions you're asked at the inquest and you won't tell too much."

"'Little Birds are hiding Crimes in carpetbags—'"

"If the public gets the idea this is part of the Armstrong kidnaping there'll be another awful howl. And we can't prove it was. There's a lot of questions to be answered—"

"Why, if she knew anything about that kidnaping, didn't she tell it?"

"That's number one. Your first guess would be that she was paid to keep still. If she was, she didn't spend any of the money and she salted it away where we haven't traced it yet. I don't believe she was bought off. I think she didn't realize the importance of what she did know."

"Or if there was ever anything she thought needed explanation, that was forthcoming?"

"Well, she liked those people. Dumont's attractive and so is Holaday, besides being nearer her age."

"Then question number two seems to be: how did she discover she had suppressed important evidence? If she wasn't simply bought off, her own ignorance is about the only thing that would protect her for more than a year. And when she realized she did know something, why didn't she talk?"

"From what Miss Bond said, I'd guess this fellow warned her she'd be letting herself in for trouble if she did. Well, she had her professional reputation to think of. Being mixed up in the kidnaping at all hadn't done it any good. Admitting she'd kept her mouth shut for a year wouldn't do it any more," Sullivan said. "But I'll bet she'd have come to us finally."

"If the man Miss Bond heard her talking to didn't kill her, how did her murderer learn that she was dangerous?"

"Don't I wish I knew! If we can't prove she was in touch with Dumont or one of the others lately, the simplest way out of it is to say that the fellow we know was there killed her. And I'd guess his name was Smith. Though it might have been Dumont or Holaday or . . . Oh well, I'll be getting along."

"But still he answered with a sigh: 'Excelsior!' And we aren't to change our plans?"

"Oh, it would be too bad for you to have to do that," Sullivan said heartily. "You may have to wait till about Tuesday of next week to leave, but I'll fix it so you can."

"I think he wants us to go away," Valerie said, closing the door after seeing Sullivan to it. Michael grinned.

"Feminine intuition working overtime? Certainly he wants us out of the way."

"On second thought, I'm not sure that I blame him. When you're pitchforked into something like this you can't help being interested in it. At least *you* can't. And the inspector doesn't want to have to keep an eye on you to be certain your interest is purely academic."

"I'm done meddling. I don't want to come to resemble one of those old maids of detective fiction who's forever popping up where the police least expect or want her to be. Besides, since I don't know any of the principals in this case— Yes, dear," he admitted as Valerie smiled, "that last remark does give me away."

He walked over to the windows and opened them. "That pipe of Sullivan's is entitled to an old-age pension. 'Grow old along with me! The best is yet to be.' . . . . Shall we leave the place to air and take a ride?"

"I'd like to. Particularly if you'll drive by the Armstrong house. I haven't been by it for months, and while I know it's silly, I'd like to look at it again. . . ."

When they had reached the block of California Street dominated by the house and drove slowly by it, Valerie compared it to a large gray animal crouching in the grass. "More like a three-tiered cake," Michael said. "All it lacks is a curly inscription in white icing."

"Well . . . yes. Just the same, those front balustrades do look like paws and the servants' quarters like a tail. This street is so well lighted I see why they thought it was improbable anyone entered the boy's room by a ladder. And ladders leave marks, don't they?"

"Usually."

"But the kidnaper must have had a car. And if he took the boy away in it . . ."

"There's some sort of back driveway that comes in at the servants' quarters from Laguna," Michael said. "The idea was that he took the boy away by that back exit, having parked his car on Laguna, near that alley." He nodded toward a man strolling along the street in front of the huge gray house. "Six will get you ten that's a cop. It's very difficult to loiter convincingly in a residential district like this."

He drove on, so slowly that cars behind them hooted impatiently and then swept past them. Valerie waited, studying his profile thoughtfully. Once she had pronounced the harsh angles of nose, jaw and cheekbones "definitely ugly." Well, perhaps they were, but it was a long time since she had thought so, though she still considered his eyelashes ridiculous.

"It's a man's world," she said with apparent irrelevance. "We suffer permanent waves while eight out of ten men firmly repress their naturally curly hair. Well? Are we going virtuously home or are we going to do something Inspector Sullivan wouldn't approve of?"

"There is something about Sullivan that makes me want to do whatever he wouldn't approve of," Michael admitted. "And I was wondering if Birdie Crow still owns the Trilby Hotel."

"Birdie? Is that one of your improvisations? And is it Trilby for Svengali's Trilby?"

"No, it's Trilby for a hundred-to-one shot Birdie backed. And I should think her last name accounts for her first, though she does have a soft and dovelike voice. You can live at the Trilby for three-fifty per week or twelve dollars by the month."

"Is this superior hostelry in the Mission?"

"Ellis near Fillmore."

"Then we've only to turn back to Fillmore and over to Ellis—"

"What makes you think it's the sort of place I'd take you?" Michael said.

"Oh. Is it a—"

"No, dear. Birdie's never been a madam. It's a hotel in name only; in other words, a dump. Several men have been killed there resisting arrest but Birdie's never been pulled in herself. It won't harm you to meet her and I've a notion you'd object violently if I took you home first."

"Very violently," Valerie agreed. When he had turned the car and headed it back toward Fillmore she asked: "At what stage in your career did you live at the Trilby?"

"After I'd stopped driving a wildcat taxi in the Mission and before I joined the ranks of the private chauffeurs." The windshield was sweating as gray fog swirled against it. He set its wiper going before he said impatiently: "I wish Edith Parnell had been anything but one of these damn fools that insist on thinking well of their fellow men. There's not much you can do for people like that except try to protect them—"

"As rudely as possible," Valerie said, smiling. "But I wish myself that we'd let her talk to us. Though I don't see what you expect to learn from talking to your Birdie Crow about Ted Smith."

Michael turned from Fillmore into Ellis. "I'd rather talk to Mr. Smith himself. And as Birdie follows the very sound principle of never telling the police any more than she has to, she might have some idea where he is now."

He stopped the car before a tall gray house distinguished from others in the block only by the small sign over its front door. There was no lobby inside. A narrow, dimly lighted hall led to an equally narrow and more shadowy stairway. A door near the front of the house was labeled OFFICE and, standing ajar, gave a view of the hall and lower steps.

Miss Crow greeted Michael as casually as if it had been eight days instead of eight years since they had met. "I don't know," she said severely, "that you should bring your wife here. I doubt if she ever set foot in a dump like this before."

"What makes you think she's not addicted to slumming parties?" Michael said.

"No, she looks like a nice kid. Dames out slumming are usually half swacked. I don't approve of people drinking," Birdie said austerely.

All she needs to look as if she spent her life exhorting people at street-corner revivals is a blue scoop-shovel bonnet, Valerie thought. Birdie nodded toward the immense teapot on the table near her.

"Have a cup of tea with me? I drink too much but I have to stay up late to keep an eye on things."

"Your tea is too powerful a brew for me," Michael said as Birdie poured a cup of the mahogany liquid for Valerie. "Have you backed another Trilby lately?"

Birdie snorted disgustedly. "I was at Bay Meadows on getaway day and every horse I picked ran out on me. What's on your mind, Dundas?"

"Didn't a young fellow named Ted Smith stay here for a while?"

"Sure. I knew who he was. I liked him and I wish he'd stayed on. He was in kind of a dangerous state of mind. Feeling the whole world was against him, you know? And with his record there's guys who'd let him make himself useful. You know what I mean?"

"Then you don't know where he went when he left here?"

"No. He just cleared out and left me a suitcase and a note saying he'd come back and get it. He didn't owe me anything and I don't think he wanted to. You'd know about that too," Birdie said slyly. "You always had scruples about being beholden to a woman for anything, even a square meal."

Michael reddened. "There are cheaper places than this to live," he said hastily. "I suppose he went to one of them. Did you tell the police about the suitcase?"

"Lord, no! They'd have grabbed it and he could hock it for a dollar or two. You can look through it but there's just old clothes in it."

"Why," Valerie said, unable longer to suppress the question, "don't you ask why Michael's interested in Mr. Smith?"

Birdie shrugged. "Maybe he'd tell me the truth and maybe just some yarn it'd be a pleasure to believe even if I knew it wasn't true. Anyway, I knew him a long time before you did, dearie, and there's no danger in talking to him. He wouldn't turn Smith over to the cops unless he should be. I read about that nurse being killed and I had the cops here looking for Smith again this morning."

"I suppose they went over his room? Did you rent it again after he left?"

"Unh-uh. Business is bad. I cleaned it though; but if you think I or the cops could've missed anything you're welcome to look."

"I don't hope you missed anything, Birdie. Still . . . What room did he have?"

"Third floor back on the right. You go up if you want anything. I don't think the fellow that came this afternoon is in but—"

"What fellow?"

"I'm telling you. He came here looking for Smith. Said when he last heard from him he was at Mrs. Easter's boardinghouse. And he was: Kate Easter sent him here because he was looking for something cheaper."

Birdie picked up the teapot and shook it thoughtfully. "This fellow—Roland's his name—says he worked with Smith at a riding academy and Smith did work in one. He's not a cop: I can smell them a mile off. But he might be a Fed. Those boys are good. I had one here for ten days and didn't spot him. I'll never hear the last of that."

"You think he might be waiting here for Smith?"

"Well, I told him I kind of expected Smith to come back here. If he's a Fed I don't want him to think I care if he's around. And if he's Smith's friend he might as well pay me rent as anyone else. Lord, I got to live. He wanted a room some-wheres so I gave him my third floor back on the left. I just thought you'd want to keep an eye out for him."

"I will." Passing Valerie, Michael put a hand lightly on her shoulder for an instant. "And you," he said to Birdie, "have my permission to answer any questions my wife may want to ask you about the dim and distant past."

CHAPTER 6

Birdie still practiced rigid economy where electricity was concerned, he thought, climbing the second flight of stairs. The globe in the third-floor hall was the smallest money could buy. He turned silently toward the back of the house. He had seen too many back bedrooms in establishments like this not to know what the one Smith had occupied would be like.

A bed with a flat hard mattress over weak springs but—give Birdie credit—at least passably clean and not verminous. One straight chair and a bureau with a cracked mirror. He was not particularly interested in that bedroom but he would like to see Mr. Smith's friend if he was in his room.

A thin streak of light showed under the door of one of the two back bedrooms. The fellow must have slipped past Birdie—not an easy thing to do. Michael started to knock and then stopped. He could simply tell the truth; that he was anxious to get in touch with Smith.

But he, like Birdie, objected to parting with any more information than was necessary. The old stall: "Doesn't Jim Brown—" No; a name like Mc-Gruder would be more convincing. "Doesn't Jim McGruder live here? The landlady said . . ." Etcetera, et cetera.

He raised his hand again. And dropped it again, this time to the doorknob. His fingers tightened on the worn brass. For someone was moving about on the other side of the door; walking back and forth across the room. Humming as he walked: "'Alouette, gentille Alouette, Alouette . . .'"

Michael looked quickly down at the door. If the key happened to be on the outside . . . The key wasn't. He thought: I've no authority even to try to detain this fellow simply because he hums "Alouette." If I scare him away Sullivan won't forget it or allow me to. Whereas if I call him . . .

And having come to this reasonable conclusion, he knocked on the door. He would at least have a look at the man.

"Well?" said a flat voice.

Michael, explaining apologetically that he was looking for Jim McGruder, decided he had wasted time. The man's face was so much like so many hundreds of other faces. A middle-aged man with

a brownish, short-clipped mustache, a nose neither markedly long nor short, eyes not quite blue,
not quite gray. Perhaps he was more tanned than
the average San Franciscan and the nail on the
middle finger of the right hand was badly discolored. His suit was dark, conservative. . . .

"So I guess he must be on the second floor," Michael finished. "Though I'd have sworn the landlady said the third. Sorry to have bothered you."

"Don't mention it," the man said civilly. "I'm
new here so I wouldn't know."

He closed the door. Michael sauntered back toward the stairs, down the first flight slowly enough
and the second at breakneck speed. There was no
one in Birdie's office. The teapot was gone from
the table and he guessed that she and Valerie were
in the kitchen.

He picked up the telephone and then hesitated. Sullivan should be at home now but you never
knew. He would prefer to talk to Sullivan and
no one else but if he wasted time trying to find
him . . .

"Put that phone down," the flat voice said. Michael whirled about, still holding the telephone.
He looked at the man who called himself Roland
and then at the gun in his hand. The steadiness
of that hand and the cold unwinking stare of the
nondescript eyes were not encouraging but:

"Can't a fellow phone his girl?" Michael protested. "I mean, if you're in a hurry to use the
phone—"

Roland reached out and smashed the gun down
on his wrist. Its barrel cut a deep gash across his
hand. His fingers turned numb. Roland caught
the telephone as he dropped it; set it carefully on
its stand and drew a knife from his pocket.

"You came in with a girl." He tossed the knife
onto the fringed red cloth that covered Birdie's
tea table. "Cut the wire. And don't upset anything
when you do it. If you make too much noise the
women might come running in here. And that,"
Roland said with a complete absence of anger,
"might be too bad for them. Cut the wire."

Michael finished wrapping a handkerchief
about his hand. He looked at the knife; an old one
with large nicks in its pearl handle. He had time
to be surprised at his reluctance to pick it up. He
thought he knew a killer when he saw one and
he rather prided himself upon having learned to
yield more or less gracefully when the odds were
against him. But it seemed that even ten years of
self-discipline hadn't subdued a naturally explo-
sive temper. . . .

"Cut the wire," said Mr. Roland for the third
time and still without emphasis.

Michael picked up the knife. He sawed savagely at the wire, thinking: This weapon would be all the Saint needed to conquer ten armed thugs. Or Bulldog Drummond. No, dear old Bulldog would dispose of them with his bare hands. . . .

"Don't take so long about it," Roland said.

"Considering I've only one hand to work with, I'm doing rather well." Michael looked at the blood-soaked handkerchief and sought relief in the Spanish of Cervantes: "'Those who play with cats must expect to be scratched.'"

"Talk English. If I thought you were anything but an interfering busybody I'd let you have it. I don't like snoopers, so suppose you tell me why you were."

Michael yanked at the weakened telephone wire, eying Roland warily. That glance ended in a conviction that this, of all times in his life, was the one when a plausible lie was vitally necessary. "Oh, all right," he said hastily. "My wife and I are chasing her brother. I don't know how she ever came to have a lug like that for a brother, and he's got a nice wife too. . . ."

He restrained a freakish impulse to endow his newly created brother-in-law with six little ones and perhaps a seventh in the offing.

"But he's a periodical," he went on. "And he holes up in places like this. And his wife nearly

goes nuts, so it's up to us to find him. One of his
pals saw him on Fillmore today and suggested we
look here. Miss Crow says she don't know him;
that you're her only new roomer and you certainly
weren't soused.

"She seems all right but some of these dames
aren't and he don't always use his own name. So she
said I could go up and look at you. It's not a thing
you like to tell strangers about," Michael ended
sadly. "And I just hurried down to telephone his
wife because we promised we would right away.
She's—"

From down the hall Birdie could be heard saying: "You watch that toast, Mrs. Dundas, and I'll
just run upstairs. . . ."

Roland waited until the sound of footsteps on
the thinly carpeted stairs died away. And, waiting,
regarded Michael thoughtfully. The trouble was,
Michael decided dispassionately, that his appearance didn't match his language. That lapse into
Spanish had been a mistake. Neither did he look
a good Samaritan. He hoped Mr. Roland was not
too keen a student of human nature, but his muscles tensed unconsciously.

"I've got to get out of here," Roland said abruptly. "And I'd rather have things quiet around this
joint for quite a while. . . ."

Michael saw it coming and there was nothing at all he could do about it. Except, in the brief instant before blackness washed over him, to try to be thankful for a rap over the head instead of a bullet in the intestines.

The old family doctor dropped in Thursday afternoon "because," he said, "I happened to be driving by." Ariadne suspected he'd been asked to come, probably by Basil, perhaps by Daniel. He talked of Edith Parnell, putting his stethoscope away and rummaging through the jumbled contents of his scuffed brown bag.

"I had a detective asking me questions, and the idea Parnell had a lover who killed her is as ridiculous as the theory she knew something about Freddie's kidnaping and didn't tell it—"

Ariadne fastened the collar of her dress. "But she was killed."

"I know!" Dr. Monroe said testily. "But she's not the first fool woman who's opened her door to a killer. Of course she wasn't attacked, but she did fight and he may have had to run for it."

"Doctor, when Freddie was kidnaped, did you talk to her about it?"

"Of course. I knew she liked all of you. If there was some little thing she'd noticed but thought couldn't be important she might keep still to be obliging. But she swore she didn't know anything and hadn't seen anything."

"But if she realized just lately that she really had, do you think she'd have hesitated to tell it now?"

"Well, she wasn't so busy this last year. Well-to-do people with children turned thumbs down on her several times. Getting mixed up in the case again wouldn't have helped her."

"You never told anyone about sewing Freddie's head up after Phil knocked him down, Doctor."

"Wasn't important. Fool idea people have, that children are always lovable and loved just because they are children. I've often wanted to tan Freddie's bottom myself. And speaking of Phil: I'd hate to see you marry him."

"Marry Phil! He's younger than I am—"

"Not so much younger and you've always gotten along better with him than anyone else. He's fond of you. And he doesn't inherit anything when the estate's settled but you do. Hortense wouldn't oppose it too much for that reason. Don't let yourself drift into it just because you see too much of each other and not enough of other young people. I knew Eve Burris, his mother, and his grandfather. Burris wasn't a drinking man but some people called him a rascal. Basil was right to break with him but handing Phil over to Hortense, with his heredity, was a mistake."

"You needn't worry about me. I'll never drift into marrying Phil—or anyone else."

"So? I was afraid of that and it won't work out either, Ariadne. But I know there's no use arguing with women about things like that. Well, here's something to help you sleep. Don't give Phil any of it. Most of this stuff shouldn't be habit-forming but I'm not taking any chances with him. I suppose you know he got into Parnell's stock?"

"No, but now I see why he bothered to be nice to her sometimes. He took her picture sitting by my bed. It turned out very well and of course it pleased her."

"I remember. But you've got to get out more. Take up tennis or swimming again, or riding. You don't have to worry over what a horse may be thinking about you. And while it would be better if you all got away from each other as well as the city, I'm in favor of your going to the mountains. It will be particularly good for you, and I don't see why the trip should be given up."

Neither, apparently, did the others. That night Jonathan abandoned his study and joined them in what was known as the "reading room," where he sat wrapping bits of brightly colored silk about his trout pole and brushing them with shellac.

Basil was looking over an assortment of flies while Phil read the *Amateur Photographer*.

Hortense was struggling with a very long biography of a very unimportant person. She held the book almost at arm's length, not only because she was farsighted but as a protest against Daniel's gaily jacketed *Cinderella in Sable*.

Jonathan grinned at Ariadne as she sat watching him. "Hortense," he murmured, "thinks there's some virtue in reading dull books just because they are dull. When she wants to be particularly virtuous she reads mine— at Daniel."

Ariadne laughed and Hortense looked at them suspiciously. "Some people can sit for hours with their hands folded in their laps but I never can," she remarked. "Of course when you've been as busy all day long as I have it's a real treat to relax over a good book."

Jonathan chuckled. "The old-fashioned idea that love and literature belong to the hours after dark, Spider."

Hortense flushed. "I'm sure you don't need to be vulgar." She looked at Daniel, sunk in the most comfortable chair with the best reading lamp beside him, and addressed Phil. "Can you see, lover? Wouldn't you like to change places with me? You have a very poor light—"

"I'm all right." Phil threw his magazine to the floor. "Hell, I can take as good pictures as the ones in there."

"You can take a lot better ones. Did you get a good picture of President Roosevelt today?"

"I've told you a dozen times, I don't know! I mean," Phil said hastily as Basil raised his head, "he went by so fast it's hard to say. I shot him at a hundredth of a second so maybe I got something."

"It's nice to be a President," Ariadne said. "Since Phil turned artistic he won't take a picture of un-important people. I like landscapes with people in them too. And now that you're an expert nothing interests you but clouds and withered trees."

"That's all you know about it," Phil began, ready to resent even implied criticism. But when she smiled at him he grinned back. "Oh well, you're still just a snapshooter, Spider. That was all right while I was learning. Say, Jonathan, if you go down to Bancross I want you to ask the Townes if they ever turned up those two rolls of film I lost there."

"As I remember, you claimed at the time they were stolen," Jonathan said dryly.

"I still think the proprietor's kid, Ed, helped himself to them. I don't care about the snaps. That was when I still had the old Premo 2A and didn't know anything about composition. They were kid stuff," Phil said loftily. "I got one roll the last day we were there, just before we went back to Pluma Blanca. But I cleaned out all that junk a year ago when I got my new camera. Still, I don't like the idea of those Townes getting away with that."

"But have we been given permission to leave town?" Ariadne said. "I know Inspector Sullivan was here this morning. What did he want?"

"It was only a—routine visit," Basil said.

"He wanted to know if any of us was in the habit of singing 'Alouette,'" Jonathan added.

"'Alouette'? You taught it to me, Basil. It's a tune that runs in your head. I sang it when I was delirious," Ariadne recalled. "But what an odd thing to ask."

"I'm afraid the inspector is snatching at straws," Daniel said. "But he is very considerate. You were lying down and he said we needn't disturb you. And I think he is going to be reasonable regarding this matter of our leaving the city."

"Which means he's going to see things your way. I want to get away but I hope you're not using my health as an excuse? Did any of you ask Doctor Monroe to come to see me?"

"And if we did, why should you resent that, daughter? As a matter of fact, I had nothing to do with it. Did you, Basil?"

"I haven't—seen Monroe for some time. But he's fond of you, Ariadne."

"I suppose he is. But—whose idea was this trip? I know some or all of us have gone to Pluma Blanca for quite a few years but—"

"Well, it certainly wasn't my idea," Hortense said. "It only makes more work for me, leaving the house in order and helping everyone pack. I'd rather stay home. But Daniel likes hotel life and Jonathan likes fishing, so—"

"I'm looking forward to fishing again myself," Basil said. "I have to get new waders, Jonathan, so if there's anything you want along that line we might as well go down to Spiro's tomorrow."

"'Tomorrow, and tomorrow, and tomorrow,'" Daniel intoned. He claimed to have once carried a spear under Robert Mantell and on slight encouragement would give a creditable imitation of that actor's sonorous delivery. He wound his watch carefully; the thin platinum watch Gloria had given him on his forty-second birthday. He said, as he always did at about the same time every night:

"Well, well—bedtime again. 'Sleep that knits up the ravell'd sleave of care.' Coming, daughter? You'll never be your old self again without plenty of sleep. Good night, everyone."

Phil, falling into step with Ariadne as she started up the stairway, muttered:

"I didn't see Sullivan: I was down on Van Ness when he was here. And somehow I don't think they're telling 'the children' everything. . . ."

CHAPTER 7

Inspector Sullivan stood looking somewhat disconsolately about Edith Parnell's room while behind him Mrs. Knibbs made noises like an indignant teakettle boiling dry.

"Oh, this is the last time I'll bother you," Sullivan said. "You can rent the place now if anyone wants it."

But he made no move to go. The room was in order now. When he had come in here early Wednesday morning every drawer of the bureau had been open. There was a white drift of starched uniforms, caps, lingerie and handkerchiefs on the floor. The drawer of the old-fashioned library table had been taken out and left on the bureau. A square lacquer box had rested emptily upside down near it. . . .

But searching Edith Parnell's room and her belongings hadn't taken her murderer too long, Sullivan thought. The place was sparsely furnished and

she hadn't added anything of her own to those fur-
nishings. She'd had very few clothes, a few pieces
of inexpensive jewelry and half a dozen books.
They'd been searched; so had the tiny kitchenette.

Sullivan stared at the door that supported a wall
bed. The bed hadn't been down Wednesday morning and Edith Parnell had been fully dressed. Yet
the Bond girl swore the man she'd heard talking in
here had left about twelve-ten. Miss Bond hadn't
got into bed until twelve-thirty herself and she
was equally certain she hadn't heard a sound from
this room during those twenty minutes.

The medical examiner still stuck to it that Edith
Parnell hadn't been killed later than two o'clock,
though he admitted she might have died as early
as one-thirty. Even if you set the time of her death
at one-thirty there was still more than an hour
to be accounted for. An hour during which she
hadn't even started to get ready for bed yet hadn't
made enough noise—as she might have if she'd
still been talking to someone—to wake Miss Bond
or keep her awake.

There was no desk in the room; only the library table. Among Sullivan's very small stock of
"exhibits" was a fountain pen that seemed to have
been both filled and used recently. And half a box
of writing paper with Edith Parnell's fingerprints
on its top. The fingerprints were not old ones—

and that got you exactly nowhere. They weren't old or blurred, but who could say exactly when they had been made?

It was wonderful, Sullivan thought, what storybook detectives found out by applying mirrors to blotting paper. But if Edith Parnell had had a blotter the murderer had taken it away. He sighed and turned to Mrs. Knibbs.

"All right, I'm going. After all, this is only Friday, so you've no complaints coming and you probably won't find this room easy to rent anyway."

Maybe not, Mrs. Knibbs retorted, but she couldn't even try as long as there were cops tramping in and out of it. Sullivan grinned feebly, went out to his car and headed for Green Street.

It struck him that neither Michael nor Valerie appeared overjoyed to see him. Not being a sensitive soul, he merely chose a comfortable chair and asked for a drink.

"How are you feeling?" he said.

Michael scowled at his bandaged right hand. "All right."

"Well, at least the bump on your head don't show and you were damn lucky not to have a real concussion—"

"And what have you been doing, Inspector?" Valerie said hastily, handing him an oversized highball. She gave Michael its twin and reserved for herself a glass filled with ice cubes and a fizzy, impossibly pink liquid.

"I've been taking a last look at Miss Parnell's room. And kind of musing, you might say. . . ." Sullivan repeated to them the surmises he hadn't shared with Mrs. Knibbs. "She did stay up and there must have been a reason for that. She may have been writing a letter. On the other hand, she may have been waiting for that guy to come back."

"Or been expecting someone else to call on her," Michael said. "You didn't tell us her room was searched."

"Well, it was. And of course we explain that— to the public—by saying her lover wanted to get back any letters he might have written her. There weren't any worth-while fingerprints in the room. You know, I can't help wondering who she was thinking about when she said that sometimes a woman like her believes she's found a real friend and then usually finds out different. That is, if she was thinking of one particular instance or just several when things turned out that way. Because Dumont and Holaday are attractive and Holaday would be about the right age for her. So would Armstrong, but he's a funny-looking duck. We never turned up any women in any of their lives, though."

"According to Mrs. Knibbs, Miss Parnell sometimes blossomed forth in festive raiment and went downtown to lunch. Presumably with someone."

"Well, the Holaday girl asked her out once. And she might have meant a woman friend as well as a man. Mrs. Knibbs said she hadn't gone lately. But we're covering that angle, only there are a lot of restaurants in this town and so far we've had no luck."

"Neither have you found Mr. Roland," Valerie pointed out.

"Mrs. Dundas, there are hundreds of guys that look like the description of him. And he had a good start before you called us. If you'd called us right away—"

"Inspector, when I walked into that office of Birdie's my first thought was a doctor, not a policeman. I didn't stop to think that you could have brought one with you. There was the only husband I have bleeding profusely and dead to the world. How could I know who was responsible for that? Why should Birdie immediately be suspicious of Roland? Why—"

Sullivan hastily retreated to more tenable ground. "Oh, I know it was an awful shock. But it's too bad Birdie didn't phone us, too, when she ran out to call a doctor."

"She didn't want to leave me alone too long. And I like her very much. And it wasn't much more than half an hour before Michael was able to say something about Roland."

"Oh, I guess it wouldn't have mattered anyway," Sullivan said quickly. "That suitcase he brought to Birdie's had almost nothing in it. It's no good to us. The only thing we did find out was that some fellow did turn up at Mrs. Easter's boardinghouse, asking after Ted Smith—"

"Whom you haven't found either," Valerie said nastily.

"And she suggested he try the Trilby. Mrs. Easter didn't have her glasses on, couldn't see the guy too well and wasn't interested anyway. And that's as far back as we've got, though you can take my word we've questioned everybody that might have known him. His fingerprints didn't do us any good. I was at the Armstrong house yesterday. I didn't see Miss Holaday or Philip Dumont. Seems he's one of these camera hounds and was down trying to get a picture of the President.

"Well, the fact that Roland hummed 'Alouette' was about the most definite thing I could say about him. They all just looked blank. Dumont said he knew the song and some others like it because his father was Canadian. I tried it on Mrs. Knibbs and Miss Elston and they thought they recognized it. Miss Bond wasn't so sure but she only heard a snatch of it whistled. Of course Miss Elston heard someone whistling as well as humming it."

"As I pointed out to you, whistling isn't the same thing as humming. And by the way, wasn't Richard Burris Dumont's first father-in-law?" Michael said.

"Sure. Why?"

"One of his former employees, a man named Wales, makes costume jewelry that we sell in the shop. I don't know why he and Burris parted company but Wales doesn't speak too highly of Burris."

"We always had our suspicions he was a high-class fence. That may be one reason why he and Dumont broke up. Did this Wales ever mention Dumont?"

"No. He may never have known him."

"Well, as I said before, Dumont seems like a nice guy. And so do Holaday and Armstrong, though I'd hate to say how many years it's been since they've done a real day's work. For a wonder they'd held onto their legacies up to the time the boy was kidnaped. Their annuities are so small they couldn't live on 'em in the style they've been used to. But it was Gloria Dumont's wish that they both always be given a home there."

"I wonder what Frederick Armstrong, Jr's ideas about that would have been when he came of age?" Michael said.

Sullivan sighed heavily. "I wonder. And they're howling their heads off, wanting to leave the city. I guess we'll have to let them go. Their doctor made a point of telling me Miss Holaday needs to get away. They'd planned going before the Parnell woman was killed and we haven't been able to connect them with her death in any way. That Armstrong money still carries some weight and old Blake's been to see the D.A. to speak his piece on the subject, so I think we'll probably let 'em go Sunday."

"And what about us?" Valerie said. "Of course our name carries no weight—"

"Look, Mrs. Dundas: what's the matter? You act like I'd done something—"

"She's been putting up with my bad temper for two days," Michael said. "Now she's relieving her feelings by telling you off."

"Oh, I see. But you oughtn't to get burned up over what happened Wednesday night. From what you say about Roland, you're lucky it was no worse. And of course," Sullivan said mildly, "you shouldn't have been trying to find Smith."

"He thought you needed help," Valerie remarked sweetly.

"I do, but not along that line. Any suggestions?"

"Why don't you find out when it was that Miss Parnell bleached her hair?" Michael said.

"You're a great help! Well, I really came to tell you the inquest's Monday and you can leave the next day if you want to. It'll be cut and dried. Where is it you're going? If we pick up Roland you may have to come home."

"We're going to spend at least one night in Brookdale with a Mr. and Mrs. Allan. The River-side Hotel in Reno will get us after that and I'll drop you a line from there."

"The Allan that's sheriff up there? I know a private dick here that thinks they don't come any smarter. But working up there in the backwoods is one thing. He wouldn't find it so easy down here. Look: had you already planned going there?"

"Of course we had. I can show you Mrs. Allan's letters if you're doubtful," Valerie said. "But why should you be?"

"Because Pluma Blanca Inn, where Dumont and his gang are going, happens to be very near Brookdale."

"Is it? I didn't know that, but since you mention it," Michael said perversely, "a detour by way of Pluma Blanca might be interesting."

"Listen, you two: you keep out of this business! You go on your vacation, Michael, and—and stick to your dressmaking."

Inspector Sullivan was to regret this remark, though he never quite traced subsequent events to it. He picked up his glass and drank, missing the spark of primitive rage in Michael's blue eyes, happily unconscious he had been superlatively tactless.

Horace J. Trimmer, representing N-Dure, Aluminum Wares Like Iron, had intended leaving the Hotel Marysville soon after Sunday's sunset. In that way he would avoid the valley heat between Marysville and Oroville but still arrive in Reno not too long after midnight.

But Mr. Trimmer allowed himself to be persuaded to take a hand in the poker game in the room occupied by Witmar of Long-Life Silk Hosiery. Mr. Trimmer was a consistent winner, and as he had often tried to explain to Mrs. Trimmer, you can't quit too early when you're winning.

It was, therefore, after midnight when Mr. Trimmer drove out of the little river town. He had his winnings —twenty-four dollars and sixty-five cents—in his pocket and a stale taste of beer in his mouth. He was drowsy, too, but the still hot air promised another sweltering day and he wanted to be somewhere in the mountains before the sun came up.

He was sensible enough to drive slowly and now and then he talked to himself. "If you happen to see a good auto camp you could stop and get a little sleep, Horace." He liked to be called Horace but many people were unkind enough to call him "Horrie."

"The thing is," said Mr. Trimmer to Horace, "to get through Oroville before morning. Hottest place in the Sacramento Valley."

He drove on, nodding over the wheel, jerking himself erect and nodding again. He left Oroville behind and started up the white highway paralleling the riotous Feather River. He was some miles along it—how many he didn't know—when a shadow disputed his way, standing out in the middle of the road, waving its arms.

Mr. Trimmer was still driving slowly but if his head had not been muzzy from beer he would not have taken his foot off the accelerator while he stuck his head out of the car. The shadow proved to have form and substance and legs as well as arms. A solid body landed on the running board and something unpleasantly round and hard dug into Mr. Trimmer's ribs.

"See here, you can't I mean, I haven't any m-money," Mr. Trimmer stuttered. "Only f-five dollars—"

What he later described as a hoarse ferocious voice growled: "Shut up!" as its owner yanked open the back door and crawled into the rear of the car. The gun now pressed suggestively against the back of Mr. Trimmer's neck. "Just drive and cut out the talking."

Mr. Trimmer, no longer sleepy, drove. He wondered at what point along the way the man holding the gun would pull its trigger, dump his lifeless body into the road and go on with the car and sample cases of N-Dure. Or at the very least, take his money, kick him out of the car and leave him afoot in this terrifying wilderness.

Mr. Trimmer did not quite weep but he sniffled, prayed incoherently—and drove. He let out one small yelp as the gun suddenly pressed harder against his scrawny neck, but the voice behind him said:

"Let me out here. All right, get going!"

Mr. Trimmer went and did not look back. He kept going until he reached the small town of Brookdale, where the hotel was still open. Mr. Trimmer was burping violently; he took large quantities of sodium bicarbonate and went to bed. But in the morning, minus his nervous indigestion, Mr. Trimmer began to think rather well of himself.

He had not, after all, lost his money, his car or his life, probably because he had not allowed himself to be intimidated. And, by George, something should be done about things like this!

What Mr. Trimmer did was to call on the county sheriff before leaving Brookdale. The sheriff was a tall, amiable Mr. Allan, who made Mr. Trimmer feel not quite so heroic. But he took down Mr. Trimmer's description: a man built like a gorilla with a hoarse, ferocious-sounding voice and a gun as large—judging from Mr. Trimmer's gestures—as the big fish that got away.

Mr. Allan wanted to know whether Mr. Trimmer had any idea where he set the fellow down. He didn't? Well, it was very kind of Mr. Trimmer to let them know about it but he had better not slow down the next time someone tried to stop him late at night.

Mr. Trimmer went on to Reno and the sheriff remarked to his redheaded wife that "business is lookin' up. A guy got held up for a ride last night. Of course it probably happened in Butte County out of my jurisdiction but it's right excitin'."

"I hope," Eleanor said severely, "that after more than a year and a half of comparative peace and quiet you're not hoping for excitement when I want you to help me entertain guests."

"Are they coming?"

"They'll be in sometime tomorrow. Michael has to appear at that inquest today, though Valerie didn't tell me anything except that they talked to the woman the night she was killed. It seems some people can't avoid getting mixed up in murder cases."

"Were they mixed up in another one?"

"Darling, I told you Valerie was engaged to one of these perennial collegians—that's what she called him herself. Well, the man she did marry is about as far from that type as she could get. I like him but I imagine he's usually a cultivated taste."

"Yeah? Why?" Rocky said lazily.

"Oh, mainly because he doesn't suffer fools gladly, I suppose. He's half Argentinian: his mother was, I mean. Started out as a dancer but always found plenty of men besides her husband who were willing to support her. She taught him to walk with three books on his head without spilling the books."

"That," Rocky said gravely, "is cert'nly very interesting—and important." Eleanor, he thought, sowed information the same way she did flower seeds: hit or miss, sacrificing order to her love of massed color.

"It accounts for the fact that the way he holds his shoulders makes you instinctively straighten yours."

"Comfor'ble sort of cuss to have aroun'."

"Well, anyway, his mother died and Michael was shipped back from Europe to a very Scotchy grandfather he didn't get along with. And ran off when he was twenty and more or less pulled himself up by his own bootstraps."

"To be a dressmaker."

"Couturier, please. And you needn't sniff. I know you think couturiers must be sweet little pansies with perfumed hair but do try to conceal the fact. Because Mr. Dundas is a trifle touchy on the subject of his profession. And thoroughly hard-boiled in his quiet way."

Rocky yawned. "Yes, and those hard-boiled guys usually have a soft streak in them a mile wide— somewheres."

"Valerie is his. This man she was engaged to killed her stepsister and it was really Michael who proved he did. She told me all about it—and him."

"I wonder why?"

"Oh, I pumped her," Eleanor said shamelessly. "And when I met her she was perpetually exasperated because Michael seemed to think she must still be carrying a torch for the other man. I suppose he was afraid of rebound. But it wouldn't have been, even then, because she never really loved Howard even if she thought she did once."

Rocky yawned again. "That's nice."

"It's too early for you to be sleepy. You're getting lazy and if you don't get more exercise you'll
get fat. I won't love you if you do. Fat blonds are
so much worse than any other kind of fat man."

Rocky rose to the bait. "I weigh just what I did
when I got my full growth. What's Valerie like?"

"Oh, you'll like her. She's very much like me
except that she's a good deal younger. And very
pretty. Not spectacularly, but she has lovely ha-
zel eyes and she's all brown and gold. Her hair, I
mean—"

"Well, I hope they turn out more congenial
than the last couple you asked up here. The man
that was a diehard Republican and didn't eat anything but nuts and all those veg'tables stewed up
an' the water strained off."

"Potassium broth," Eleanor said, giggling. "But
I didn't know he'd be like that. I don't often inflict
people like that on you. And I haven't turned into
a devoted-mother-who-neglects-her-husband-for-
her-child, have I? In fact I'm a pretty swell wife."

"Few white men and no n—s at all have wives
like you," Rocky said drowsily. "And I'll bet you
somethin'. I'll bet in spite of the way they soft-ped-
aled that Parnell woman's death in the papers, one
of these days the Armstrong kidnaping case will
come to life again just like a hatful of firecrackers
someone throws a match into."

CHAPTER 8

They came through the valley in the middle of the morning and reached Oroville at noon. The wind was from the north, a scorching, energy-sapping wind. When it died down for an instant heat waves flickered across fields and orchards and the piles of sterile sand and rock left by the gold dredgers near Oroville.

Michael unfastened another button on his shirt. "Do you want to eat something here?"

"I don't ever want to eat." Valerie pulled her limp dress away from her shoulders. "My nose is a pink marshmallow. Let's go on. But if we had started—"

"If we had started earlier we would have avoided this. But let me remind you, light of my eyes, that it was you who wanted to get out of the fog to someplace where they have summer in July."

"I know," Valerie said serenely. "Let me mop up your forehead, darling. Why don't you read Mr.

Carnegie and Mr. Wash Young and train yourself to rise above petty annoyances?"

"Petty!" Michael scowled at her. "I'll take my Turkish baths at Hamman's if you don't mind. Just don't talk to me for a while. You always rise so exasperatingly above petty annoyances. I suppose we'll get out of this eventually. . . ."

But for miles the road was unshaded and great white cliffs caught the sun's rays and threw them glaringly back over the highway. Michael drove with eyes half closed, having curtly refused to take Valerie's sunglasses. The dark green of surrounding forests and the nearness of hurrying, splashing water was only an aggravation. By the time they reached Brookdale he had a savage headache and his eyeballs felt as if they had been peeled and dried in the sun.

Therefore it was exasperating to see Mr. Allan rise from a comfortable chair on a shady porch, unwilted, vigorous and hospitable. "It's one of these large hearty persons," Michael thought unjustly and momentarily evaded what he imagined was going to be a bone-crushing handshake.

"The left if you don't mind," he said.

Rocky glanced at the wide strip of adhesive he still wore across his right hand. "Accident?"

"I was driving in a nail," Michael said perfunctorily, "and missed the nail."

Rocky watched him open the car door and pull out their bags, using his left hand. His eyebrows rose slightly but: "That's too bad," he said, picking up one of the bags. "You folks must be starved."

"We've waited for you," Eleanor said. "And everything is cold, including the drinks, which are also long."

Being a forthright person, when the weather and beauties of the Feather River canyon were disposed of Rocky said: "We don't get the city papers till later this afternoon, though I don't suppose the accounts of the inquest on that Parnell woman will be worth readin'. Did you tell all you knew at the inquest?"

"I gave strictly a command performance. Then locked my memory and gave away the keys—to Inspector Sullivan," Michael said blandly. "So if you don't mind, let's discuss the state of the nation."

Rocky was relieved, as the meal progressed, to discover that at least Mr. Dundas was neither a Republican nor a vegetarian. He was aware he had been snubbed. The fellow had a damned aggravating way of saying: "If you don't mind?" He might as well add: "And the hell with it if you do!" But Valerie seemed like a nice kid. Rocky eyed her paternally and began to plan for their entertainment.

"We could take a hike up the side of Bald Mountain—" Eleanor groaned. "Oh, you girls can stay here."

"I'm afraid I'm not equal to that sort of hike," Michael said humbly.

"What about fishing? It's pretty good now."

"But so fatiguing. One has to scramble over rocks and through brush and risk falling into the water. You see, I don't swim very well either."

Valerie wished that he were close enough to her to be kicked. The truth was that he was an excellent swimmer. He's in one of those contrary moods when he persists in putting his worst foot forward, she thought. Though why Mr. Allan should have that effect on him is more than a mere woman can understand.

"Well," Rocky said, "the deer season's not open yet but there's some game you can kill—"

Michael shuddered. "Slaughter our little woodland friends? Besides," he added truthfully, "I couldn't hit a cow at six paces. I'm afraid I'm hopelessly unathletic, Mr. Allan."

"Does that include dancin'?" Rocky said politely. "Because we wanted to take you down to a dance at Pluma Blanca tonight— What's the matter?"

Michael and Valerie continued to look at each other. Then Valerie laughed and Michael shrugged.

"We're just puppets and someone is jerking the strings, *niña*."

"Then you know the Dumonts and Holadays are there?" Rocky drawled. "But this is a long-standin' invitation. Ev'ry year Suzy Cochrane gives a party her last night at the inn. We've never gone but we thought we would this year if you're not too tired. Suzy's parties start late, though they do last till train time, which is about 5 A.M. now."

"And you wouldn't by any chance like to have a look at the Dumonts and Holadays?" Eleanor suggested.

"You know we both would, honey. God knows we talked enough about that case last year—"

A pig-tailed Chinese in padded slippers and an apron crackling with starch brought in dessert. "This is Sing Toy," Eleanor said and explained when he had gone: "He's what people refer to almost reverently as 'an old-fashioned Chinese.' At least he has the proper characteristics, though he's not over fifty-five. Rocky rescued him from a lumber camp where he was cooking—"

"Or did I rescue the camp from him? And there's nothin' old-fashioned about his sal'ry."

"He's worth it. He does everything and looks after the baby besides. You should have seen him in the early stages, surrounded by charts, baby books and formulas," Eleanor laughed. "If I dared test the bath water with my elbow instead of a thermometer he'd growl: "Missy want to scald baby? Missy let Sing Toy do.'"

"He can talk English if he wants to," Rocky said. "Only it adds to his value to be picturesque. But it's somethin' to have someone aroun' you feel safe to leave a kid with, though he may grow up talkin a mixture of pidgin English an' Cantonese. If he ever talks at all, which I doubt."

"It's a darling baby," Valerie said thoughtfully. Michael grinned at her.

"'Two are better than one; because they have a good reward for their labor.' But we've only been married six months, my dear." Valerie turned scarlet. "She's not really embarrassed. Blushing is something she's never outgrown, along with her fondness for highly colored nonalcoholic drinks."

Valerie ignored him. "I think it would be fun to go to that dance. But what should we wear, Eleanor? Isn't that inn terribly swanky?"

"So swanky that half the crowd will be frightfully horsy or too, too casual in simple little sport frocks such as Gisele charges fifty dollars for."

"Buy cheap and sell high," Michael said. "Pray demand will exceed supply, soak the rich and insult your customers judiciously."

"That head saleslady of yours does the last perfectly. One glance from her and you feel everything you have on should go to the Salvation Army."

"Maybe he trained her pers'nally, honey," Rocky said amiably. "And the rich aren't the only ones you soak, seems to me. I nearly had heart failure when Eleanor fin'lly let me see the check for that green suit she got from you. But maybe it was worth it. She never looked better in anything. Not that I know anything about women's clothes and it's a mystery to me how anyone can make head or tail of 'em but—"

"But you do know what you like?" Michael suggested suavely.

Rocky, on the point of saying just that, swallowed hastily. "Well, that's the way most men feel about it—"

"And a lot of good it does them," Eleanor broke in. "The truth is, my pet, that women don't dress for men but for other women. Let's go into the living room. . . ."

This, she thought, is going to be one of these visits that adds to the hostess's gray hairs. I should have known. Well, you can always discuss a baby without his resenting it, and mine apparently craves company.

She invaded the nursery and bore Robert Edward Lee Allan, Jr into the living room. "Only it's

such a lot of name for one baby that we call him
Shay," she said. "On account of a shay is a very
small engine with a very loud whistle. It makes
just as much noise as a malley. Go to the nice
lady, Shay, and don't pull her hair when you get
there."

Valerie held out her hands but young Mr. Allan
disdained her. He staggered over to Michael and
tried to ascend his legs.

"Well I'll be damned," Rocky said. "And he's a
snooty brat if there ever was one."

"Ah, but they say children and dogs always
know, Mr. Allan." Michael picked the baby up.
"He detects the mother in me."

"You do that very well," Eleanor said, "except
that you should hold him on your left arm to leave
your right free."

"He's left-handed, honey."

"Is he? I hadn't noticed."

"You'd have to be to hit your right hand with a
hammer, drivin' a nail. Only people don't gen'rally
hit themselves near the wrist but on the thumb."

Michael's lips twitched. "Suppose I said I ran
a needle into my hand while whipping up a little
frock for Valerie?"

"I wouldn't believe that either," Rocky drawled.
"I don't know much about dr—couturiers but I
was always under the impression they left the

sewin' to someone else. And anyone would know you were left-handed by watchin' or shaking hands with you."

"I take baby now," Sing Toy announced. "Time baby have bath. And boss got to go to Bancloss."

"The hell you say! What's wrong at Bancross?"

"Boy call up, say boss come to Bancloss. I say boss have company, come when cool—"

"Give you six months more an I can retire," Rocky muttered. "You could spare time from runnin' us to look after law and order too. Was it Ed Towne?"

Sing Toy nodded. "But he say boss better come. Dead man in cabin there. Not murder—"

"Suicide? He would pick the hottest day of the year to do it. Well, I'm glad you decided I should know about it."

"No trouble," Sing Toy said impassively, took the baby from Michael and bore him protesting from the room. Rocky, staring after them, asked pensively:

"Honey, am I wrong in thinkin' you and I were responsible for that kid's being here? Or did he just spring full grown out of Sing Toy's brain?" He got up. "Well, I reckon I'll have to trot down to Bancross."

"I might have known it," Eleanor said. "We never will get to one of Suzy's parties."

"Oh, I reckon we can go. I won't bother the cor'ner; he's conducting a fun'ral over at Indian Walley. But will you answer the phone instead of leavin' it to Sing Toy? We got to assert ourselves while we still can."

He turned to Michael. "Considering how far you've driven already today, I reckon you'd rather stay with the girls?"

Although Valerie, at least, knew that was what Michael would have preferred, he rose promptly. "Oh no; I'll tag along, if you don't mind?"

"I don't. Only suicides have a bad habit of makin' pretty much a mess of themselves, one way or another—"

"Well, perhaps Eleanor could lend me some smelling salts," Michael said provokingly. "But I wouldn't think of looking at your corpse. Corpses distress me. I'm just going along for the ride and to see how these things are handled in the—er—"

"'Backwoods' is the word," Rocky snapped. "All right, let's start."

They were nearing Bancross before either of them spoke again. Then Rocky said, half to himself: "I believe this is the first time I was ever called to Bancross officially. I haven't even been there to fish for more than a year. It's off the main highway, and before that was finished the easiest thing was to come in by train. So it wasn't a popular resort then, and now folks just whiz by it."

"I remember a road turning off over a bridge—"

"Yeah, that's it. The Townes don't care so long as they make a living and some people keep coming back because they like a place that's not too crowded or fash'nable. This is it."

They went across an old red bridge, turned a corner and were at the beginning of Bancross's one street; a wide dusty road shaded by apple trees. There were twelve flimsy cottages with cracked coats of thin stucco, a general store and post office, a hotel that was merely a sprawling shingled cottage, a gasoline pump and blacksmith shop.

The river and highway were below the town, and the railroad tracks and a small tan station on the hills above. A long freight train was squirming around the tracks now like a fat black snake, its engine, out of sight around a curve, hissing dismally.

The place was hot enough, pinned at the foot of bare steep cliffs, though there were water sprinklers going all along the road. The town's one new building, a long yellowish affair labeled CLUB-HOUSE, was nearest them when Rocky stopped the car. A lanky, towheaded boy wearing very tight blue jeans and the remains of a tan shirt got up from a chair on the porch and hurried over to the car.

"I didn't know if that Chink understood what I was saying. It's that guy— Oh, I guess you never met him. Well, he came back here early Friday morning and now he's blown the top off his head out at Holy Joe's cabin."

"Very inconsid'rate of him. This is Ed Towne— Mr. Dundas." Rocky glanced toward the clubhouse. Inside a man with a round bald head and a compensating clump of reddish mustache appeared to be dozing behind the soda fountain. "Your dad's taking it calm enough."

"You know Pop. He just sets. He got more het up over some groc'ries and a shovel being stole from the store Sunday night. But not excited enough to put a better lock on the place. But we would rather the cottagers didn't get wise to this. You know how they are."

"Yeah, they'd be underfoot in no time. You hang onto the running board, Ed."

Rocky turned the car again, continued on past the road to the bridge and along a narrow rutted track through the woods. The fenders tore through bushes overhanging the road or scraped against fallen tree trunks and protruding rocks.

"Where does this lead to?" Michael asked.

"Oh, nowhere much. We get our wood around here. . . ."

Ed waved his hand vaguely toward the forest to the right of the road. The river was to its left, in some places separated from them only by a dense growth of underbrush and willow. Now and then they passed men shoveling red dirt and gravel into battered buckets or merely leaning for the moment on their shovels, their bare shoulders, burned mahogany-brown, glistening with sweat.

To all of them young Mr. Towne said: "Hi!" and to Rocky: "There's a lot of snipers along here this summer. Hi there! How's it comin'?"

The solidly built young fellow laboriously wresting a shovelful of rocks from a shallow hole said amiably: "All right, I guess," and ducked his head to wipe his face on a salmon-pink arm.

"Damned hot work on a day like this," Rocky said absently. "What happened to Holy Joe's cabin after he got to thinking he'd been appointed God's prophet on earth and we lugged him away to the bughouse?"

"Joe was just a squatter. He was an old prospector that went nuts. He built this place," Ed explained to Michael. "It didn't really belong to anyone and about three years ago this guy Roche turned up. He had a little money and Pop said he could use the cabin. He'd been sick, he told us.

"I never liked him myself. I had a dog that went for him after Roche kicked him. Roche had ta run for it and then Towser just disappeared and I always did think Roche shot him. And here's something funny: he came back in a new car and the name inside is 'Rolfe' instead of Roche. He used to have this old see-dan but his uncle left him some money so he—"

Ed stopped, staring at Michael, who was looking out at the trees, whistling shrilly. "W-where did you learn that?" he stammered. "I—I mean what m-makes you whistle it right now? Because that's what we've always called Roche's song."

Rocky stopped the car in a small clearing from which a path led to a tipsy shack halfway up the hill. He turned to look at Michael.

"That," he said, "might, and probably will, be explained as just coincidence. You stay here, Ed. Oh yes, you will! You're still green around the gills from lookin' at him once. You sit and admire nature for a while. . . ."

CHAPTER 9

Michael stood looking down at what was left of the dead man's face. He lay on his back on a low camp cot, his right arm hanging over its edge, fingers touching the floor. Michael dropped to one knee to study those fingers. He glanced at the gun lying within an inch of them and stood up.

"In life he was neither lovely nor pleasant and death has not changed him," he observed. "But what a pity!"

"What's a pity?"

"I had hoped," Michael said gently, "someday to catch up with Mr. Roche, alias Roland, alias Rolfe. It might interest you to know that the gun with which he presumably shot himself is not the one he carried Wednesday night."

"No? How do you know?"

"Oh . . ." Michael yanked at one end of the tape across his hand and showed Rocky the half-healed gash beneath it. "I don't know anything about guns but I do know the one he did that with had more barrel than the one on the floor has."

"That's as interestin' as the position of this cot and the way he's dressed."

There were no windows in the cabin. With the late afternoon sun beating down on its thin roof it was almost unbearably hot inside. The cot was close to the door; not so close that they had not been able to enter the cabin without moving it, but so placed that when the door was open Roche's head and shoulders were opposite it. He was stripped to the waist, and coat, vest and shirt were hanging over a straight chair near the one homemade pine table.

"Holy Joe always slept outside in the summer," Rocky said. "But if I was going to kill myself I don't think I'd care much whether I did it where I could get what breeze there might be." He pointed to a large rock on the floor near the door. "I'd guess that's a door prop. But of course Ed said this guy got here Friday morning, so he slept here more than one night."

"I'm not an expert on stages of dissolution but he's certainly been dead some time."

"No doubt about that. And if he was this unpleasant in life he must've been mighty disagreeable. Will it take you long to tell me about him?"

"That depends on how much I tell you," Michael said coolly.

Rocky counted ten—three times. Any time they give a prize for sheer orneriness he'll win hands down, he thought. And said pleasantly:

"I don't know how much you could tell me."

"'Anger and pride are both unwise, Vinegar never catches flies,'" Michael murmured. "Of course I must tell you what I can about Roche. But if I also tell you about Edith Parnell, that will take some time. And I had a good deal of information from Inspector Sullivan that he'd probably prefer I didn't pass on."

"And you're a friend of his?"

"We might pass for friends but I'm not feeling too friendly toward him just now. He forgot to exact any promises and this death is your business—so far. It might be interesting to see what you do with it."

"In other words, you've no objections to helpin' me just to spite Sullivan? But that suits me. I'll look aroun' in here and then we'll talk outside. The fingerprints will have to wait. I didn't come prepared for anything more 'n an open-and-shut suicide."

Michael sat down in the one old-fashioned rocking chair while Rocky opened a suitcase lying on the floor. It was obviously new and fairly expensive, not locked but in no unusual state of disorder. There was a tight roll of soiled clothing—underwear and two shirts—but none of these had been laundered and all the other garments were new and unworn.

"Damn nice shirts," Rocky said. "And eight of 'em, all new. Besides the other new stuff and the suitcase."

"Ergo, Mr. Roche did not lack ready cash. Q.E.D."

Rocky moved over to the table and picked up a paper plate not quite scraped clean. "Caviar or I don't know the stinkin' stuff. He seems to 've had expensive tastes, judging by the groc'ries he brought up here."

In a large box by the stove were scraps of paper and kindling, eight more paper plates, a dozen or so empty cans and jars that had held chicken, caviar, ham, fruits, marrons glacés, imported cheeses and anchovies. Three of the plates were splotched with grease and the yellow of egg yolks.

A box nailed against the wall accommodated what was left of bacon, eggs, coffee and bread, an empty matchbox and several unopened tins of food. There was a half-empty pint bottle of whisky on the table, a tin cup with a quarter inch of

black coffee in it and a granite coffeepot heavy
with dry grounds.

Rocky put the whisky bottle and tin cup carefully aside and considered the rest of the litter on
the table. There was a large flashlight, a kerosene
lamp, a battered tin ash tray overflowing with cigarette stubs, a Sacramento *Bee* dated Monday, July
11. In the center of the table a withered spray of
tiger lilies lay across three red hot-water bags that
had been slit down their middles.

"Always believe at least six impossible things
before breakfast," Rocky muttered. His eyes nar-
rowed speculatively. "I remember reading about
someone who— Well, we'll see. It looks like he
was in Sacramento Monday, at least. And you saw
him Wednesday night? Did he have a mustache
then?"

"Yes. I noticed that he was rather tanned. Also
that the nail on the middle finger of his right
hand was badly discolored—as this man's is. And
he carried a knife with a pearl handle that had a
good many nicks in it."

"I'll go through his pockets in a minute. I
thought he must 've had a mustache. His upper
lip's still whiter than the rest of his face. Well, Ed
says he came here early Friday mornin'. He apparently had three breakfasts and six cold meals. If

he ate breakfast here Friday that would take you through Sunday night and I wouldn't doubt he's been dead that long."

He picked up Roche's coat and vest. There was nothing in their pockets but an Eversharp pencil, a new Hamilton watch, a scrap of paper on which a list of supplies had been written, a soiled handkerchief and a nearly empty pack of cigarettes.

Without moving the body he managed to get his hand into Roche's trouser pockets. He drew out another handkerchief, a penny box of matches with two matches in it and a pearl-handled knife.

"This the one?"

"It looks as if it might be," Michael said cautiously.

Rocky laid the knife on the table and found Roche's car keys and billfold in another pocket. "Three hundred in nice clean bills and a driver's license made out to George Rolfe. He probably got it same time as the car. You can go quite a distance on three hundred if it's not hot money."

"Hot money?" Michael said obtusely.

"Oh sure, I'm jumpin' at conclusions. But if you've got such a long story to tell about Edith Parnell, who was connected with the Armstrong case and— Oh well, let it go. Will you grab this guy's feet? Lorenzo won't care if we move him.

He's the cor'ner. I guess you'll have to give up
your chair to him for a while."

He returned to the cot and threw back the dirty
blankets Roche had laid on. "Um-hum," he said
complacently. "He's probably got a ridge across
his back from sleepin' on this."

He opened the broad leather money belt that
had been concealed beneath the blankets. It was
stuffed to fullest capacity with limp, soiled bills:
fives, tens and twenties.

"But mainly twenties," Rocky said. "I won't
bother to count it now. It's the Armstrong ransom; I know the series numbers by heart." He added disgustedly: "I've waited a year, like ev'ryone
else, for some of it to turn up. And here it was all
the time, right under my nose."

"You think he left it here?"

"Buried somewheres near here. What else were
these hot-water bags for? They'd be waterproof,
and there's some dirt and pine needles sticking to
them. And why are they slit?"

"You could get the bills into them by rolling
them tightly and using something to poke them
down," Michael admitted. "But you'd have to slit
them to get the money out. Certainly, since he obviously had enough money to live on, he'd be a fool
to carry the ransom bills with him. I wonder . . ."

"What?"

"Where he got the money that made it possible for him to get along for a year without having to use any of the ransom?"

"The money Ed said his uncle left him—"

"Do you think so?"

"Why," Mr. Allan inquired politely, "don't you just say I'm a damn fool? That's the impression you manage to convey. Did anybody ever tell you you've got a very expressive voice?

Michael grinned. "I've heard comments to that effect. And you don't believe in Mr. Roche's uncle any more than you think he was overcome with remorse for his sins and killed himself."

"Well, for God's sake, don't you tell anyone that! Let's lay him out all pretty for Lorenzo. . . . An' for a person that corpses 'distress,' you seem right at home with this one. That's good enough. Lorenzo ain't particular. I guess the stove's all there is left to look at."

Michael followed and watched while he removed the lids. Instead of the fine gray wood ash he had expected, there were several handfuls of crinkly black flakes. "Some kind of paper," Rocky said, poking at it cautiously. "He did a good job. It'd take a wizard to make anything of this. I wonder what it was?"

"Possibly, among other things, a letter Edith Parnell sat up to write."

"Think so? Say, did Roche have a record?"

"Sullivan said his fingerprints hadn't helped them."

"Well, he still might be— Hey! Here's something he missed!"

He stared covetously into the firebox, looked at his own big hands and then at Michael's long slim fingers. "You get it out. I don't want to lose any of it. See what I mean? It's a match folder—"

"Furnished by the Pluma Blanca Inn to its guests," Michael finished. He carried the half-burned bit of cardboard over to the table and laid it carefully on the newspaper there.

"Roche was nearly out of matches," Rocky said. "So I reckon somebody used his own to light that little bonfire and either dropped the folder in there accident'lly or threw it in without thinking because there weren't any more matches in it. And that cardboard don't burn so easy. This place is an oven. Let's go outside."

"Gladly. But would you mind finding out now what the boy knows about Roche? That, and not my encounter with him, is nearer the beginning of the story."

"I reckon you're right."

Rocky closed the door and beckoned to Ed, who was already standing looking eagerly up the hill. He walked over to a tall pine near the cabin where a small spring was guarded by a circle of stones.

"Sit down, Ed. And tell us all you know about Roche."

Well, he'd turned up early in the spring of '35, Ed began. He said he'd been sick and he did have a bad cough. He was driving an old sedan and had some money. Ed's father had been sorry for him and said he could use this cabin. So he moved in. He was a natural-born fisherman and in deer season he always got a couple of bucks. Probably, Ed added darkly, he didn't mind shooting does if they came his way.

"Didn't he ever say where he was from?"

"No, except that something he said once made me think he'd hunted and fished in Canada. And there was that song he was forever humming. It had French words and he sang 'em once, but he shut up like a clam when I spoke about it."

"Oh? Well, how'd he manage to live?"

"He did some sniping along the river and sometimes he took out quite a little gold. Then he'd take people hunting and fishing and Pop gave him odd jobs to do. He was handy with cars. He fixed the engine over in his so it'd do eighty, though you'd never guess it to look at it. He never talked much. He wasn't even polite to these guys he'd act as guide to. But you know how summer people are? They'd just call him a 'character' and put up with it as long as he took them where there was fish or deer."

"But didn't his uncle help him out?"

"Why—why, no. Come to think of it, he never even mentioned havin' a uncle till just before he left here. That was last July when he said his uncle had died and left him some money so he was goin' out for a while. He left some things here, at his own risk, and said he'd probably be back this summer. But, Rocky, why'd he kill himself? I'd never expect a guy like him to do that."

"It looks like he did, Ed. What kind of gun did he have when he lived here?"

"Oh, it was a .38 special. Awful unhandy to carry: you know that. But I'm sure he had a shoulder holster. But, Rocky, with a new car and all, why—"

Mr. Allan sighed. "I know. Well, kid, it looks like he kidnaped the Armstrong boy."

"The— Oh! . . . Oh gosh, Rocky!"

"You think that's excitin', don't you? But if you tell anyone but your dad I'll take it out of your hide. He's safe, but there's a lot of things I want to clear up without the place bein' overrun with a lot of—of reporters and summer people looking for a sensation."

"Not to mention the F.B.I.," Michael murmured. But Ed agreed loyally:

"We can handle this ourselves. Gee, why didn't I ever think of Roche when Freddie Armstrong was kidnaped? I read all I could about it, on account of having known him and—"

"You—what? You knew Freddie Armstrong?"

"Sure. At least, he was here when the rest of 'em were."

"I wish," Rocky said, "someone would take me out and kick me. Oh well! Tell me about it."

Well, first Mr. and Mrs. Dumont spent a week in one of the cabins when they hadn't been married very long. She was swell—honest! Put on overalls and went fishing and did the cooking herself. But the rest of 'em! Ed lifted his shoulders scornfully.

"They weren't along that time?"

"Oh no. And that was before Roche came here. Then after she was dead they all came; two years ago, in '36. They only stayed four days and the old maid and the young fellow kicked about the meals and hotel all the time. He was sick most the time; said it was something we served that upset his stummick, but he just made a hog of himself eatin' candy and stuff.

"And the day before he left he accused us of stealin' two rolls of film he'd taken. But you know, though I thought then he'd just mislaid 'em, afterwards I wondered if Roche could have copped them. Because he was funny about having his picture taken. He wouldn't ever let anybody do that. I've heard him make excuses when fellows he'd taken fishing wanted to. The only thing is, I didn't think it was likely Phil Dumont got far enough away from the hotel to get a picture of Roche. And Roche never hung around the hotel—"

"He didn't care for summer people?" Michael suggested.

"Well, they are an awful pest. And I've told you how he didn't put himself out for anybody, not even people we knew had money. As a matter of fact," Ed said thoughtfully, "he seemed to like that kind least of all. Used to call 'em rich bastards."

"He seems to 've been a nice guy," Rocky said.

"I always thought he was a crook but I never could get Pop to see it. And maybe his picture's in some rogues' gallery and that's why he didn't want it taken again."

"Or suppose it wasn't?" Michael said. "You realize that he was very difficult to describe? He looked like hundreds of other men; you'd hesitate even to guess how old he was. And so long as no picture of him existed he was doubly safe."

"Why—that's right." Ed decided Mr. Dundas might have something on the ball after all, even if he did talk kind of like the history teacher at Oroville High. The one who was born in England but had been here a long time. "He was awfully ordinary-looking, come to think of it."

"I reckon he realized that. Well, did the rest of the bunch make themselves disagreeable too?"

"Nope. Dumont and Armstrong had been here fishing for just one day the year before but they didn't have Roche take them out till they came to stay longer. Old Holaday didn't fish; he mostly just sat, except he'd take a walk ev'nings, usually with the kid and that guy that looked after him."

"And the girl?" Michael said.

"There wasn't no girl with them. Miss Dumont just set around and made a pest of herself, fussing. Phil Dumont did get out with his camera a little but, like I said, he had a bellyache most the time. The kid kept Smith on the run—"

"What did you think of the kid?" Rocky asked.

"I hate to say it but he was a whiny little tattle-tale. Mr. Dumont was awful nice to him but you could see Phil Dumont or his aunt couldn't stand him. Smith was with him all the time, so I never really talked to Smith."

"You're a gold mine, Ed. Which ones would you say knew Roche best? He may've got the idea of

kidnaping the boy then and kind of pumped someone to find out the things he'd need to know."

"Gee, maybe he did! Well, he knew Armstrong
and Dumont best, of course. Smith used to walk
out this way with the kid, and didn't they kind of
suspect him of being in cahoots with the kidnaper? Gosh, maybe they cooked it up that summer!"

"Maybe. What about Holaday?"

"Well, he did come out this way with Smith and
the kid. Roche was working a piece of dirt down
on the river then, and they all seemed kind of interested in that. Summer people always are. They
think," Ed said tolerantly, "that if they look close
enough they'll pick up a handful of nuggets."

"Well, you remember the youngster was kidnaped either late the last day of May or early the
first of June, last year?"

"Decoration Day was the thirtieth and a Sunday," Ed said. "So Monday, the thirty-first, was
a holiday too. One of these three-day week ends,
and there was an awful mob here. We were so busy
I couldn't say if Roche was here all the time or
not. Probably no one else could. He didn't have to
drive through town to go away; just out this road
and then turn and go across the bridge."

"But the new highway wasn't open then," Rocky
said. "So he had to go aroun' by Lake Almanor
and Red Bluff."

"That's quite a long drive?" Michael said. "But of course, with a car that would do eighty . . ."

"Yeah. The train's out. He had to have a car."

"But he did go out on the train that same week," Ed said. "The westbound came through about midnight then. I took some folks to it and Roche said his uncle in Sacramento was sick. That was—that was just into Wednesday morning, the second of June. And then he came right back on the eastbound about three the next morning. He said his uncle was better. And then in July he said he'd died and left him some money—"

"And had he by any chance gone to visit his sick uncle in May?" Michael said.

"Yep. About the middle of May, and that was the first time he'd ever mentioned his uncle."

"And you're sure he came back early this Friday?" Rocky said.

"I was starting out fishing about five and saw this car going along in front of me. So I was near enough to see Roche when he stopped here and got out. But I hung back so I wouldn't have to speak to him. I never saw him again but there was smoke coming out of the chimney Saturday and Sunday mornings. I ain't been by since then; not till this afternoon. I don't know why I felt like something was wrong but it was so kind of still. And his car's never been moved since he drove in.

You look and you'll see. So—well, I just came up and peeked in. The door was shut—"

"He didn't stay in the cabin the whole time though. He picked some tiger lilies somewhere."

"That's funny. It's getting too hot for them. There might be some left, back deep in the woods."

"What about the old graveyard?"

"Nope: not damp enough. Say, are you thinking about—about the kid's body? Because if you are, the graveyard's out. He wouldn't bury him the first place people think of when they think of bodies—"

"But no one's been buried there for years, Ed."

"Old Hezzie Slater was, a year ago this April. He'd almost always lived here and he said he wasn't going to leave. They had an awful time getting the coffin up there. Well, Mom was fond of Hezzie, so she sent me up once or twice with flowers, and ever'thing was like it should be. Besides there not ever being any tiger lilies there. But I'll find where they were blooming last week, if you want me to."

"That's what I do want. Nobody will think anything about it if you wander aroun' the woods."

"And maybe," Ed said, "I'll find—what else you want to find."

"If you think you have, call me before you make certain. Don't dig into anything you think might be a grave. And now here's Roche's car keys. You go call my office and tell Al Sully to come right down here. We'll wait."

"My turn?" Michael inquired as Ed galloped down the hill. "'Piper, sit thee down and write in a book that all may read.' We'd never been drawn into this if I hadn't worked late and Valerie's feet hadn't hurt her. . . ."

CHAPTER 10

Rocky let him tell his story without interrupting. "I wish," he remarked, "that all witnesses knew how to begin at the beginning, go straight through to the end and then stop. Did you consider Roche dang'rous?"

"Did I— What do you think? It's true I never fight if I can avoid it. Or give away weight. But I dislike being threatened and in the course of a varied career I have picked up a number of extremely unsportsmanlike tricks that I never hesitate to use when I'm forced to fight. But men who flourish guns usually fall into three classes: those who haven't nerve enough to shoot, those who shoot wildly and the ones like Roche who very calmly and coolly plug you in the guts while you're flinging yourself at them. I've seen one or two killers and I've also heard that belly wounds are extremely unpleasant."

Rocky grinned. "You know, now that I'm gettin' used to it, I'm beginning to like to listen to you talk. But you misunderstood me. You'd have been a fool to do anything but what you did do. What I really meant was would you have felt safe pickin' Roche to do your dirty work for you?"

"If I ever engage in murder I'll attend to it myself. I would consider Roche's habit of humming 'Alouette' rather dangerous. But leaving that out of it, I'm sure he was an extremely efficient employee who would never become rattled in emergencies. That is, if he was an employee."

"Oh hell! I'll bet a year's sal'ry he was. It's interestin' that he was looking for Ted Smith that night in the city."

"Do you think so?"

"Don't you? But you evidently scared him away, though he took his time coming here. That looks like he was careful and not easily rattled."

"Do you remember that part of *Through the Looking Glass* where Alice tries to get out of the house?" Michael said abruptly. "No matter how often she started out on the path that seemed to lead away from it, she always found herself walking back to the house or even in at the front door. We left the city—"

"To get away from it and just get back into it again? Well, I know how you feel but you'd decided to come here before you ever ran into the Parnell woman. And Roche had to come back here," Rocky said sensibly, "regardless of what you did—"

He stopped as Roche's car appeared. Ed, racing up the hill again, reported:

"Al Sully ain't had his dinner yet. I tried to argue with him but—"

"Let me guess. Mr. Sully's goin' to eat first." Mr. Allan disposed of Mr. Sully in a few well-chosen words. "I'm going to take the gun and a few things from the cabin and look at the walls and floor. Then could you stay and watch till Al gets here, Ed? I'll call him myself from the clubhouse. Then you can go back in Roche's car. I'll have Lorenzo come down and get the body tonight. It can't lie aroun' till morning."

"'Forty dollars I will fine you, For I couldn't well confine you, As already you've been lying 'round too long,'" Michael said.

"That's no lie. I won't come back with Lorenzo tonight, Ed. There's some things I'll be busy doin' in Brookdale. Uh—fingerprints and so on," Rocky said vaguely.

"Mahomet, having come to the mountain, is bearing it away with him," Michael drawled.

Rocky's ears reddened. He could bring his fingerprinting apparatus back here tonight instead of carrying articles to it but he had other plans. He addressed Ed pointedly:

"I'll explain to your dad and you keep your mouth shut!"

"So help me, Rocky, I'm dumb as an oyster! And I'll get out first thing in the morning to look for—for tiger lilies. And anybody that wants in here will have to get by me."

Ed set his jaw, tightened the belt of his jeans and wondered why Mr. Dundas, brushing pine needles from his shoulders, should murmur:

"'Then out spake brave Horatius, The Captain of the Gate . . .'"

It was past six-thirty when Rocky got into the car. He returned Ed's wave with a bleat of the horn and put his foot on the starter. He wanted to get in touch with Al Sully as quickly as possible but still he stopped when they came to the first of the diggings along the road.

In response to his "Hey, there!" a muffled voice said: "Coming." There was a sound of rocks slipping into water and then the rustle of underbrush before the thickset young fellow appeared, whistling into the towel with which he was drying his face and short-clipped hair.

"What's up?"

"Fellow killed himself in that cabin back there. You hear any shots lately?"

"Not in the daytime. And at night—I sleep!"

"Been sniping here long?"

"Sn— Oh, just a few days. My partner and I were over on the Yuba River but that was too crowded. He's out fishing. Did you want to see him? He usually don't get back till after dark. But if he heard anything he didn't tell me, and I think he would have." The young man winced as he patted his forehead gently with the dirty towel. "You see, we don't have much to talk about so we talk about anything."

"Well, would a car comin' in here late Sunday night or early Monday mornin' wake you?"

"After a day of this nothing would wake me." He tucked his khaki shirt under his trousers. "And we'd hiked ten miles Sunday—"

"O.K. I'll be back tomorrow mornin' and talk to your partner then."

The same questions asked of the other snipers drew negative answers except from a gaunt man who admitted with a bitter smile to being "an expert accountant, temporarily unemployed. I did think I heard a car come along here very late Sunday night. I was too tired even to sleep well. But as to hearing any shot—"

"No, you wouldn't, this far from the cabin. Well, I'll talk to you again tomorrow. I'm in a hurry right now."

Rocky returned to the car, after telephoning to Al Sully, with an unaccustomed set look of exasperation about his mouth.

"If anyone should ask what I want for Christmas, one vig'rous deputy with just av'rage intelligence would do," he said. And when they were fairly on the road back toward Brookdale: "You think I ought to get in touch with all the authorities right away," he began combatively.

"I refuse to quarrel with you, Mr. Allan. I think you don't want to notify them. And if you don't, who am I to beard the lion in his den, the Douglas in his halls?"

"Which is one way of callin' me a big frog in a small puddle. But I do know my puddle from top to bottom. And I can't help thinking it's luck that bunch should be over at Pluma Blanca right now."

"Luck?"

"Oh, not just coincidence but luck for me. We can go over there tonight without anyone knowin' we know Roche is dead. I can always say I was too dumb to see right away that he was mixed up in the kidnaping. Though there's the ransom—"

"You could find that hidden in the cabin—tomorrow morning."

"I could say so. But you saw me find it."

"Did I? I don't remember."

"That'll do all right. Well, if you won't argue, what do you really think of the idea?"

"Won't everyone at Pluma Blanca know who you are?"

"Yeah, but we were going to Suzy's party anyway, which she may have mentioned."

"Since the Dumonts and Holadays are in a state of semi-mourning, will they be among those present?"

"If you knew Suzy like I know Suzy! She'll know 'em by now and insist on them enjoyin' themselves. She wants people to. And Mower, the manager there, will play ball with me. One time he had a Mr. and Mrs. Jones stayin' there. And Mr. Jones' wife turned up with her little fo'ty-four and went root-toot-toot at the lady that was passin' as Mrs. Jones. She didn't kill her and we hushed it up. Mower would rather I'd talk to the help privately anyway. . . .

"I was thinkin'," Rocky said presently as they neared Brookdale, "that it's too bad we've only got one bathroom. But I'll give you first crack at the shower. You don't seem to 've burned any."

"Very little. I don't, easily."

"Damn! Oh, not because you don't sunburn," Rocky said, laughing. "I was on the point of thinkin' what it was I noticed that wasn't right. Only I was in a hurry—"

"Was it anything in the cabin? Were any shots fired there beside the one that killed Roche?"

"Not that I could find and the walls are pretty flimsy. It wasn't anything to do with the cabin. Maybe my brains will take a new lease on life when we've had supper.

"That is," he added, "if Eleanor gives me a chance to eat after she's heard the news." And later, finally pushing his plate aside, he complained: "Honey, I can't concentrate on food when you watch me like you hoped every mouthful would be my last."

"You've eaten enough to keep you from fainting through lack of nourishment," Eleanor retorted. "Valerie and I have been very, very patient and now we want to know all about it."

"So do I—"

"Don't put on an act for me, darling. And don't let Michael cramp your style. You know I was almost morbidly interested in that kidnaping. Perhaps because of what would delicately be called my condition. I'd lie around and wonder if I *could* get any bulkier," Eleanor said indelicately. "And envy the lowly rabbit and read the newspapers."

"I know. And we agreed the thing must have been very carefully planned. It would have looked pretty suspicious if he'd been kidnaped as soon as his mother died. There was plenty of time before he'd come of age. But of course the older he got, the harder it would be to dispose of him. So three years was about right. By then the world thought of him as a millionaire baby that might be kidnaped.

"Then the fact that the authorities never turned up one clue that pointed even to an ord'nary kidnaper workin' alone showed somebody was plenty smart. And since none of the ransom money was spent, that proves whoever got it didn't have to take that chance."

"Considering the state of Roche's finances while he lived at Bancross, it seems he must have received some sort of down payment," Michael said. "But where did it come from? It must have been a fairly substantial sum, yet that angle was thoroughly investigated and no one concerned, apparently, had made any unusual expenditure that couldn't be accounted for."

"That bothers me. Maybe he was paid when we'll presume the plan was first made. But I can't believe anyone would be fool enough to pay even a retainin' fee a whole year ahead. Because even if we hadn't found that match folder from the inn I'd still assume the business was planned by one of the relatives. And they all came in contact with Roche in '36. But no one acted hastily.

"Maybe Roche was determined no connection with them should ever be traced to him. He did go away before the kidnaping, but if he went to meet his boss and make the final arrangements I'll bet he was never near the house in San Francisco except the night the job was done. Or at least he wouldn't risk goin' there to talk to him.

"You've got to admire the way they just set tight and didn't talk or even act—again. They didn't even fall out like thieves usually do. Not for a year, anyway. A year to give that hot money a chance to cool off, I reckon.

"And besides Roche havin' the money, the question of time works out all right. It helps explain the whole timetable of the case too. Because drivin' around by Red Bluff like he had to then would take him about twelve hours. Say he took the boy's body away about midnight of the thirty-first. He'd be back in Bancross by noon and out of the city and more crowded highways by night.

"No one in Bancross would pay any attention to his car or what he had in it. After dark he had time to dispose of the body and still catch the train back to the city when it came through. Figurin', probably, that was safer than another trip in his car. He'd get into the city early in the mornin', the right time to make the phone call they had, telling how to deliver the ransom.

"Basil Dumont paid it early that evenin'. That always seemed to me a funny hour to pick, but now we know it was because Roche wanted to catch the train back to Bancross about seven-thirty. So before they'd even announced the boy was gone, Roche was back in Bancross again with the fifty grand."

"I know it's a great satisfaction to you to have all that settled in your mind," Eleanor said. "But it doesn't really get you anywhere. Besides, you admit Roche seems to have killed himself."

"'Appears to.' And I consider that more luck because we can call it suicide to the cor'ner's jury tomorrow. And there's no direct physical evidence he didn't kill himself except the gun used wasn't the one he used to have. But he'd changed his name, had a fairly new car, outfitted himself from head to foot with new clothes and shaved off his mustache. He had enough money without the ransom to go quite a ways.

"It would be a lot safer to try to unload that now. You'd even guess he knew someone—in the East, maybe—who'd help him do it. From what Michael says about him you can't imagine him killing himself through remorse, and the person that hired him wouldn't dare squeal on him. The authorities never even knew he existed till you ran into him, and even after that they still didn't manage to pick him up."

"But if he was ready to clear out and there was nothing to prevent his doing it, why did he come up here?" Valerie said.

"To dig up his money. And he was tanned enough that after he shaved off his mustache he needed to hide out for a few days till his face was all one color."

"Suicides usually leave notes. And if he'd killed himself you'd think he would have left one saying where the boy's body would be found—"

"Whereas the last thing in the world he'd want so long as he intended to go on livin' was for that body to be found," Rocky said.

"But someone does want it discovered," Michael pointed out. "Which is probably as good a motive for Roche's death as any. You find him dead and the ransom with him, and you immediately begin looking for the child's body. Roche, alive, would never have said where it was and someone is becoming impatient to prove the boy is dead so that the estate can be settled."

"Yeah, a year's a long time to be patient. Well, about the Parnell woman—I know Sullivan said she apparently hadn't collected blackmail—"

"I'm sure she hadn't," Valerie said. "I've thought about her a lot lately. She was very easily flattered and so anxious to be liked that she'd go out of her way to be obliging. Which only made people despise her a little. My mother and stepsister were always very willing to let her relieve them of all practical worries so that they could give their full attention to their grief."

Her tone of quiet cynicism made Rocky look at her sharply and decide she was grown up after all.

She went on: "Maxine, for instance, was pleasant to such people only when it paid her to be, but Miss Parnell never realized that. And two women had found my stepfather sufficiently charming to be willing to support him. Miss Parnell was quite coquettish toward him until he was really ill. Then she was all the nurse and a very good one. I can easily imagine her thinking, 'These people have been so nice to me: why should I add to their troubles by telling the police something that can't be important?' Though I do think she'd be more apt to protect a man than a woman in that way."

"All right. But how the hell did she discover it was important? When you talked to her she must 've known something about Roche or she wouldn't have sung 'Alouette.' So—"

The door between the kitchen and dining room swung open and Sing Toy thrust his head into the room. "You stop talkee about murder," he said severely. "Is velly late: you got catchee shave, change clothes, get to party. I got washee dish, clean kitchen. You not talkee no more."

"It's only nine," Eleanor said. "And I have heard Mrs. Cochrane's parties are not well started by eleven."

"Go early, not stay too late, catchum sleep," Sing Toy persisted. "Boss got to go to Bancloss velly early. You get dlessed now. And not come home drunk and wake baby." He nodded majestically, terminating the audience.

"That old heathen always knows ever'thing, though I'll admit he never tells any of it," Rocky said. "And we might as well do like he says or he'll just start clearin' away."

"Yes, but take your time. As you said, we must assert ourselves," Eleanor reminded him. "And there's no use in our getting there too early."

CHAPTER 11

When she had pulled her dress over her head and smoothed it down over her hips, Valerie backed over to the chair where Michael had been lounging for the past fifteen minutes.

"What do you think—now?" she said.

"About what?" Michael kissed her bare shoulders, tightened the long black velvet ribbon about her waist and spun her around to face him. "It's to be tied in front, dear, not in back. Why do so many women want large bows waggling over their fannies?"

"To hide them. Or maybe to draw attention to them. And you know what I mean."

"If you're referring to Mr. Allan—what do you think of him?"

"He's very good-looking. But hasn't he peculiar eyes? With his yellow hair he should have your eyes, but his are so light they're almost yellow. And he does appear so even-tempered and amiable that you're inclined not to take him too seriously. As a detective, I mean."

"Which I imagine is exactly what Mr. Allan wants," Michael said dryly. He pulled the black velvet rosette he had made into place. "The affable homespun sleuth who doesn't quite know what it's all about but is going to plod along, doing his duty."

"But of course Mr. Dundas saw through that pose at once?"

"I don't think it's a deliberate pose, impertinence. We got off to a bad start," Michael said candidly. "He was so exasperatingly hearty and unwilted by the heat. Besides, as you know, I dislike being towered over."

Valerie sat down on his knee. "Mr. Allan can't help that."

"But as you once told me, my ego has as many prickles as a cactus. I'll grant you he's even-tempered and his temper was sorely tried," Michael said with a wholly unrepentant grin. "But the joke was equally on me. He waits until he sees his opening and then—touché! Rise up, my love, my fair one, before I get housemaid's knee. I think they must be ready by now."

"Um-m!" Eleanor said, of Valerie's full-skirted dress of white dotted swiss trimmed with narrow black velvet ribbon. "It must be nice to have all of Gisele's to choose from. And of course you would be one of these strange creatures who doesn't care much about clothes. But see, Rocky: I'm right. She looks about sixteen and very wide-eyed—"

"We were debatin' which of you is to work on which Mr. Dumont," Rocky explained.

"And I say Valerie should concentrate on the elder."

"What makes you think he likes 'em young, honey?"

"Oh, it's just that I think Valerie's too near Philip Dumont's age to captivate him. That needs an experienced glamorous older woman like me," Eleanor said modestly.

"Black satin would be more suitable to that role than printed seersucker, don't you think?" Michael said.

"Yes, but I won't swelter, even for a good cause. And you surely didn't tie that rosette yourself, Valerie?" Eleanor said with a dissatisfied look at her own sash. "If you did, I wish you'd do this one over."

"I—I can try—"

"She's a poor liar," Michael said. He sauntered over to Eleanor. "Permítame, señora? As a matter of fact, the pleasure is all mine. This lopsided production of yours"—he untied the sash—"distressed me. And tell your husband that impersonality toward living models is as much a habit of mind with a couturier as an artist."

"As a matter of fact," Rocky said, "I'd forgotten you were one—for quite a while." And having been as unconsciously tactful as Inspector Sullivan had been otherwise, he stood up. "I'd like to know which of that gang was so anxious to get to Pluma Blanca. Come on, let's get going."

Hortense, who disliked Mrs. Cochrane, had insisted it wouldn't be "suitable" for them to accept her invitation. Daniel remarked, glancing toward Phil, that if they behaved "suitably" it would be quite "suitable" for them to attend any public or private function in the hotel.

If they had meant to remain in seclusion they should not have come here. Certainly people knew who they were, and for that very reason they should show the world they were not skulking in their tents like Agamemnon.

"It was Achilles in my schooldays," Jonathan said, lovingly rearranging flies in a leather case. "I'll look in if I'm not too tired tomorrow evening. But there's no reason Hortense should go if she thinks she won't enjoy it."

"I see no reason why we shouldn't all go," Basil said. "After all, in the eyes of the world we are in no way affected by Miss Parnell's death. You'd like to go, wouldn't you, Ariadne?"

"I— Oh yes. Yes, of course," Ariadne said hastily, wondering if he had been issuing a warning or only stating something that was entirely true. "Yes, I'd like to go."

But we'll still be a family party, she thought. The inn was only half filled and mainly with middle-aged married couples. The only two young bachelors were attached to the daughters of another large family party. But she liked to dance with Basil—and Phil—and with Mrs. Cochrane as a catalyzer even the mixed crowd she had commanded to her farewell party might coalesce into friendliness and hilarity.

For the first time in a year Ariadne took some pains with her dressing. The result didn't please her: her face still looked white and thin under her light brown flyaway hair. Her eyes, she considered disgustedly, were too much like her father's—too pale a gray and too prominent. But the effect as a whole was not too bad. "If there were any young men about, they'd dance with me," she thought. "Why not? Won't I inherit a quarter million dollars . . ."

Mrs. Cochrane had taken over a small ball-room, installed a makeshift bar in one corner and a four-piece orchestra from Reno in another. She had also provided balloons, serpentine and paper hats.

Having personally placed a gilt crown on Ariadne's head and a fireman's hat on Phil's, she bade them "run along and have a walloping good time. Young things like you should. Anybody you want to meet, just tell me—if you think an introduction's necessary. It isn't. . . . Well, Slim Powell! You old horse thief!"

She galloped away to greet a man with a weather-beaten brown face, ill at ease in a wrinkled suit, clinging to his broad-brimmed hat.

"This is Slim, folks—the best broncobuster in two states. Slim, come have a drink."

She led the way to the bar, trailing orange chiffon draperies, scattering hospitable diamond-and-platinum gestures to right and left.

"She's nuts, if you ask me," Phil said. "Dance, Spider?"

"Of course. But I think she's grand."

"Well, she does things in a big way." Phil looked approvingly at the bar. "Plenty of champagne—"

"Phil, please don't—don't drink too much. Not just because it's free." Ariadne laughed unconvincingly. "I expect you to dance with me, you know."

"Oh, I can take it or leave it alone. You don't need to worry about me. I like to have you, though."

His arm tightened about her waist. That doesn't mean anything, Ariadne told herself quickly. It's just Phil. And Dr. Monroe is too apt to think he knows his patients better than they know themselves. . . .

"And while I shouldn't have brought it up at the table the other morning, you ought to forget Ted. I don't know that he did help Freddie's kidnaper but you know someone in the house almost had to and he's the most likely one—"

"I did hope we'd forget—everything tonight! I don't know where you got the idea Ted cared anything about me—"

"He did. Why not, considering he was just a high-toned servant and looking out for himself?"

"I had no prospects then. Well, you're unfair to him," Ariadne retorted to Phil's unpleasant grin. "If you think he was willing to see Freddie kidnaped with the idea of marrying me afterward you're—you're crazy! I liked him but I never even thought of being in love with him."

"All right; I just wanted to know," Phil muttered. And as Mrs. Cochrane glittered past again, headed for some unhappy wallflower with an equally unhappy prospective partner in tow: "Jeez, I should think she'd put those rocks in a safe instead of throwing temptation in everyone's way."

"Perhaps they're well insured. Or they may be imitations. Her husband is a diamond broker anyway."

"Dad doesn't think they're imitations. Not what she had on last night when he was talking to her. And he learned something, working for my grandfather, you know. I see you aren't wearing your bracelet tonight. Spider."

"I forgot to put it on. I wanted to show it to Mr. Cochrane. You know he was interested in it when he noticed it at dinner last night. But it's too loose on my wrist—"

"Just as well not to wear it here. If you lost it you'd probably never find it again. Well, here comes Dad," Phil said as the music stopped. "And if I don't do my duty by Hortense I'll hear about it for a week. She didn't want to come—oh no! But of course she wouldn't stay away. I'll be back."

"And you'll—remember? It worries Basil so to have you—"

"Oh, that's it? Just because it worries dear Basil!"

"Oh no, Phil! But he isn't as patient as he used to be, and you know when he does lose his temper—"

"He won't lose it with me. And I could tell you why. Did you notice he seems to have gotten some mail today? One letter anyway. Maybe you think he'd tell you who it was from—"

"It's simply no use trying to be decent to you," Ariadne said, biting her lip. "I wanted to have a good time tonight and you've already spoiled it."

"If you hadn't said you—"

"Your aunt is waiting for you, Phil," Basil said. "Please dance with her at least once. . . . Was he making a nuisance of himself, Ariadne?"

"We got to—to quarreling. We so often do, you know."

"Yes, but you have more influence over him than you realize. And in spite of his pose of being very hardboiled about the—the whole thing, it has affected his nerves. They aren't too—stable. And you can do a great deal for him."

"I would like to. I've always felt," Ariadne said deliberately, "as if he were my younger brother. A rather troublesome one, but most younger brothers are, aren't they?"

"I believe so. I'm—sure Phil is a typical younger brother in that respect."

He smiled, but Basil's smile, nowadays, reminded you of a piece of machinery badly in need of a thorough overhauling. And that habit of hesitating, searching for the proper word, was growing on him.

"I hope he hasn't spoiled this for you, Ariadne. I'd thought you already looked better. As if you might have slept better here—"

"I slept wonderfully last night and well enough the first night we were here. But I'm afraid the Sunday quiet was too much for you, Basil. Did you take a walk or were you only looking for cigarettes?"

"Looking— I'm afraid I don't know what you mean."

"Oh, wasn't it you who went outside Sunday night? I thought I recognized your walk. The hall isn't carpeted, you know."

"Why no, Ariadne, I wasn't out of my room all night."

He was lying, Ariadne thought, though she couldn't see why he should bother to. And this afternoon he had been reading a letter, frowning over it but looking as if he were a little amused by it. When she came up behind him he had started nervously and thrust the folded violet-colored page quickly into his pocket.

"I see Jonathan is here after all," she said.

"Jon— Oh—oh yes. Arthur Barnhart, who wrote *Sash and Saber,* is here. His field is Civil War history but Jonathan wanted to meet him. Wait: I'll take you by them—"

Jonathan, his glasses and his nose bedewed with perspiration and enthusiasm, sat astride one of the chairs near the door, facing a big round-shouldered man with a square, bluish-black jaw.

". . . never satisfactorily explained either," Barnhart was saying. "At least, not to Jackson's admirers. He certainly was not well—"

"'Fever and a general feeling of debility,' he said," Jonathan contributed. "He should have allowed himself more time for the march from the valley. Lee was willing to allow him more. Lee was always beautifully reasonable. Whereas Charles Lee—too bad to speak of him and Robert Edward in the same breath, isn't it?—was only consistently inconsistent. For years he has been called a traitor but—"

Basil guided Ariadne back to the center of the floor, smiling again; his old boyish grin. "Depend on Jonathan. If you began to discuss the culture of roses with him, he'd still manage to lead you to the strange conduct of Charles Lee at the battle of Monmouth."

"And whether or not Washington really did swear at him. Jonathan says not but I'd rather believe Washington did—"

She stopped because Basil wasn't listening to her. The guarded look was on his face once more while he watched Mrs. Cochrane hilariously take four new arrivals to her heart. The man in front was tall and blond. Ariadne heard his drawled answer to Mrs. Cochrane's greeting:

"Yes, we fin'lly got here, Suzy. Came to keep an eye on your jewl'ry store and brought Mr. and Mrs. Dundas with us."

"That," Basil said, "is the sheriff of the county. And a man named Dundas was to testify at the inquest on Edith Parnell. I—will you excuse me, Ariadne? I should—should look for—for Phil. . . ."

CHAPTER 12

There were stags after all. "Mrs. Cochrane," as her admiring husband said, "always thinks of everything," and she was completely democratic. Ariadne danced with a railroad doctor from the nearby town of Merton, a barnstorming aviator from Reno and a forest ranger. The floor was crowded, all the chairs around it filled, and a number of men who were not dancing had their elbows permanently imbedded on the bar.

Phil had been there once, just after the Allans and Dundases arrived. He was gone now; Ariadne had not seen him for some time. Hortense, sitting out by a pink matron who rattled on interminably regarding "Betty and Junior," fidgeted in her chair and twisted about, striving for a better view of the porches outside.

People strolled out there to smoke or for the fresh air no longer obtainable inside. Mr. Barnhart and Jonathan had gone out some time ago.

Standing for a minute by a window, Ariadne heard
him saying:

"The evidence points to sunstroke. It does
strange things to one's mental processes. Lafayette was exhausted and Hamilton seemed slightly
unbalanced. And Sir Henry Clinton said . . ."

Ariadne smiled wanly. Jonathan at least was
enjoying himself on Monmouth's battlefield. For
that matter, her father wasn't doing badly. He was
dancing with the redheaded Mrs. Allan and, from
his look of trouble bravely borne, telling her all
about himself. Mr. Allan apparently did not care
to dance. He must be outside or talking to Mrs.
Cochrane. . . .

But here was Mrs. Cochrane and the slight dark
man with the peculiar white streak in his black
hair. "Be a good child and dance with Mr. Dundas. He doesn't want to drag me around the floor
even if he is polite enough to ask me, so I'm offer-
ing you as a substitute."

He was, as she had suspected from watching
him with his wife, an extraordinarily good dancer.
He didn't try to make talk but Ariadne felt uneasily that he was studying her whenever she wasn't
looking at him. She said finally:

"You're—you're staying in Brookdale, aren't
you? Have you been there long?"

"Only long enough to wash off the dust and get ready to come here. We'd intended leaving the city last Saturday but we were—we were unavoidably delayed."

"By an inquest?" Ariadne said. He looked at her sharply and then smiled.

"Yes. Since you don't pretend not to know that, I won't pretend not to know who you are. And I thought perhaps you'd rather I didn't mention Edith Parnell."

"N-no. It does seem that someone should regret her death. Oh, not regret exactly, but—"

"Mourn for her? 'In quiet she reposes; Ah, would that I did so too!'"

Ariadne flushed. "That was what I was thinking but you make it sound—silly."

"I'm sorry," he said quickly. "I see too much of people who think it's clever to talk like that. And unfortunately my one meeting with Miss Parnell led me to think her a rather tiresome person. I imagine you did too, or you wouldn't feel guilty because you can't really regret her death."

"I'm afraid that's so. She was very good to me. She wasn't one of these impersonal nurses. She did far more than she had to. But—and I'm not clever myself—she wasn't a very stimulating companion. She was—well, the sort of person you showed the family photograph album to."

"In that case," Mr. Dundas suggested, smiling again, "she must have been too polite to protest."

"Oh, she would be. But something like that would entertain her; she'd feel grateful to you for making an effort to do so and would be a very appreciative audience. And then you wouldn't have to try to make talk or listen to her talk. But if you only met her once, why did you have to testify at the inquest? Unless you and your wife were the 'friends' the newspapers spoke of who saw her the night she was killed?"

"We were and it's customary to call such witnesses. But we were not friends of hers. My wife's stepfather died of pneumonia and Miss Parnell was his nurse. But Valerie would not have recognized her if she hadn't spoken first. It seems she had bleached her hair since Valerie last saw her."

"I know. She did that after she left us and it was a shock to me when I saw her again. She wasn't really gray: her hair was just sort of drab. She had some rather—gaudy new clothes too. But—didn't she say anything that helped the police when you told them about it? I shouldn't keep harping on the subject but—"

"Why not? But she simply talked over old times with Valerie. She'd been drinking but she'd only achieved a state of intense refinement. We took her home and that was the end of it. Except that

I think we would have felt we wanted to get out of the city then even if we hadn't already planned to. We've been trying for a long time to visit the Allans. We considered spending one week here but —well, what does one do here aside from paying an astounding price to breathe the mountain air?"

Ariadne laughed. "I wonder sometimes. Well, the men fish. But as Mr. Armstrong says, the trout don't bite any better because you're staying at Pluma Blanca instead of a tourist camp."

"I've always understood trout are singularly democratic. And while I admit I never have the slightest desire to 'rough it,' I find pseudo-rusticity at much more than Palace Hotel prices a trifle irritating."

"It's amusing when you stop to think of it. I do like really to camp out, and Mr. Armstrong and Mr. Dumont have been known to 'rough it.' But I've noticed that when they're done fishing they don't object to a very good dinner here instead of bacon, beans and trout over a campfire."

"Or to a Simmons Beauty Rest instead of a bed of pine boughs?"

"And a tub instead of a very cold mountain stream. My father," Ariadne said, "is at least quite honest about it. He doesn't like to fish and he does like to be comfortable."

"He likes to come here?"

"Oh, we feel more or less at home here. You know how it is: you talk of going to some new place but always decide not to risk it."

"And how do you pass the time?" Mr. Dundas asked politely.

"I'm afraid Miss Dumont and I don't get our money's worth. But at least I'm good at doing nothing while she finds it hard to relax away from home. She's a very good housekeeper," Ariadne added hastily. "Which I never would be. My system would be to strip the house periodically instead of hoarding things that 'might be useful.' Then there'd be so much less house to keep. . . . I suppose I'll take up riding again, though there's no place to ride to here. And Phil Dumont is an amateur photographer."

"There seems to be an ever-increasing number of them. You can't walk about the city without running into at least half a dozen camera hounds trailing possible shots."

"Oh, but Phil is no longer a mere snapshooter," Ariadne laughed. "He takes only two pictures where most people would snap two rolls. And that involves a good deal of squinting and trying after what he calls 'angles.' He almost stands on his head sometimes. It's a very serious business. And he has no use for anything he took before he got the camera he has now, just before Freddie— That is, even as souvenirs. That's the main value of a snapshot to me, and Phil used to take very good ones of people, though he always leaned toward the 'quaint' even then. However, he got rid of his boyish efforts."

"Not wanting to be reminded of his guilty past?" Mr. Dundas said perfunctorily. "I think there is going to be an intermission. Would you like to go outside?"

Jonathan was still perched on the porch railing but it was Mr. Allan who was talking to Mr. Barnhart now. "I'm glad to hear you're havin' such a good season at Slacktown."

"The murders we had up there two years ago put the place on the map," Mr. Barnhart said dryly. "But I understand you've had an unexciting life for some time."

"A few guys still fall off trains and a hobo breaks into a groc'ry store now and then. Or a fellow stops to tell me he's been held up in another county and wants me to do somethin' about it."

"I suppose you assured him that steps would be taken?"

"Oh sure, the usual"—the drawling voice did not quite stop but it changed from lazy tolerance to something like disgust with the next word— "line. We all make mistakes sometimes and can't be in two places at once. Mr. Armstrong and Mr. Barnhart—Mr. Dundas. And I reckon this is Miss Holaday?"

"You've been lucky, Spider." Jonathan smiled at Ariadne. "You haven't had to dance with me. But for once I envy Daniel. He's been dancing with Mrs. Allan and Mrs. Dundas and what more could man ask?"

"In that case I'm entitled to dance with his daughter," Mr. Allan said. "If you aren't too tired? They seem to be tunin' up again."

He also seemed disinclined to talk unless she wished to, but Ariadne did not feel he was watching her as Mr. Dundas had. She suspected he was not thinking of her at all. What had he meant by saying, "We all make mistakes sometimes and can't be in two places at once"? A fellow had complained of being held up in another county . . .

They were near one of the doors now and she found herself looking at Phil. He was very thoroughly drunk. He threw out a thin arm, tapped Mr. Allan on the shoulder and seized her wrist.

"Thought you wanted to dance with me? Jus' giving me the run-around again, hunh?"

"You don't want to dance with him, do you?" Mr. Allan said calmly. "No? Then if you'll excuse me . . ."

His large capable hand settled on Phil's coat collar. "The lady," he said softly, "don't want to be annoyed. Shh!"

His other hand went over Phil's mouth and a knee in his back shunted him out the door. Ariadne's face burned red though it was so quietly done that only the people nearest them knew what had happened. But Phil couldn't be left to Mr. Allan.

She caught up her ruffled yellow skirt and ran after them. Mr. Allan had marched Phil away into a clump of trees off the main driveway and was listening placidly to what he had to say, though most of his remarks verged on the unprintable. When Phil was interrupted by a fit of hiccoughing he said:

"How'd you like to get tossed in the swimmin' pool? A little cold water— Oh, Miss Holaday! Why don't you let me handle this?"

"You shouldn't have to."

"I've had plenty of experience with plain an' fancy drunks, ma'am. He'll have to sleep it off. If you'll tell me where to take him—"

"Not goin' to bed," Phil said loudly. "You keep your nose out of this. Who're you—" He stopped, squinting. "Why, goddamned if it isn't the sh-sher'ff. Look, Spider. That's a joke. I guess I could

make his eyes pop out if I wanted to. Give a hick
sher'ff the lowdown—"

"On how you swiped a couple of bottles from
the bar an' sneaked off with 'em?" Mr. Allan said
mildly.

"Hah! Lissen to him. He don't hear about things
up here. Don' know about Freddie. Snivelin' little
brat, just waitin' to turn us all out—"

"Oh, Phil, please! Won't you go to bed?" Ariadne burst into hysterical tears and Phil blinked
at her owlishly.

"Cry, baby, cry! She don't want me to talk.
Might say too much about my old man. Ques'ion
is, ish my ol' man her ol' man or is— Never min'.
Likes Jon'than too. Likes ever'body but me. I know
too much. I go out late. Get aroun' an' see thingsh
but don' tell all I s—see—"

Basil had come up to them so quietly that they
hardly heard him before he caught Phil by the
shoulders and shook him until his head wabbled
like an apple on a string.

"Go to bed before you make any more of a fool
of yourself! Ariadne, don't cry! You're tired—"

"Sc-scared," Phil said thickly. "Ask her why.
Ask her why she's c-cryin'. No: she won't talk.
Don't dare to—"

Basil hit him, one short thudding blow in the
jaw, and held him up as his body went limp. "Kind
of a Spartan father, aren't you?" Mr. Allan drawled.

Basil's eyes, as always when he was angry, were blank. "We won't trouble you any longer. I can manage by myself."

"Her too? I think I'd better stick aroun'. Look, Miss Holaday, you can't go back inside if you don't quit cryin'."

His voice suddenly lacked assurance. He'd rather deal with Phil or a dozen like him than with one hysterical woman, Ariadne thought. This seemed so very funny that she had to lean against a tree trunk to keep from being shaken to pieces by her laughter.

"Oh, good Lord! Look, Miss Holaday—you've got to stop. It may be better to laugh than cry but I don't see why—"

"Don't shout at her," a woman's voice said. It was a beautifully matter-of-fact voice and Mrs. Allan's shoulder a friendly one to cry on. "I couldn't help hearing the—disturbance."

"She's—she's tired and she hasn't been—been well," Basil stammered. "And—this has upset her."

"I don't want to cry! It's just crying itself!"

"Then don't try to stop and you will," Mrs. Allan said calmly. "Let's walk up to your room. And why don't you let Rocky help you, Mr. Dumont? It certainly would be better to make it look as if he were walking between you than for either of you to carry him."

A boardwalk with electric lights strung at intervals above it led from the hotel to a half circle of log chalets facing a slope of lawn broken by tall pines scorning striped lounging chairs and swings. Their chalet was the second along the walk. There were four upstairs bedrooms, three more downstairs and a narrow living room across the front of the house.

Phil was on the second floor with Daniel and Hortense, but Basil nodded toward the door nearest the stairway. "In here, please, where I can look after him during the night. Mr. Armstrong and I took downstairs rooms by request since we're the fishermen and the others don't care to be waked at sunrise. . . ."

The bedroom door closed after him and Rocky. Ariadne had reached the stage where she wiped her eyes and laughed shakily.

"I chose the ground floor, too, though not by request," she said. "This way— I'd like to wash my face since I'm here."

She went over to the washstand in one corner of the room. Mrs. Allan stood looking thoughtfully at a photograph of Gloria on the bureau.

"I don't believe I ever saw that picture of your sister."

"They've never printed it. The ones in the newspapers always make her look like a blonde show girl. Or gold digger, and she wasn't," Ariadne said bitterly, sitting down on the bed. "She was the grandest person I ever knew except maybe Frederick. He was a little like Mrs. Cochrane. Some people laughed at him but he didn't care: he wouldn't pretend to be what he wasn't. And Gloria really did love him. She— Oh, good Lord! That's Hortense in the hall!"

She flung herself across the bed. "I took this bedroom to get away from her—and Father. They keep fussing about my health—or he does. Hortense just lectures me: she says if I'll just make an effort and stop brooding I'll be all right, and Father wants me to drink eggnogs and I hate eggnogs—"

"I won't let Miss Dumont come in here," Mrs. Allan promised. She glanced at Ariadne's clenched hands. "Do you happen to have any phenobarbital? It wouldn't hurt you to take some. I used to be a nurse, you see. That's why I'm so bossy."

"There's some in that top bureau drawer. I'll get it."

"You lie still." Mrs. Allan opened the drawer and laughed. "I'm glad to see someone besides me doesn't keep her bureau drawers in order."

"Why, what do you mean?" Ariadne got up hastily. "I haven't been here long enough to mess them up—"

"No?" Mrs. Allan stood aside. "Nevertheless, this looks as if it had been stirred up with a stick."

The handkerchiefs that should have been in a neat pile were strewn over the drawer along with powder from an open box, sheets of Kleenex, new and used powder puffs and an assortment of aspirin and other tablets. Ariadne picked up one of the handkerchiefs and then let it fall back into the drawer.

"They were looking for my bracelet; the one Gloria gave me. It was stuck in among the handkerchiefs. So of course they found it."

CHAPTER 13

Philip Dumont groaned and muttered incoherently. He opened his eyes, looked at his father with bewildered resentment, turned his face into the pillow and went to sleep.

"He'll be all right now," Basil Dumont said, pulling off his son's shoes. "It was good of you to help me."

"Oh, it was a pleasure," Rocky said ironically. "But if you hadn't turned up I might not have known how to—handle him."

He turned toward the door and dodged hastily, just managing to avoid collision with the woman who had been pointed out to him as Hortense Dumont. She very ostentatiously presented a thin back for his inspection and addressed Basil.

"Why didn't you call me instead of asking help from a stranger? Phil would have listened to me—"

"I doubt it. Mr. Allan didn't ask to be dragged into this. He was dancing with Ariadne and Mr. Cochrane told me that Phil—"

"I saw the whole thing. If Ariadne had handled him properly he wouldn't have made any trouble. Why shouldn't she dance with him? By the time I got across the dance floor you'd disappeared. Of course Jonathan wasn't around and Daniel is making a fool of himself dancing with women young enough to be his daughters—"

"Don't you think, Hortense, that speaking so frankly before a stranger is more unsuitable than asking his help?"

Hortense flushed unbecomingly and fingered her pearls. "Phil is just like my own child, Mr. Allan. If he wasn't so high-strung he wouldn't do things like this." She tiptoed over to the bed and laid her hand on Phil's forehead. "Poor, poor boy—"

"For God's sake, Hortense! What good does it do for me to be harsh with him when you . . . Please go back to the dance. I'll stay here but we shouldn't all leave early."

"Your boy's by no means the only one that's got plastered tonight," Rocky observed. "And— Oh, hello, honey. Is Miss Holaday feelin' better now?"

"No," Eleanor said flatly. "Someone's turned a bureau drawer inside out and taken a very valuable bracelet."

"The one Gloria gave her? There, I said she wasn't fit to be trusted with valuable property,"

Hortense said. "That was worth thousands of dollars."

Jonathan Armstrong, coming up behind Eleanor as she stood in the doorway, removed his pipe from his mouth and whistled. "Perhaps she's mislaid it. She did once before."

"No, it's a plain case of theft."

"I hate for her to lose it," Basil said slowly. "But I wish it could be handled quietly."

"Suzy Cochrane'd have a fit if I searched her guests," Rocky said. "She'd rather pay you the price of the bracelet."

"It's nobody's fault but Ariadne's and we certainly aren't going to make a fuss about it," Hortense said. "If we speak to the manager and he keeps his eyes open he'll probably find the servant who took it."

"Well, I reckon I'd better talk to Miss Holaday," Rocky decided. "Then I'll see Mower—"

"You go with him, Basil." Hortense sat down in a chair close to the bed. "I'll stay here and watch Phil."

Rocky, with a final glance at her face as she sat gazing down at the boy, thought: Now what does that look remind me of? and followed Eleanor down the hall to Ariadne's bedroom. He was relieved to find her quite calm now and no more anxious than the others to interrupt Mrs. Cochrane's party.

"Of course I shouldn't have brought the bracelet up here. I hide it at home, but I've lots of
hiding places in my bedroom there and this one is
rather bare."

"One of the maids may've seen it, though they
don't gen'rally meddle with things in a bureau,"
Rocky said.

"Oh, it was there when I left my room after I'd
dressed tonight. I waited for the others out on the
porch and no maid came in here before we left.
One turned the beds down while I was dressing.
But I wore the bracelet at dinner last night and
Mr. Cochrane said, when we were out on the porch
at the hotel afterwards, that he'd like to examine
it sometime. He speaks quite loudly, you know, so
he did draw people's attention to it."

"And things are disorganized here tonight,"
Basil said.

"Yes, they are," Rocky agreed. "It'd always be
safer to take it at night, but I reckon ord'narily
you'd come back here fairly early after dinner?"

"We did until tonight. And last night I had
my purse under my pillow and the bracelet in it,"
Ariadne said. "It's too large for me and I slipped
it off and into my purse when we were walking
back from the hotel last night. So you see no one
could get it then and I didn't leave the chalet at
all today. I had to alter my dress and I thought I'd

better rest this afternoon. I didn't want to bother with a purse tonight so I put what money I had in with my stockings—and it's still there—and the bracelet under my handkerchiefs. I should have taken it all to the hotel safe but it wasn't so valuable that—"

"Not valuable? Frederick told me he paid something like forty thousand dollars for it," Jonathan said.

"Oh, Jonathan—no!"

"Oh, Spider—yes! My dear girl, there are four large diamonds in it besides the sapphires—"

"I didn't suppose they were good ones. Gloria didn't tell me. She—she just said: 'H-here's something to remind you of me and Frederick.' He'd given her so much jewelry I thought this was one of the inexpensive pieces—"

"Frederick didn't buy inexpensive things. That one was distressingly gaudy but not cheap." Jonathan drew reflectively on his pipe. "I left some money in my room, too, but it wasn't taken. What about fingerprints, Allan?"

"Eleanor's, Miss Holaday's and a lot of others would be on the doorknob. And probably the bureau too. You try not to touch the bureau any more 'n you have to, Miss Holaday. I'll get down here tomorrow and go over it, and meanwhile I'll talk to Mower and get him to check on the servants."

The glacial blonde who until now had been no-
table only for an unbelievable refinement of manner could be heard declaring passionately that she
"jus' mus' have a penguin." She clutched the coat
lapels of the stout gentleman who for this week
had made her free of his bed, his board and his
name. "Jus' gotta have a penguin, Papa. Can I have
a penguim? Hunh? He can live in the bathtub, see?
An' I will get a li'le icesh bag an' put icesh in it
an' put it on his head an' take him out walkin'.
Don' wanna dog; gotta have a pemguim—"

"Attend to it firs' thing in the mornin'," Papa
said firmly. She lowered her head to his shirt front
and spilled grateful tears down it while at the bar
a fervent brunette pinned pretzels in her hair and
assured an encouraging audience that she was prepared to do a sword dance—if someone would
find a sword. Or if there were no swords, butcher
knives would do.

The musicians had disappeared and Mrs. Cochrane recommended the buffet supper with a tire-
lessness deserving of better results. A barbershop
quartette cheered her and swung into "For She's a
Jolly Good Fellow." A group of parlor athletes in-
vited her to pick up a handkerchief from the floor
with her teeth, standing on one foot with hands
outstretched. Or, alternatively, to cross her legs

and walk on her knees. "I'm too fat for that," said Suzy Cochrane. "But I'll show you one. . . . Hi there, Rocky! You ought to get in on this. Didn't you used to tear telephone books in two?"

"I'm gettin' old and feeble, Suzy. Have you seen Mr. and Mrs. Dundas lately?"

"They're outside. Bring 'em in to supper. Now you—" She singled out the young man who could cross his eyes and wriggle his ears at the same time. "You give me your hand. I won't hurt you."

Rocky grinned, walking away. Suzy had started life in a Nevada mining camp and she knew a trick or two. Her partner in this one would probably sail through the air with the greatest of ease and land on the floor in a manner far from graceful.

He found Michael and Valerie sitting on a bench under a pine tree, smoking. "Well?" Michael said, standing up.

"It isn't. I wanted to pull out of here right away."

"Why?" Valerie asked. "And where did you disappear to almost as soon as we arrived?"

"Oh, talkin' to Mower and the servants. This gang came up on the train so they've got no car here. But they've all been here before and know the setup. A lot of people just leave their cars outside if they're out late and don't want to ring the bell to get the garage attendant up after midnight. There's a young fellow named Swanson who's sparkin' a girl here so they've been getting in late.

"He left his roadster outside Sunday night—with the keys in it. Love's like that. He told the garageman he figured someone borrowed it later that night because the gas was almost gone Monday morning. I got a look at the car and the fenders are plenty scratched, though Swanson hadn't mentioned that to the garageman, and he's been along brushy roads himself. And of course the car's been cleaned up since then and a lot of different people have driven it."

"I suppose," Michael said, "that if there hadn't been a car handy on Sunday night the trip to Bancross would have been postponed until there was."

"I don't imagine they'd tried to set any definite time for meeting—if they'd agreed to meet in Bancross. Well, I examined their rooms in the chalet and didn't find anything suspicious. Of course there's fresh matches put in the rooms every day. No one saw the car bein' driven out or anyone sneakin' out or into the Dumont chalet. So the trip must 've been made after one o'clock or later. With no traffic on the roads and drivin' fast, you can make it to Bancross in three quarters of an hour. I was goin' to prove that if this other hadn't come up."

"What other?" Valerie said.

"Did you notice I had a little set-to with Phil Dumont?"

"Oh yes. Everyone has been discussing that."

"Well, Ariadne had hysterics and Eleanor just happened along—like she does. She took her over to her room and discovered someone's stolen a very valuable bracelet from her. So I've got to take steps. Mower will pass out. If you opened up his heart you'd find 'No Undesirable Publicity' on it."

"How valuable was the bracelet?" Michael said.

"Worth about forty grand. She said she didn't know it was. Armstrong said she'd mislaid it once. She wore it at dinner last night and Cochrane was loudly int'rested in it. So all the hired help and a lot of guests had their attention drawn to it. Hell! I haven't got time to waste on that kind of thing."

"You haven't said why you wanted to go back to Bancross tonight," Valerie reminded him. "Not just to prove you can do it in three quarters of an hour—"

"I was goin' to look into that little matter of some groc'ries being taken from Adam Towne's store."

"But why should that be more important than—"

"If you don't mind," Michael said abruptly, "could we talk to Cochrane before you see Mower?"

"Sure. But why? I'm going to ask him who-all was around last night—" Michael shook his head. "That's not what you have in mind? All right, do it your own way. Let's go find him. . . .

"You wait out here," he suggested when they had reached the hotel. "I'll take Valerie in to Eleanor and bring Cochrane out."

The dance floor was almost deserted and Mr. and Mrs. Cochrane were herding a few stragglers toward the supper room. Cochrane, at Rocky's whispered request, nodded and went along with him to where Michael was leaning against a porch pillar.

"Mr. Dundas has an idea he wants you to confirm and I'll be mighty grateful if you'll tell him what—what you think."

"Did you suspect that bracelet of Miss Holaday's was an imitation?" Michael asked.

Cochrane, a small man with a large head and larger voice, fingered his lower lip reflectively. "I don't see how you guessed that but I did. I'm naturally curious about such things and I knew that if those stones were genuine it must be a very valuable piece of jewelry. That little girl didn't strike me as the sort who'd wear anything so ornate if the stones were simply glass—"

"As it happens, she doesn't seem to have thought about that," Rocky said. "She valued it just because her sister gave it to her. And only wore it for that reason, I imagine."

"Oh, I see. Well, I'm fairly certain those aren't genuine diamonds and sapphires. There are so many smaller stones besides I couldn't get a really good look at the larger ones."

"The entire family was present when you spoke about the bracelet?" Michael said.

"Yes. Besides a lot of other people near them. Why?"

"The bracelet has been mislaid," Michael said. "Mr. Allan was wondering what measures to take for its recovery."

"So? I wouldn't worry about it, Rocky. Miss Holaday wouldn't be the first woman who was wearing a copy she thought was an original. She might as well be ignorant and happy. I won't talk. Only I'd like to know what made you think of that, Mr. Dundas?"

"Oh—my mother collected jewelry—as an investment. And while she always knew when she was wearing copies the men who had given her the originals did not. Or that they had perhaps been converted into cash."

Cochrane stared at him curiously. "Well, I've known that to happen too."

"Did you also happen to know Dumont's first father-in-law?"

"Burris?" Cochrane snorted. "I spoke to him when we met. Damned rascal. They said he'd buy stones from you without asking too many inconvenient questions if he knew you. There were even people who suggested he engineered a holdup or two to collect insurance on what was stolen. And by the way! There was a fellow named Hogue who worked for him who's an artist along his line. That is, he could copy anything you took to him. About the only one in the city I know of who could. He has his own shop since Burris died. And in this day of Woolworth and costume jewelry, who knows if the diamonds or sapphires in a bracelet are real?"

"And what do you think of Miss Dumont's pearls?" Michael asked. "Or have you noticed them?"

"I always notice pearls and I took a good look at those inside the hotel. I'd say they were fairly good ones. Worth about ten thousand or so—perhaps. I might be mistaken: I didn't really examine them. Well, I'd better be getting back to Suzy. And don't worry about me talking. I won't."

"Nice guy," Rocky said. "Well, you do have inspirations."

"Not entirely inspiration. What I said about my mother was true. But Sullivan's opinion of Burris was about the same as Cochrane's, though he didn't mention Hogue. And another man who used to work for Burris doesn't speak highly of him either. I think he—Wales—may have known Hogue too."

"Yeah? Well, any more suggestions?"

"Only that you ask Miss Holaday when it was that she mislaid that bracelet before and how long it was before she did find it."

"I get you. I'm sorry for her—but I'm takin' the gloves off now."

CHAPTER 14

Most of the guests had already eaten and swarmed on to new fields. Mrs. Cochrane was still so busy diffusing hospitality that Eleanor and Valerie escaped from her table to one where no one else was sitting.

"We might keep places for our wandering boys tonight," Eleanor said, consuming scrambled eggs. "And again, we might not. At least you've had the pleasure of dancing with your own husband more than once—and dancing with him is a pleasure. But what on earth has put it into Rocky's head to go back to Bancross again tonight?"

"You ask him and see if you get any more answer— Oh, Lord! Here comes God's gift to women again," Valerie muttered disrespectfully. "In fact the whole gang."

"I wanted to express my appreciation for your kindness toward my little girl, Mrs. Allan," Daniel Holaday said. "May we sit down? Thank you.

I'm afraid she's not too well and gives way to her feelings rather easily."

"I'd say she repressed them too much, if anything," Eleanor said brusquely. "And that she acted very sensibly."

"As a mere man I must defer to a woman's judgment. But I'm afraid not everyone would make allowances for her as you are doing. She is rather inclined to make mountains out of molehills—"

Valerie smiled at Ariadne. "I've never been able to understand why parents are privileged to make impertinent remarks about their children, always with the excuse that they have their best interests at heart," she said.

Daniel glanced uncertainly toward Eleanor as if he felt these outrageous sentiments should rightly have come from her and not anyone who looked as young and ingenuous as Valerie. Then: "When you are older and have had more experience—" he began.

"I've had plenty of experience," Valerie said coolly. "My maiden name was Sheridan, if that means anything to you? I see it does." She turned to Ariadne again. "Some of us are lucky enough to learn before we're very old that people don't often change. There's no use breaking your heart hoping they will or trying to make them over yourself.

You'd better take them as they are. Take them or leave them alone, and it's usually wisest to leave them alone."

"I never heard such nonsense," Hortense said feebly. She had not been allowed to be self-sacrificing since Jonathan had promised to keep an eye on Philip. "I'm sure it would be a queer world if we didn't do our duty by those nearest and dearest to us. And I certainly can't understand you, Mrs. Dundas. Talking like you do about—about such things."

"Some of us embrace martyrdom," Eleanor said, looking at Daniel. "And others of us evade it—"

She stopped as Rocky and Michael came up to the table, thinking, Oh dear! and he told us not to antagonize them. And then decided, It doesn't matter after all, seeing Rocky survey the group with a too affable smile.

"Miss Holaday, when was it you mislaid that bracelet of yours before? 'Mislaid' was Mr. Armstrong's word—"

"It was mine too," Ariadne said steadily. "It wasn't where I thought I'd put it, but two or three days later I came across it in a drawer where I thought I'd looked two or three times. As to the time, it was the last of March: Easter vacation. I wouldn't have been home otherwise."

"You took the bracelet to school with you?"

"Yes. It was—suggested I leave it at home but it was never mislaid—at Mills."

"And you haven't had a jeweler look at it since it was mislaid? No? Well then—"

"Really, Mr. Allan, while we want to co-operate in every way, I can't see—"

"If you can't, you'll be happier if you don't, Mr. Holaday. And you don't need to bother tryin' not to touch the bureau, Miss Holaday. There won't be any fingerprints but yours and my wife's on it. And I'm sure you-all will agree there's no use me wastin' my valuable time making any more inquiries about the bracelet."

"That would be like looking for a needle in a haystack. Least said, soonest mended. We don't want a fuss and experience is the best teacher," Daniel said nobly. "Ariadne won't be so careless again."

"No, I don't imagine she will," Rocky drawled. "If you girls are through eating, let's get started to Bancross."

"Bancross?" Eleanor repeated. "Must we?"

"Oh, I reckon we'd better," Rocky said carelessly. "You don't mind, do you?"

He spoke to Eleanor but he was watching Basil Dumont. For Michael, looking inexpressibly bored, was humming "Alouette" and Dumont's face was suddenly the color of putty.

"And so where are we?" Rocky said, clearing a dry throat.

"Just past Brookdale, proceeding to Bancross," Eleanor answered. "And if your murderer drove as you do, he must also have suicidal tendencies."

"He prob'ly drove faster because he didn't have two women to explain things to. Or any passengers in the back seat."

"What makes you think we're still here?" Michael said grimly.

"Oh, I kind of sense a disapproving attitude from back there."

"There are more ways of kicking a car around a curve than anyone ever taught you, Mr. Allan."

"Then teach him just one of them," Eleanor begged, clutching the side of the car. "He has lead in his foot—on an accelerator. How is Valerie bearing up?"

"Valerie has a miraculous gift for sleep—except very early in the morning."

Valerie lifted her head from his shoulder. "I was only cat-napping. And it's very interesting that Ariadne's bracelet was probably an imitation—but what of it?"

"Someone in that little family group was responsible for its being made," Eleanor guessed. "And took it before Mr. Cochrane could look at it carefully."

"Yeah, isn't that luck for you? Ariadne'd never have questioned it being the original and then they come up to a place where an expert wants to give it the once-over," Rocky said.

"And you think that's why it wasn't taken before?"

"Honey, why provide an imitation except so she wouldn't know the real one was gone? And when you had, why steal it and maybe have the police called in?"

"It's odd, don't you think, that Miss Holaday didn't report its loss to the police when it was missing before?" Michael said.

"Maybe she just didn't want to be too hasty. But there was no use stealin' the imitation till you had to, to keep someone like Cochrane from spotting it. With the girl in her room most of yesterday there wasn't much chance to grab it. It'd be safer to do it while the dance was goin' on."

"The entire family party was present when we arrived. And you went to their chalet very soon."

"And was there quite a while. Suzy Cochrane says they were only there for two dances before we came. After that Miss Dumont set the same place all evenin' till Phil began to act up. Barnhart says he and Armstrong talked from the time Armstrong got there—"

"Until Armstrong left us after you took Miss Holaday inside. He apologized for having talked Barnhart into a state of coma; said he was going to get his pipe, take a stroll and go to bed."

"His pipe? That's interestin'. Phil Dumont was presumably getting soused. Maybe he danced one of those first two dances with Ariadne. But after that—"

"He was dancing with Miss Dumont when we arrived," Eleanor said. "Mr. Dumont was dancing with Ariadne and my impression is that he danced every dance after that, mostly with various wall-flowers. What do you think, Valerie?"

"I think you're right. Anyway, my trying to fascinate him was so much waste effort. Also I'll alibi Mr. Holaday, what time you can't. At least my mangled feet will. And so you think that bracelet might answer the problem of Roche's living expenses for the last year?"

"Why not?" Rocky said. "Only thing we've found that begins to. Could you get about five grand for a bracelet like that, Michael?"

"Yes. I know a few pawnbrokers. And Dumont did work for his father-in-law. And Cochrane did think Miss Dumont's pearls are fairly valuable."

"So what? You mean she could have pawned them?"

"I suppose so, but I was really only thinking it's odd she should have pearls like that."

"I've had to revise my ideas," Eleanor complained. "I'd been thinking of the entire group as gilded rich, and people like that never seem real to me. I should have remembered that Frederick Armstrong was one of these self-made men, and from what Ariadne said, having money didn't spoil him. You talked most to her, Michael. Did you get any results?"

"Miss Parnell bleached her hair after the kidnaping."

Rocky snorted but: "I see what you're drivin' at," he admitted. "And whose idea was it to come up here?"

"I don't think the girl knows. Perhaps no one does except the person who first suggested they should get away from the city."

"Power of suggestion, you mean? Yes, and some people are pretty suggestible. Besides there bein' nothing at all unusual about them comin' up here. Did she seem suspicious of you?"

"She was doubtful. And I made the mistake of being a trifle flippant regarding the fact that Edith Parnell went unmourned to her grave. That's for your future reference. She's a nice child and unexpectedly free from pretense and the so-called social graces. When I became very frank and communicative"—Rocky snorted again—"she relaxed. We discussed Philip Dumont's mania for photography. But he disposed of what she called his 'boyish' efforts some time ago. He makes a serious business of it now. And while it's probably not important, she did suggest that though they may sometimes give an appearance to the contrary, Armstrong and Dumont do not object to more or less luxurious surroundings."

"I'll bet they don't," Eleanor said. "I've seldom seen anyone I detested more heartily than Daniel Holaday. Did she mention him in connection with a taste for luxury, Michael?"

"She said he admits that he likes to be 'comfortable.'"

"Just like one of these insufferable Persian cats who takes the best chair, must have cream, not milk—and looks at you as if he were doing you a favor to accept favors," Valerie said. "He reminds me of my mother. So, though he's no doubt very glad the boy's out of the way, I do doubt that he risked his own skin to get rid of him."

"I can't see any of 'em as men of action," Rocky said. "But of course Roche was really the active agent. I liked Armstrong but historians are funny sometimes. They take such a long view of things they're apt to think one life more or less don't matter one way or the other."

"That's true," Michael said, "except that they seldom carry their detachment to its logical conclusion and admit their own lives or lifework are also unimportant."

"Well, I think the evening was decidedly worthwhile," Eleanor said. "Philip Dumont's outburst was interesting too."

"Yes, though he was pretty well lit. On the other hand, Dumont certainly didn't waste any time shuttin' him off," Rocky remarked. "Look: what'd Miss Dumont remind me of when she was looking down at Phil Dumont?"

"Lioness guarding her young."

"That's it. Well, they were at least tryin' to act natural and unconcerned, which they wouldn't have had to do if I'd just gone down to tell 'em the ransom has turned up. And it won't hurt them to wonder for a while why we had to come down here tonight and why Michael whistled 'Alouette.'"

"By special request from Mr. Allan. And an unnecessarily theatrical performance, I think," Michael said austerely.

"I thought it was rather effective. However," Eleanor said as they turned onto the old red bridge over the river at Bancross, "the time has certainly come to tell us why we are here instead of home in bed as we should be."

Rocky looked at his watch by the dashboard light. "Not quite three quarters of an hour to where we turn off. . . ."

He turned. Eleanor's teeth nipped her tongue as they lurched in and out of the first chuckhole. "And it's only about an hour and a half from Brookdale to Reno! And a six weeks sojourn there with you paying all expenses and alimony to come—"

"'Oh, it's roundup time in Reno but there ain't no dogies there,'" Michael sang. "'There's lots of pretty ladies with orange-colored hair. Yo-de-lay-de, lay-de, lay-de!'"

"Well, honey, we're here because someone stole some groceries and a shovel from the store. And because I wonder why someone held up a travelin' salesman just for a ride and why a fellow who claims to 've been sniping over on the Yuba River before he came here has got a fresh new sunburn."

Underbrush scraped stiffly against the car's fenders and not far away the river purred contentedly in its bed. Michael's voice, when he spoke, was sad as the wind in pine and willow.

"Mr. Allan, I am groveling."

"I don't know what it's all about," Valerie said. "And Rocky didn't tell us about the traveling salesman. Is it one of those stories?"

Rocky chuckled. "Unh-unh. I didn't tell you because I was too dumb to see it was important. . . . This must be about it."

He took a flashlight from a pocket of the car. "You stay here. I don't want any more noise than's necessary."

"Now," Eleanor said, "you tell us!"

Michael shook his head. "It's his bright thought. Let him tell you."

Eleanor shrugged resignedly and closed her eyes. "I wonder if my baby's all right? Oh, I don't forget him, whatever all the old tabbies in Brookdale think. The next one isn't going to have a sheriff for a father!"

"Doesn't he ever worry?" Valerie asked.

"Rocky? Heavens, no! And I thought he'd be one of these helpful fathers. But it took six months to persuade him babies don't break if you touch them and now he can't understand why it takes them so long to acquire teeth and a vocabulary."

Michael laughed; then: "I think I'll shake several dozen assorted kinks out of my anatomy," he said, opening the car door.

"Me too." Valerie scrambled after him. "Eleanor?"

"N-no. No, I'll just take a nap. . . ."

CHAPTER 15

They walked along the road, their feet making a soft squashing sound in the deep mountain dust. Valerie, trying to hold her long skirt out of it, whispered:

"I don't see how she can sit there so calmly with him off chasing someone—if he is."

"I don't think he's in any danger."

"I know. You'd have gone with him if you had. Just the same, I couldn't stand it. I'm glad Roche is dead because now you can never try to catch up with him."

Michael grinned. "Are you suggesting I'm inclined to be a trifle vindictive?"

"Oh no. Just that you and a grudge resemble a hen setting on one precious egg. And while I haven't mentioned it, my nerves were permanently shattered by the late incident at the Trilby Hotel. Also I behaved very well," Valerie said aggrievedly, "and I've received no credit for it."

"Your self-control was truly remarkable, my dear."

Valerie looked at him suspiciously. "I was speaking of my self-control during your convalescence, not of the way I conducted myself while Birdie was trying to get a doctor. But you were supposed to be unconscious."

"I could hear before my tongue would work. I gathered that when you had tracked down my murderer you would demand a grave both wide and deep with tombstones at your head and feet—"

"This," Valerie said coldly, "is another time when flippancy is not appreciated. . . . No, I don't want to be kissed. I'm—I'm not amused."

"Oh, but you will be, darling, if you'll only abandon yourself to the moment and let nature take its course."

"Michael!" Valerie laughed helplessly and yielded to his arms and lips. "I might as well remember what I couldn't help saying to Ariadne Holaday and not try to change you—"

"You two don't need to whisper," Rocky said from the darkness. "He's gone. He did some cooking: remains of sev'ral fires and a lot of tin cans. He hadn't any sluice box on the stream so he wasn't mining and I guess the partner he spoke of never existed except in his mind."

He raised his voice. "Eleanor! Turn on the lights and drive the car down this way. I'll tell you where to stop."

It was, he remarked as they walked in front of the car's lights toward the cabin, one of the warmest nights he'd ever seen in the mountains. Expecting it would be was one reason he'd told Al Sully to put a padlock on the cabin door and then keep guard outside.

Another reason for the padlock was evident without his stating it when he turned his flashlight on his deputy. Mr. Sully lay on his back on a blanket, gun and torch by his side, mouth open and a small fire siren apparently concealed in his throat.

"See? I cert'nly inherited two of the sleepin'est deputies one sheriff ever handed over to another."

"'"Isn't he a lovely sight?" said Tweedledum.'"

"Yeah, isn't he? Well, nobody's disturbed the padlock." Rocky came back from the cabin door and kicked Mr. Sully awake. "I hate to spoil your nap but did you see any of the snipers along the river when you came in? Or anyone else aroun' here lately?"

Mr. Sully sheepishly laid his gun down on the blanket again. "You kind of startled me. I ain't seen a soul since I got here except Lorenzo when he took the body away. And all I saw of them snipers was I kind of heard some of 'em talking and the smoke from their fires."

"Did you see— Oh well, you wouldn't. I'll be down early so's you can go home and get your sleep, Al. And take it easy in the meantime," Rocky said solicitously.

When they had bumped back over the track through the woods and were crossing the bridge again he patted Eleanor's knee conciliatingly.

"Don't tap your foot at me, honey. I'm going to tell you. That fellow that was held up for a ride didn't know just where he let his passenger off, but from what he did say, it could easily have been about here. That was Sunday night. Or early Monday mornin' if you want to be particular. And that was the time someone stole some groc'ries and a shovel from the store. And the sniper nearest the cabin claimed he'd been on the Yuba Pass before he came here but he had a bright new sunburn and it took him a minute to guess what I meant by 'sniping.'"

"That's very interesting," Eleanor said politely. "Go on."

"Go on? Well, he's cleared out and he wasn't really sniping and—" Rocky groaned. "You tell her, Michael. I've talked till my throat's dry."

"You'll correct me if I'm wrong? There was one man who tried Miss Parnell's door some time before she came home on the night she was killed. He was humming 'Alouette' and ran away when he was noticed. There was a man with a 'young voice' who talked to her much later that night and he whistled, according to Miss Bond, a funny tune. There was someone on the Sunday night before that who entered the house, whistling 'Alouette,' and Miss Bond thought that Miss Parnell was talking to someone in her room that Sunday night.

"You might argue that all those someones equal only one man. But Roche did not whistle. He hummed and he did not have a 'young voice.' And Miss Bond insists the man who did left Miss Parnell alive. From their conversation they were not on bad terms but simply shared some sort of knowledge. And the general tone of that discussion suggested they were not discussing it for the first time. *And* it was on Monday night that Miss Parnell first tried to console herself by getting swacked."

"In other words there were two men who came to see her," Valerie said. "One was Roche and you think he killed her. The other—"

"Was Ted Smith, I think. I believe Sullivan thought there were two men concerned but he had been unable to prove anyone from the Armstrong house had visited her very lately. Until he knew of Roche's existence he couldn't assign him to the role of the second man."

"We've wondered how the Parnell woman found out she knew anything important," Rocky said. "Even if she was in touch with the Dumonts and Holadays without anyone knowin' it, I can't imagine any of them enlightening her. Or that Roche would. I doubt if he ever saw her, and someone probably had to tell him where she lived. Since he had a Monday's Sacramento *Bee* the possibilities are against him being in San Francisco Sunday night. But by Monday she was upset so it looks like the man she talked to Sunday was responsible for that. And Roche hung around the city trying to find Ted Smith.

"When I think I could just have reached out and grabbed that guy this evening! Smith may have been in cahoots with Roche. But while he had a good reason for clearing out of the city after Miss Parnell was killed, if he had been seeing her, he apparently already meant to leave. The Bond woman heard Miss Parnell say something about 'if you've made up your mind to go.'"

"You're only guessing your sniper was Smith," Eleanor said. "You didn't recognize him."

"From newspaper pictures? Be reas'nable, honey. He's changed the way he cuts his hair: I remember his pictures that well. Ed might have recognized him but he didn't really talk to him. And why did the guy lie the way he did and then clear out? And why hadn't the police picked Smith up unless he's not in the city? And if he isn't, where—"

"All right. But you still have not proved any criminal connection between Roche and the group at Pluma Blanca."

"My best pal an' severest critic! Never mind, we're almost home. You've always said Sing Toy could be trusted with a dozen babies and in a few minutes you can satisfy yourself he can be trusted with ours. You'n Valerie can sleep late in the mornin'. We'll have to get an early start. Will six o'clock be all right?"

"Válgame Dios! You didn't— Did you say six o'clock?"

"Oh, I should think that'd be early enough. Though if you want to make it five—"

"Five! Hell!" said Mr. Dundas bitterly, shocked into Anglo-Saxon.

Lorenzo Sloane, clearing his throat ceremoniously, intimated it was time the six good men and true declared the deceased had taken his own life. Which the six did, adjourning from the small dance hall toward the soda fountain, agreeing it was sure going to be a sizzler today and how about a good cold bottle of beer?

Ed Towne, according to his father, had been up and away for more than an hour before they arrived in Bancross. Al Sully was pointedly awake when they got to the cabin and yawned himself away after his halfhearted offer to "stay and help" was refused. Rocky had gone to work with camera and fingerprinting apparatus.

His cheerful comments fell on barren soil and slowly withered. He suggested finally that perhaps Michael might like to lie down and take a nap. Michael looked unenthusiastically at the cot and said he wasn't sleepy, thank you. He continued to sit in the rocking chair with his eyes half closed until the coroner arrived.

Lorenzo Sloane brought a message from Dr. Bradley. He was to tell Rocky that Roche had been dead about forty-eight hours and killed about six after his last meal. The bullet had come from the only gun Rocky had seen fit to turn over to him. That was all he had to say except that if Rocky sent him any more corpses during this hot spell the doctor would appreciate his delivering them before they were half spoiled.

"That's all right," Rocky said. "The time of death, I mean. Well, shall we get it over, Lorenzo?"

"We'd better. Shall I bury him? You got his fingerprints this morning. Of course you say he only had a little silver in his pockets—"

"Keep him on ice for a while. But the county will bury him if no relatives show up."

Rocky thought of the two hundred dollars in Roche's billfold. But tell a jury a man had that much ready cash and they'd wonder why the hell he killed himself. Even Lorenzo would ask embarrassing questions. As it was, his one idea was to hurry through the inquest and back to Brookdale as quickly as possible. . . .

Back in the cabin after Lorenzo had done just that, Rocky produced a packet of envelopes and began clearing the table of all articles small enough to go into them.

"I didn't let Lorenzo see the hot-water bags," he admitted.

"No fingerprints but Roche's anywhere, I suppose?"

"Just his, aroun' here and on the money belt and billfold. I got his prints at Lorenzo's fun'ral parlors this mornin'. That's why I kept you waiting outside the office: I wanted to check them against the things I left there last night. But it's a damn discouragin' lot of exhibits. Nothing you can get your teeth into."

"Even so, you know far more about the Armstrong kidnaping than anyone else has learned in more than a year."

"Anyone who had the facts could figure out what Roche's movements must have been. Or how Edith Parnell found out she'd been suppressing evidence. But we still don't know what it was she knew or who hired Roche—or anything really worthwhile," Rocky said gloomily. "What d'you suppose, besides the letter Miss Parnell may 've written, could have been burned here?"

"Oh . . . It's possible Roche and his employer exchanged a few letters, though why anyone would be fool enough to put anything into writing—"

"They do though, and in this case they may almost have had to write. Bein' very careful what they said, I reckon. Still, I'll bet Roche would hang onto the letters he got and his employer might keep Roche's—"

"Until Roche was dead, when they could all be safely burned. If the gun in his hand wasn't Roche's, where do you think his is?"

"Somewhere in the river between here and Pluma Blanca, I hope. I mean I hope no one thinks he still needs a gun. I don't think he'd risk keeping Roche's though, and I'll bet we never trace the one we found here back to him. Well, Roche must have felt pretty safe—"

"Men of action don't always think too highly of those who prefer to sit still and exercise their little gray cells without agitating themselves physically, do they?" Michael said gravely.

Rocky flushed. "I like to sit still and just think sometimes myself," he said and was annoyed by the brief flash of amusement in Michael's eyes. "But that's one way of putting it. But it was luck for whoever killed Roche to be able to sneak up on him asleep right in the doorway. There's where the weather took a hand in the game. Let's carry this junk out to the car. I'm through here and when I do two or three more little jobs we'll go home to lunch."

The first of Rocky's "little jobs" took the form of an interview with the sniper who was by profession an expert accountant. The man—his name was Gowland— answered Rocky's question without hesitation.

"That young fellow started working down there Monday morning. He didn't have any partner and, judging by his talk, he was a greenhorn. I walked down that way last night and he's gone."

"I thought he must be. Well, thanks anyway."

He drove on, parked before the clubhouse again and went in to ask Adam Towne for a list of the groceries that had been stolen from his store.

"Three cans of beans, a package of crackers, two cans of peaches, two of corned beef and two sardines," Mr. Towne said promptly. "And a shovel and a can of coffee."

"Oh. That's not enough to— There don't happen to be any cars missing aroun' here this morning?"

"Not that I've heard. I always warn the cottagers not to leave them unlocked."

"Good idea. Was Ed coming home for lunch?"

"Nope, he took a san'wich with him. But he did figger on coming back by three or four to report to you."

"If I'm not here then, have him call me at home or the office. We'll be seeing you. . . . You might as well drive," Rocky suggested as they left the clubhouse. "I'll be getting in and out and it'll save time. We'll go down to the cottages first. . . ."

Michael, waiting in the car, heard him ask a large pink lady in orange slacks if she had been "bothered lately by any bums asking for a handout."

"Why no, not a one. And I certainly wouldn't give any of them anything if they did ask," the woman said with a militant wave of the embryonic knitted garment she was working on. "What I say: a man can always get work if he really wants to work."

Michael grinned sardonically and smoked two cigarettes while Rocky went on down the row of cottages to the sixth and last, crossed the road and worked his way back through the six on that side.

"No dice," he said. "And God it's hot! Why do people come on vacations just to sit on porches and knit? Keep along this road till you get to the station."

The station was a small tan box at the end of a narrow twisting road. Above the cliffs the forests were coolly green but there was not a tree any-where near the railroad tracks.

Rocky went into the station but the telegraph instruments were clacking loudly and Michael could not hear what he and the first-trick oper-ator were saying to each other. Finally he came back, wiping his face on a wilted sleeve.

"Awful in there. That guy says I'm lucky I quit railroadin'. He wouldn't know. Well, an east- and westbound had a meet here last night. That's bad. Drive on out of town and turn down the highway. Stop at the first house you see."

They stopped at four houses and a new auto camp before Rocky gave the order to turn back toward Bancross and Brookdale. "We've come ten miles. That's enough," he said as if that were a complete explanation of their activities. "Go straight back through to the first house on the other side of the Bancross bridge."

The last house at which they stopped, some ten miles from Bancross, was built so near the highway that Rocky did not have to get out of the car to speak to the elderly man squatting on its steps.

"Hi there, Charlie! Your car isn't missin', is it? No? That's good. And nobody's asked you for a handout the last day or two?"

Charlie shook his head and shifted a wad of tobacco from one cheek to another. "Thanks," Rocky said hastily. "Give him five minutes more and he might start talkin'," he added to Michael. "No, you drive on home. I'll admit you're a damn good driver." He grinned wearily. "I reckon you don't ever brag without reason. Let's get home and then I suppose after we've had somethin' to eat we'll have to think what to do next."

CHAPTER 16

But when they had eaten lunch he showed no disposition to do anything but sit still and talk to Valerie—without mentioning Roche or the Armstrong kidnaping. He discussed Howard Hughes and Douglas Corrigan at some length while Valerie smiled at him receptively and wondered why Michael looked as if he were laughing to himself.

"While your husband and my wife are putting aviation in its place, couldn't you and I amuse ourselves by admiring your son?" he said finally, turning to Eleanor. "After all, the little things in life . . ."

"I have also been put in my place in that connection. Sing Toy says he must catchee nap. Those loud shrieks you politely ignored were Shay's opinion of Sing Toy but he'll catchee nap or else. And you wouldn't be trying to win your way to a mother's heart, would you?"

"As a matter of fact, I like babies. Also puppies and kittens—"

"All small, helpless creatures," Valerie said significantly, looking at Rocky. He grinned. "Sister, I may not be small but I'm feelin' plenty helpless right now. I know what I ought to do but I don't want to do it. And your husband knows it, damn—"

"Not before the ladies, Mr. Allan!"

"Oh, don't mind us," Valerie said. "We aren't ladies: just wives."

"'I believe there are no ladies present?' 'No, said General Grant, but there are gentlemen!'" Rocky snorted impolitely. "I am only a peaceable private citizen," Michael continued virtuously. "How should I know what etiquette or professional ethics calls for in a situation of this kind?"

"Oh, so that's it?" Eleanor said. "Well, you don't come up for re-election until '40 and we can always go to Texas and live with your father if you lose your job."

"That's two years off. And right now I can't set aroun' here any longer."

"I was wondering when you'd realize that. After sending poor Ed out to comb the woods you don't seem at all anxious to hear what he may have discovered. And while I may be wrong about that too, I've always understood a body is an accepted feature of a murder case."

"We've got Roche's, honey. And I know where the kid's body is," Rocky said placidly. "I just sent Ed out to keep him busy—and happy. And out of my way."

"I should have known! Like the time you sent Jazz Mitchell and your father to tear up the floors of all the houses in Slacktown. But do you know or do you just think you do?"

"Oh, I only think I do. Don't you, Michael?"

"No, I certainly do not. Should I?"

"You might have a hunch if you'd listened to what Ed said. And I didn't send him out just to get him from underfoot. I'd like to know where Roche picked those tiger lilies. It might turn out to be important. Though I imagine he'd just been digging up the ransom and where he hid it don't matter."

"Then you don't think he buried it with the boy's body?" Valerie said.

"Why would he? We agreed he certainly wouldn't want the body found so he wouldn't want to have to risk going back to the grave to get his money. . . . Well, it's almost three, so we'd better get down to Bancross and see what Ed's done. That won't take long. You girls be good."

"I suppose I'm just a bird brain," Valerie said when the men had gone, "but I don't know what Rocky should do that he doesn't want to do."

"He should get in touch with the F.B.I. and the city police—as he very well knows. And so does Michael."

"But I doubt if Michael wants him to. I wonder if Rocky realizes that?"

"He'll find out. And it won't hurt him not to know at once. He's been in danger of becoming complacent. It's been a long time since anyone around here has done more than listen with bated breath to his pronouncements and admire them. So Michael's very good for him."

Valerie laughed. "That goes both ways. They're really very funny together even if they don't realize it."

"Oh, Michael probably does. Rocky would if he thought about it, but he isn't much given to self-analysis. Of course they're funny: men always are, with their precious masculine dignity and reserve." Eleanor got up, pulled the shades to the window sill and turned on an electric fan. "Bancross is a good deal lower than Brookdale and it's hot enough here. I'm glad I'm not out on the highway."

She would have been inclined to an even stronger expression of gratitude if she had seen her

husband and Mr. Dundas wrestling with the spare
wheel halfway between Bancross and Brookdale,
at a point on the highway ungraced by even one
small tree.

After Rocky's brief and bitter comment: "First
puncture I've had in six months," they were wise
enough not to talk at all. Except when Rocky,
hurrying to be through, dropped an essential nut
into the dust by the road. And his comments, as
he groped for it, could not be classed as conver-
sational.

"Haste makes waste, as our Mr. Holaday would
no doubt tell you." Michael took off his shirt and
threw it into the car. "And mad dogs and Englishmen go out in the midday sun."

Rocky set his teeth as he sifted red dirt between his fingers. He decided it wasn't up to him
to warn Michael he'd get a hell of a sunburn in no
time if he left his shirt off. He had removed his
own some time ago but he was already well tanned
and Michael should have sense enough to see that.

He scooped up another handful of dust and
found the washer in it. They got the wheel on, re-
leased the jack and were rewarded by a reproach-
ful "suzz-z-z" as the spare also went flat.

"Goddam it to hell! If I've told that fellow in
the garage once I've told him fifty times to be sure

the spare's all right! Now I suppose we'll find out
he hasn't left any extra tubes . . ."

The offending garage mechanic had but it took
them an hour to finish a job that should have been
done in fifteen minutes. It was then after four
o'clock and Rocky said abruptly:

"I'll be damned if I'm going to dig up any
corpses till it's cooler."

He drove on for several miles until the murmur
of the stream could be heard faintly; turned onto
a little-used track through the trees and parked at
the end of it.

"There's kind of a cove down here with a strip
of sand halfway like a beach. I'll warn you the
water's cold but I'm going to get some of this dirt
off me before I go on. You needn't mention this to
Eleanor. She'd have a lot to say about people who
go in swimming without cooling off first."

Presently, watching Michael out in the middle of the stream where the current was swift, he
smiled sardonically. "That's a nice crawl stroke
you've got," he said mildly when Michael returned
to the cove. "So why did you claim you couldn't
swim very well? It seems kind of unnecessary—
and childish."

Michael grimaced. "That's a direct hit, Mr. Allan. It was childish." He climbed out to the narrow
strip of pebbly sand that edged the water. "But

you're so damned condescending at times and in your own amiable way. I couldn't resist trying to plumb the depths of your condescension. Moses leading a tenderfoot around the wilderness. But I can't remember your warning me against that current out there."

"I'm not as gullible as I was twenty-four hours ago. If you'd done a belly flop off that rock there instead of a very good swan dive, I'd have told you. Look: considerin' Sullivan kind of confided in you, don't you ever feel like you ought to let him in on this?"

"But suppose you wouldn't allow me to?"

"I couldn't keep you from it."

"You could very easily detain me in your county bastille."

"You're my guest," Rocky said stiffly

"So it's true what they say about Dixie? Our Southern hospitality . . . That was uncalled for," Michael decided. "I'm sorry."

"O.K. But I'll bet that tongue of yours has gotten you into plenty of trouble."

"And out of it, Mr. Allan."

"For God's sake quit callin' me Mr. Allan! And you haven't answered my question."

"During our last conversation the inspector was a trifle tactless. However, it goes deeper and farther back than that. Sullivan does not often make hasty arrests, but about eight years ago he did make one."

"You? It's a long time to hold a grudge."

"I don't hold it against him," Michael said coolly, "but I'd have had him up for false arrest if I could have afforded to. And that's one reason I won't go out of my way to let him know what's going on here. If you knew his opinion of—uh—small-town peace officers—"

"Don't bother to put it so nicely. Just say 'back-woods sheriff.' And I know just about what Sullivan said: I've heard it plenty of times."

"And don't like it?" Michael suggested.

"Why would I? I get tired of being called 'a fool for luck.' I admit I've had my share but I need it."

"Yes, from what I've seen of your supporting cast, you do. And a cast-iron constitution besides. Haven't you even one deputy who is not actively stupid?"

"I've got one in Merton who's not lazy and don't scare easy. But I didn't pick him for his intellectual brilliance. I sent him over to Pluma Blanca this mornin'," Rocky added casually. "He can pass as a guest—so long as he don't talk. I wouldn't like that bunch to clear out without warnin'. So long as they stay there I'm in no hurry to talk to 'em again. Let them wonder for a while how much we know."

"And in the meantime?"

"Oh, I suppose when I've seen Ed I'll give in and begin sendin' telegrams. I wouldn't care," Rocky said defensively, "if it wasn't that once I do that, it's out of my hands. The place'll be overrun with Feds. And what can they do that I can't?"

"'What has Mrs. Simpson got, That you and I, my gel, have not . . .' I agree with you, strange as it may seem. The difficulty is that you can't contact the Sacramento and San Francisco police without notifying the federal agents too. Yet the police might be able to help you."

"They could trace Roche's movements in Sacramento—in time. And eventually he might be traced back to wherever he came from: Canada maybe. But I doubt if what he did before he came here is important. And if they never even discovered he existed in their first investigation, why should I hope for much along that line now? The bracelet's a good lead and I suppose they can find out if it was pawned or if there was an imitation made. So far as Smith's concerned, I doubt if he'll head back toward the city. I can send out descriptions of him east and west of here without anybody thinking much of it."

"I had an idea you thought he might still be somewhere near here."

"It's slow going on foot and folks don't care about picking up hitchhikers. Hopping a freight last night was his best bet. If he did, he's miles away by now and probably hiding out in some jungle. But if he's still aroun' he must be pretty hungry by now. Like most city fellows, he didn't bury his tin cans. Ever'thing Adam Towne told us was stolen is accounted for down where Smith camped. That's why I thought if he tried to get away on foot he might have asked for a handout somewhere."

"There's no jungle attached to Brookdale?"

"No real one. The bums don't like to stop here. The tourists won't feed 'em and neither will the Townes, so the place has a bad name with the 'bos. I suppose Smith 'd keep to himself anyway. Well"—he stood up— "we might as well wash off this sand and be on our way. And if you don't mind a word of advice from Moses, put your shirt back on or you'll be howlin' for sunburn lotion by the middle of the night."

In the clubhouse Mr. Towne had just turned off his electric fan and added six personally emptied bottles of beer to the stack behind the soda fountain.

"Nothing like beer on a hot day. Doesn't take your appetite away, either. I was just going—" From the direction of the hotel a bell clanged loudly. "There! I was just goin' to supper. You boys join us?"

"Thanks. But where's Ed? Over there?"

"Oh, now, I forgot about him. He come in about four and phoned Brookdale but they said you'd started for here. So he thought maybe you'd drove out to the cabin and he went to see. Ought to 've been back by now: it's five-thirty. But when my boy Ed gets int'rested in anything he don't mind about meals."

"Well, we had a late lunch and it's too hot to eat anyway. We'll go bring Ed back," Rocky said. "He probably is figurin' I'll come after him. If we don't get back right off don't you worry. . . ."

"Even your prospectors—snipers—appear to have called it a day," Michael remarked, looking toward the deserted diggings along the road.

"Yeah, or gone fishin'. They start now and work their way back when the sun's off the water. . . . Damn!" Rocky stared up toward the cabin. "Ed don't seem to be here. He must 've beat it back through the woods and just missed us. Ed! Hey, Ed! Wa-hoo-o!"

"'And it's just grand for calling pigs!' Shall we go up?"

"I guess we better. He might've gone to sleep inside."

The door was swinging a little open on its leather hinges. The sun was beginning to drop behind the mountains but it died hard, and the cabin's crazy roof of flattened tin cans and tarpaper almost visibly radiated heat.

"Give Roche another day in there an' Doc Bradley'd had somethin' to complain about," Rocky murmured and kicked the door open. They saw the sagging cot then, that it had hidden, and Ed Towne motionless on the dirty blankets, blood drying in a great smear across his freckled forehead.

CHAPTER 17

Rocky started forward, swearing. The door swung shut. Michael was first to see the man who had stood behind it: a thickset young fellow in stained khaki trousers and a torn blue shirt. Face, throat and forearms were burned red; even his square hairy hands and the finger crooked about the trigger of an automatic.

"All right, take it easy! And reach! You heard me! I mean you, Sheriff. Stay where you are—"

"*Arriba las manos,* Mr. Allan," Michael said softly, raising his own hands. "It's Cactus Bill, the Pecos Killer."

Rocky, already halfway back to the door, checked himself with difficulty and raised his hands a grudging six inches.

"I see you been having a bite to eat," he said, glancing toward a plate that held scraps of chicken, ham and fruit. "It's going to be a damn expensive meal. Did you kill him?"

"I had to hit him when he came walking in here but it's just a scalp wound. You can look after him. I hoped you'd come up here when I heard you yell. Are the keys in your car? I'm borrowing it for a while."

"He talks from the corner of his mouth," Michael said admiringly. "Did it take you long to learn to slide the words out like that?"

"I can get along without your bright chatter. You guys take off your shoes. Yes, and your pants—"

"Oh, not in public, Mr. Smith! You are Mr. Smith, aren't you? The shoes if you like but not the trousers. I appeal to your finer feelings—"

"I'll appeal to one or two of your feelings in a minute. And you'd better strip clean while you're at it. You won't catch cold." Mr. Smith grinned unpleasantly. "And it'll keep you here quite a while."

"We should have settled for shoes and trousers," Michael said sadly. "After all, a shirt, if properly adjusted—"

"I thought about that."

Rocky lowered his hands. "You think about ever'thing, don't you? So you think about what I'm going to do when I catch up with you. And how you're goin' to get my clothes off me."

"Listen, tough guy . . . You get over against that table!" This was to Michael, who backed obediently. "You know what you can do with the end of a gun, don't you? I don't want to kill any sheriffs but how'd you like to have that handsome pan of yours messed up?"

"Qué estás tonto!" Michael said sharply as Rocky thrust his hands into his pockets and stood motionless and waiting. "Don't be a fool. You must make allowances for my friend, Mr. Smith. He doesn't look at this matter sensibly, as I do."

"Sensibly!" Rocky flared. "Why you—"

"Tsk-tsk! Just give him time and he'll come to it. May I sit down? It's difficult to take off your shoes, standing."

"All right—but get 'em off. And you back over by him, Sheriff. How about it? I wouldn't mind raking the skin off your face. Hell! What's some skin or a broken nose—"

"Between friends?" Michael said helpfully. He dropped one shoe to the floor. "We could be friends if you didn't take entirely the wrong attitude."

"Hand that— No, just kick that shoe over here."

Michael looked regretfully at the shoe. "It's my favorite pair. My feet are so tender. I suppose you couldn't drop them off by the side of the road?"

Mr. Smith grinned. "O.K., toots."

"And could we have one can of something to eat? We haven't had any lunch," Michael said pathetically. He pulled off his other shoe and balanced it in his right hand.

"Help yourself. Well, Sheriff—how about your shoes? You wouldn't want to go home to your wife looking like a piece of raw meat."

"Certainly he doesn't. And don't talk about raw meat. Could we have this tin of ham?"

"O.K.—O.K.'" Smith's eyes were on the shoe in Michael's right hand. "Well? Yeah, tough guy, I thought you'd come to it."

Rocky bent down slowly and untied his shoe-laces. He heard Smith bark: "And drop that: don't throw it!" His muscles tensed. Under his arm he could see Michael appearing grieved and misunderstood. He dropped the shoe from his right hand, reaching with his left for the tinned ham.

"Kick it over—" Mr. Smith began. The command went forever unfinished. Michael's left arm snapped back. He threw the can with a whiplash motion and flung himself to the floor.

A bullet whined into the flimsy walls before the heavy tin struck Mr. Smith squarely between the eyes. Rocky's head with all his weight behind it in Mr. Smith's stomach completed his ruin. He hit the floor with a crash that loosened his grip on the automatic and made the table and everything on it skip convulsively. A fist like a small pile driver connected with Mr. Smith's chin. Mr.

Smith, having found perfect peace, relaxed and let the rest of the world go by.

"Nice goin'," Rocky said briefly. "You had me fooled for a minute. My temper got the best of my common sense. Tough guy, huh?" He looked longingly at Mr. Smith's stubbly jaw. "If I didn't want you to be able to talk . . ."

Michael raised his head from protecting arms and got to his feet. "I'm not so sure he's really tough. Just a little overwrought, I think."

"Overwrought, hell! D'you think he wouldn't 've made hamburger out of my face?"

"Oh yes. And that you would have been fool enough to let him. And he had a nervous finger on this trigger." Michael tossed the gun onto the table. "And I meant it when I said you didn't look at this matter sensibly. If you'd ever had to depend on your wits instead of your strong right arm—"

"Oh, don't rub it in! There's nothing wrong with your left arm, incident'lly. Hopelessly unathletic, did you say? I'm goin' to get some water and see what I can do for Ed."

When Mr. Smith opened his eyes the sheriff was wrapping a wet cloth around Ed Towne's head. The slight dark man who had talked so foolishly and then turned out to be a southpaw was whistling softly and cleaning his fingernails with the end of a match. Mr. Smith closed his eyes but not quickly enough. The dark man looked at him and smiled slowly.

"Our little playmate is awake. Do you know, I've always wanted to meet a man named Smith."

"I've heard of guys named Smith," the sheriff said thoughtfully. "Only till now they've been the same as purple cows with me. And this turns out to be a Ted Smith, too. Well, we always welcome celebrities up here but we're curious—"

"Manners, Mr. Allan, manners!"

"Oh, we're just crude sons of the soil. With hearts of gold, of course." The sheriff beamed on Mr. Smith with an amiability that should have been encouraging—and wasn't. "So we ask questions."

Ted Smith struggled to his feet and got his back against the door. "I'm not talking," he said.

"To ev'ry man upon this earth most ever'thing comes soon or late. I not only meet a guy named Smith but he says: 'I'm not talking.' What do I say?"

"'Come clean, you lug! Why'd you bump him off?'" Michael suggested. "Or you might beat hell out of him. That's only a suggestion on my part. If that takes long enough to fatigue you unduly, I can no doubt think of something else to vary the monotony. In fact this match end puts me in mind of something. The movies are so educative. . . ."

Mr. Smith began to have all the sensations of an unhappy mouse being batted back and forth from one playful cat to another. He had for some time considered himself a tough guy but it was hard to be tough with a beehive in your head and a very bad case of sunburn.

He ran his tongue over his lips. The sheriff looked good-natured except for those yellow cat-eyes that looked right through you. He could certainly beat you up without its bothering him any. But he wouldn't light matches under a guy's fingernails, and there was something about the other man's expression that made Mr. Smith think he probably would if he thought it was necessary.

Michael pulled out a cigarette, struck a match and watched its tiny flame admiringly. "Of course he's young and probably has no mother to guide him. He shouldn't charge about the country trying to slay dragons without a sword. Though it was Andromache who was left to the dragon's mercy, wasn't it? Not Ariadne."

"I thought it was a sea serpent, but that don't matter."

"You leave her out of it!" Mr. Smith said. "She's got nothing to do with it—"

"Do you hear that, Mr. Allan? Chivalry is not dead."

"And there's still one born every minute. Why keep still to save the hides of the rest of 'em? We know Roche was just the hired man."

"You—what?"

"We know someone hired Roche to cart the boy's body away."

"But how could you— It's a trick," Smith said confusedly. "And I'm not going to be tricked into—"

"Admitting you know more 'n you should? That's what you think," Rocky said pleasantly. He walked over to Smith, yanked him off his feet with one hand and slapped his face, unhurriedly and with apparent indolence. Nevertheless Mr. Smith's head wobbled. On the other side of a yellowish mist someone was saying: "'For, infidel, know, you trod on the toe of Abdullah Boul Boul Ameer.'"

His stomach heaved warningly. He gasped: "If you don't want me to puke in here—" wrenched the door open and stumbled outside.

"I guess you're right about the overwrought nerves," Rocky said. "Though he shouldn't have eaten so much on an empty stomach. Well, with all he's been doing . . ."

"And he's been pretty well batted about by the world. One either becomes genuinely hard as a result of that or secretly a little frightened. And

Smith's sort usually assume the mannerisms of a movie tough guy to deceive themselves and everyone else."

Michael got up as Smith walked waveringly back into the cabin. "Sit down."

Mr. Smith sat down. He laid his head on his arms and groaned. "Honest to God, I must 've been crazy to ever start this! But I got to where I couldn't stand it any longer and—and I'm sorry about Ed over there."

"He's got a little concussion but he'll be all right," Rocky said. "No thanks to you."

"The heat must have gone to my head. I'd just have clipped him on the jaw ordinarily. But when he came up here and I was afraid he'd recognize me . . . Well, I had to eat and I couldn't get out of here unless I walked. I tried to hop a freight last night but the brakeman came along and—"

"All right, I can guess all that. Start at the beginning."

Mr. Smith groaned again. "Jeez, you won't believe me. But I didn't kill Miss Parnell. I wanted her alive. Roche too. And I can't even prove I didn't kill him."

"Let me worry about that. Go ahead: we haven't got all night to listen to you."

"Just as well Mr. Towne is not conscious," Michael observed. "Here, you'd better take a cigarette."

"Oh—thanks. Thanks! I've been all out since morning." Smith squared his heavy shoulders and winced involuntarily. "Well, it was like this. . . ."

When he'd had to leave his last college he'd found it pretty tough sledding, not being trained for anything but athletics. He had a lot of jobs and knew a soft one when he found it, which the one Dumont gave him was. And it might last till the kid was grown. Of course he was a spoiled, whiny little brat, though it wasn't all his fault.

"Why not?" Rocky said.

"Dumont couldn't bring himself to crack the whip even over his own kid, except once in a while he'd lose his temper. But then he'd be apologetic afterwards, and that don't do any good."

But even if he was too soft with Freddie, Dumont did see that he was well guarded, Smith went on. His testimony to that effect had been true. The first thing he lied about was the kid himself and how he felt about his relatives. He didn't like any of them but Dumont and Ariadne, and he did about as he liked with Dumont. The trouble was, Freddie knew just how things were and the first thing he'd say when he got mad at any of them was: "Wait till I'm grown up and you'll see!"

"Oh, so it was like that?" Rocky said. "Why'd he get mad?"

"Refuse him anything and he'd sulk. I was hired partly because Dumont knew his own failings, I guess. Have you met any of 'em? You have? Then I guess I don't need to try to describe them to you. But Phil Dumont hated Freddie and of course Miss Dumont would too. She's crazy about Dumont but crazier about Phil. And once Phil knocked the kid down so hard he cut his head on a chair. Then I put Phil on the floor and afterward Dumont took it out of his hide. And Miss Dumont sniffled for a week.

"Well, that's one of the things I didn't tell. Or how Freddie told tales. It was because he saw Phil sneaking in cockeyed and told Dumont that Phil went after him. And he'd get in people's rooms and stir things up. Once he made such a mess of Armstrong's papers he never did find some really important ones. And he'd mimic Miss Dumont to her face and say how homely she was— Oh well, you see what I mean?"

"Yeah. Pleasant atmosphere. And you still didn't think the kid was in any danger from them?"

"I used to wonder at first but I got used to it—and careless. And I was a sucker if there ever was one. I listened to what they all said that first morning: that we ought to keep our heads and not talk too much."

"Who said that?"

"Everyone but Armstrong and Ariadne. Dumont hesitated at first but he finally agreed that people were going to be suspicious enough and wouldn't believe what kind of kid Freddie was. And they'd make it up to me if I was discreet. That's what they called it. I fell for it. Because I didn't realize till later—"

"What?"

He didn't realize till later that he'd been drugged that night, Smith said stolidly. He was tired and he took his usual drink from the decanter in his room and went to bed. He was used to looking in at the boy two or three times every night. He managed to stagger up twice but he felt dazed with sleep. He just looked into Freddie's room, saw the hump under the bedcovers and stumbled back to bed again.

"And you didn't tell that either?" Rocky said incredulously.

"I forgot about the funny way my mouth tasted in the excitement. And I couldn't prove it, could I? By the time I got at the whisky decanter and tried what was in it, it was all right. But it may have been removed and refilled and put back again while I was asleep that night. And while we were still waiting to get the kid back I didn't like to accuse anyone. In fact I couldn't believe that I hadn't just slept a lot more soundly than usual. Then when they called the police in I couldn't make up my mind and . . . Well, since I didn't speak of it right away there was no use saying anything at all. They'd just come back at me with: 'Oh, of course that's what he *would* say to try to squirm out of it.'"

"There's something in that," Michael said.

"Sure. I was just the hired bodyguard. When they began on me I knew I was in a tight spot. I thought, 'The less you say, the better off you'll be. They expect you to start accusing everyone else, so don't do it.'"

"Along those lines, you're a man after my own heart."

"He's got somethin there," Rocky agreed. "And when did it occur to you that you might get some proof you were drugged?"

Smith stared at him. "Jeez, you tumbled to that quick! Why, not so long ago. I'd never paid much attention to the nurse, you see. But I used to go in to see Ariadne and one night a picture of a table with all those boxes and bottles on it just seemed to come to me. Jeez, what a sap! And she had missed some dope—"

"And why didn't she—"

"Because," Smith said slowly, "she thought Phil Dumont had taken it and when she told Dumont about it he asked her please not to say anything."

CHAPTER 18

"Well, when I did think of Miss Parnell I thought about how she used to be sort of coy with Dumont and Holaday," Smith went on. "But I'd better go back to the beginning. . . ."

When the police had finally let up on him he knew they were still watching him so he was careful what he did. He'd managed to see Ariadne once and he'd seen Dumont that month too. Dumont had offered to find a job for him but he'd been feeling pretty sore by then.

He hesitated, flushed deeply and added: "I'll be on the level with you: I liked Ariadne pretty well and that probably did more than anything else to keep me from talking. But I finally tumbled to the fact she don't care anything for me. And that she'd rather know the truth about things. But that's enough about that."

He couldn't get a job without references, and anyone who read his knew who he was and wouldn't hire him. So he'd just scraped along on what he'd saved—and thought. And one day he'd dug something out of his memory.

"Roche?" Rocky said.

"Yeah. Because I kept going back and back till I came to that summer and him. And then it came to me that one day about the middle of May last year I was exercisin' Freddie over at Lafayette Park. And that we passed Roche there. Well, you know what he looked like and why I didn't place him at the time? But then I began to wonder—"

"We can guess what you wondered and thought."

"Roche was a hard egg if I ever saw one. Freddie got fresh with him once, and the way he looked at him! Anyway, I'd also got my bright idea about Miss Parnell's drugstore. But I didn't hurry to her: I made sure I'd shaken off the cops first, changing my living places two or three times. I finally saw her late Sunday night. And she admitted missing quite a bit out of a bottle of stuff she said I wouldn't have tasted in whisky if I'd just gulped it down. And it would have acted the way it did with me."

Smith frowned. "It's true Phil's a bundle of nerves and had swiped some pills from her. Their doctor don't encourage him taking things like that. So of course she'd believe Dumont and keep still. But I think she knew something she wouldn't tell me. When I mentioned finally getting at the decanter again and trying the whisky and finding it all right, she looked awful funny. But I couldn't get anything out of her."

"You think she might have seen whoever carried away the doped whisky from your room?" Rocky asked.

"Well, I'd meet her in the hall myself when I'd go out after getting up to look at Freddie. But if she saw someone going in or coming out of my room that night they gave her some explanation she swallowed. She still didn't know whether to trust me or someone else. So I told her about Roche and tried to describe him. And finally I mentioned that habit he had of humming 'Alouette' and whistled it for her—"

"And she recognized it?"

Smith nodded. Ariadne had sung the song when she was delirious. And on Decoration Day Miss Parnell had taken her usual walk, late in the afternoon. She almost always walked up to California and Fillmore, over to Sacramento and back along that street. At Laguna and Sacramento she had stopped to allow several machines to go by. A man was standing on the corner, waiting and humming "Alouette."

Miss Parnell, thinking that he was a timid soul, had said kindly: "My, you take your life in your

hands every time you cross the street, don't you?"
The man had turned and glared at her. Miss Parnell's feelings were hurt. She stood on the corner
an instant longer and the man stood there, too,
not looking at her, still humming.

"Then she crossed over and went home. She was
sure it must have been Roche from my description
of him, though I'll admit he was hard to describe.
But he must have been taking a last look at the lay
of the land."

"And was she ready to believe he was the kidnaper?" Michael said.

Yes, but not that he'd been hired to do the
job. He'd seen her again the night she was killed,
Smith said. And she wasn't quite so sure by then
that Roche had played a lone hand. She was even
frightened. She kept saying she would have told
about the missing medicine if she hadn't thought
it was perfectly all right and didn't want to make
trouble for anyone.

"She still wouldn't admit she hadn't told me
everything. She said she was afraid of Roche, but
why should she be? I thought he'd either skipped
out or was hiding up here. I'd already decided to
come here and see what I could find out. I didn't
think the police would listen to me and I was fed
up with them anyway. Oh, I was a first-class sap—"

"Didn't she want to go to the police?" Rocky said.

"She mentioned that but she really hadn't made up her mind to anything. She admitted that getting her name in the papers again as having known something she hadn't told wouldn't do her any good professionally. Well, I didn't want her to go to the police—then.

"I didn't tell her I'd been to see Dumont the night before. Monday, that was. I phoned him first and someone might have listened in on that on one of the extensions—"

"How many are there? And where?"

"There's one in the kitchen and two upstairs. One in Miss Dumont's bedroom, that is, and another in a front room that was Mrs. Dumont's and hasn't been used since she died. Oh, it's open and I've used the telephone in it myself. Well, I saw Dumont late, after everyone was in bed. I won't claim no one could have listened to us. And I got a little excited and didn't talk as low as I meant to.

"To tell you the truth, I was broke and I intended getting some money from Dumont. It made me mad to see him in that place when I thought of some of the dumps I'd been living in. So I told him about Roche—"

"How'd he take that?"

"Knocked him for a loop. Though he just stared at me. Then I told him that now I could prove I'd been doped that night. That Miss Parnell could help me to. Then I said: 'And she can testify seeing Roche here just before the kidnaping.' Jeez, I wish I hadn't said it like that!"

"It's too bad you didn't make it clear all she could do was place him near the house the day before the kidnaping. But there's no use squalling about it now," Rocky said. "We can't prove yet that Roche killed her. But he seems to 've tried to get into her room Tuesday night. I reckon he wouldn't want anyone able to say he was even near the Armstrong house that Decoration Day. And you didn't put the bee on Dumont after all?"

"No. Early Wednesday I took a bus to Vallejo, all I had money for. I was dressed like a bum and I had that gun. Thought I'd need it if I ran into Roche. I got a few rides but mostly I walked. I didn't know about Miss Parnell till I read an old newspaper Thursday. It was just luck they didn't find my fingerprints in her room, I guess. Only I didn't sit down that last time or stay long and I must not have happened to handle anything there. Well, it took me five days to get to Oroville. I stayed in the jungle there till after dark Sunday night and started on here—"

"Skip it." Rocky grinned for the first time. "The guy you held up for a ride complained to me. So

I'm pretty sure you didn't kill Roche. He was dead before you could have got in here. But why the hell stick aroun' when he was?"

"I didn't know that! I—I took some stuff from the store here. I had to eat. And a shovel so I could pass as a prospector. I was so tired I just flopped down and slept till late Monday morning. Then I got a look at the car in front of this cabin. The name in it was 'Rolfe' but I figured Roche was just going to make a getaway under that name.

"I thought maybe he was waiting for someone here and I didn't want to scare him away too soon. I sat up all Monday night till three Tuesday morning, watching this place. I was going to risk coming up here that night. But when things began happening here I figured if I cleared out like a shot you'd suspect me and be after me right away. Young Towne hadn't recognized me because I'd cut my hair different and I'm thinner. I was scared stiff but I stuck around till evening. I guess I finally got kind of crazy with the heat. And sunburn too."

"'I weep for you,' the Walrus said: 'I deeply sympathize . . .'" Michael moved his own shoulders experimentally. "I've reached the itching stage myself. Your cue, señor."

"Me? I never say, 'I told you so,'" Rocky answered blandly. He went over to the cot, wet the bandage about Ed Towne's head and lifted one of his eyelids. "I guess he'll be all right before long. Can Miss Dumont drive a car, Smith?'"

"You wouldn't suppose so, but she can, though she never does."

"And which of the bunch knew Roche best?"

"Armstrong and Dumont. Holaday didn't like to go in the woods alone but he used to walk out here with Freddie and me sometimes. I can't say he didn't come along this road once he knew it and felt safe. Or that Phil didn't either."

"Have you got any notion how Roche, if he killed Miss Parnell, got her to open the door to him?"

"She was the kind of confiding, dumb bunny you could talk into things. Oh, I oughtn't to talk about her like that now—but it's true."

"And how do you think they got Freddie Armstrong out of his room without waking you up even if you were half doped?"

"That's easy. I think someone said to Freddie: 'How'd you like to give Ted a good scare tonight?' Then he fixed his bed up himself and skipped out. He'd even think it was funny to put a fake ransom note on his pillow."

"And not be suspicious of anyone who suggested it to him?"

"Hell! He was just a kid. I do think he might have wondered what Miss Dumont was up to if she'd suggested they play a joke together. But he knew Phil wanted to get even with me for slugging him that time. Of course he wouldn't expect that kind of business from Dumont because Dumont hired me. And he could fire me. But would a kid stop to reason things out? Coming from his grandfather or Armstrong, he'd think nothing of it."

"Well, I reckon that's all—"

"I found 'em," Ed Towne said thickly, trying to sit up. Rocky laid a restraining hand on his chest.

"That's all right. How do you feel?"

"My head aches." Ed tried to turn it, gave up and so did not see Smith, who appeared anxious to efface himself. "Someone hit me. Looking for you here; thought I'd wait and you'd come. . . . But I did find 'em. In my pocket—"

Rocky managed to get his hand into a pocket of the skimpy jeans and drew out a crushed and withered spray of tiger lilies.

"They'd be fresh last week. Little hollow in the hills back here. Still damp. Big rock there. Landmark, I mean. He'd dug up something there. Not a very big hole. I didn't," Ed finished apologetically, "find—anything else." He closed his eyes.

Rocky stooped and lifted him. "Never mind that. You're goin' home now. Hold the door open."

CHAPTER 19

The road along the river ended in a clearing where fishermen left their cars. They could then go as far as they wished on a well-defined path through the woods before breaking their way down through the brush to the stream.

Half a mile along that path another, almost indiscernible and known only to the old inhabitants, turned off into the hilly woodland that stretched to the railroad tracks. Up this trail mules had once teetered, pine coffins strapped to their backs, while the funeral cortege trudged dustily behind.

There were not and never had been any tombstones in the Bancross cemetery. Neat picket fences had enclosed the graves but there were only four of these left, half rotted or fallen to the ground. The one isinglass-covered nameplate of the modern mortician was an anachronism in that place. On it was the name of one Hezekiah Slater, born in 1845, deceased in 1937 in the month of April, aged 92 years.

It was dark among the trees at eight o'clock. The three men working there took turns handling shovels and flashlight, until iron grated against wood. There was a brief struggle with a coffin top, then a voice saying:

"The old fellow was Hezzie Slater. What's left beside him is Freddie Armstrong. Satisfied?"

"I'm—I'm satisfied," Smith said in a tone that suggested he was fighting nausea again. Michael took the flashlight from him, looked into the coffin again and turned away.

"Certainly it was a child. Mr. Roche seems never to have heard the dictum that youth should not mate with age."

Cold-blooded bastard, Mr. Smith thought, unable to see the expression of sick distaste in Michael's eyes. He said shakily: "W-what do we do next?"

"It's too late to do anything tonight except to put the lid back an' cover it up again," Rocky said.

Smith picked up a shovel. "All right. How did you guess you'd find him here?"

"Oh, I just thought where I'd go if I was a horse, as they say. Roche knew Hezzie was buried here and no one would think of looking in a grave that was already here. . . . All right, that's good enough. Let's get back to the car."

For an instant longer Michael kept the flashlight turned on the grave. He said slowly: "'Earth has got him whom God gave, Earth may sing, and earth shall smart! None of earth shall know his grave. They that dig with Death depart. . . .'" He turned away. Mr. Smith's sunburned back felt suddenly very cold. He shivered and mumbled protestingly:

"Jeez, I wish you wouldn't talk like that!"

"It fits," Rocky said briefly, starting down the hill. "So far as Roche was concerned. He figured nobody would find the kid."

When they reached the car, Michael, who had said nothing more during the walk back, suggested abruptly:

"You sit down and rest, Mr. Smith. I want to talk to Mr. Allan." He walked out of hearing distance, turned and faced Rocky. "What now?"

"End of the trail for me, I reckon. We've got the body. I put that off long's I could as an excuse for workin' under cover. Now I suppose I notify the fam'ly and the world. Why?"

Michael did not answer immediately. "Did you get a description of that bracelet last night?" he said finally.

"Oh sure, before I talked to you about it."

"Would you let me go back to the city tonight and trust me to find out who had it copied? Or better still, come with me?"

"You think that fellow Cochrane mentioned— Hogue—would talk?"

"Not willingly, probably. But I think Burris' other ex-employee, Wales, might help us," Michael said. "If the bracelet was pawned I'm afraid we can't discover where or by whom. The police can when it's necessary to prove it was pawned. But I doubt if that's too important now."

"No. Because Roche probably did that himself. It'd be safer for him to than anyone else. And that don't get you to the person behind him. You mean, I take it, we're to deal with Hogue under cover— semiofficially? Very semi?"

"If you care to risk it. The people of this county elect you but they wouldn't like you to appear ridiculous."

"I know. Just a backwoods cop gumming up the works by tryin' to do ever'thing himself. But I can't ask for help in San Francisco an ignore the fed'ral authorities. Did you say you wanted to start tonight? Suits me but"—Rocky grinned—"I'd have thought you'd want to go back and say good-by to Valerie first."

"I was going to suggest that you call and tell them—"

"Not me! I never can understand why, even when they know they can't argue you out of a thing, women still insist on saying what's on their minds. But I thought maybe you had Valerie better trained."

"Choose a young wife and train her? If I'd ever had any such idiotic idea I'd be sadly disillusioned by now. I do take advantage of her even temper, but she knows just how much it means when I growl at her. As you do when Eleanor is sweetly sarcastic. But they'd both have so many good reasons why we should be sane and sensible."

"Brother, you said it! Well, since I phoned Eleanor once they won't worry about us for quite a while. We could send a telegram from Oroville."

"Just to let them know we're thinking of them. Never neglect the little attentions if you wish your marriage to be successful."

"Yeah, and I hope the doghouse is big enough for two. Because it's bein' left behind that's really going to burn 'em." Rocky turned back toward the car. "What d'you suggest we do about Mr. Smith?'"

"He's your prisoner. However, there is a little motto to every nation dear: scratch my back and I'll scratch yours."

Rocky chuckled and then assumed an expression sternly official as they came up to the car. "Turn on the lights, Smith. I reckon you've been wondering what I'm going to do with you?"

"Throw me in your lousy jail, I suppose," Mr. Smith said spiritlessly.

"'Tisn't lousy and the grub's damn good. However, we're taking you to the city with us."

"I might have known—"

"Keep your pants on. You know, Roche did have an accomplice in the house and a lot of people still think it must 've been you. So I reckon you want this thing really cleared up?"

"If it isn't, there'll always be people who'll connect me with it and remember it against me."

"All right. Do you want to take your chances with us?"

"That's O.K. by me," Smith said unhesitatingly.

"We can't keep you under our wing forever," Rocky admitted. "But I'll bring you back here if you think you'd be happier in the Brookdale caboose. We won't bother about the question of jurisdiction yet and you might come in handy. But you'll have to forget anything I might tell you to. If you don't . . ." He paused, searching for a suitable threat.

"If you don't," Michael said promptly, "he's apt to forget that a traveling salesman even told him about being held up for a ride Monday morning."

"Oh. Oh, I see! My alibi for Roche's death depends on that guy's testimony about the time I held him up? You don't need to get hard-boiled," Mr. Smith said with gloomy dignity. "I know when I'm licked and I've lied so much a little more won't bother me. I'll even swear you hadn't found Freddie's body when we left here."

"He's not so dumb," Rocky said pensively. "Well, let's start. I reckon we can wait until we get to Oroville to eat. . . ."

Hortense hung Ariadne's yellow frock in the closet, put every article on the bureau in its place and drew down the window blinds. All without saying a word, but the effect Ariadne thought was the same as if she had remarked: "I'll do my duty however selfish other people are."

She guessed, too, that Hortense wouldn't go away without speaking. She didn't. She said, at the door:

"I suppose nothing I can say will persuade you it's foolish to pamper yourself this way. You're not the only one who feels badly this morning. If you would make an effort—"

"I am making an effort—not to throw the water bottle at you. Wasn't my health one excuse for our coming here? Then go away and let me be an invalid."

"Invalids don't dance till all hours. People will talk. And it was your fault Phil—acted the way

he did. I won't have you treating him like you do!
Goodness knows, I've tried to persuade him you're
not worth it—"

Ariadne raised her head from the pillow and a
hand toward the water bottle on the bedside table.
"Will you go away? And don't come back!"

Hortense went away and she didn't come back.
But in half an hour a maid appeared with a breakfast tray and Daniel.

"My daughter," Daniel chirruped, "doesn't feel
so well this morning. Yes, put it right there, my
girl. And here's something for your trouble. . . .
I'll just raise these shades. Fresh brook trout, my
dear. I ordered them for you especially."

"Did you tell them not to put a sharp knife on
the tray? I might cut my throat with it since I'm
overemotional—"

"My dear, I seem to have expressed myself most
unfortunately last night and I deeply regret that,"
Daniel said nobly. "If you were quite your old self
you wouldn't resent my very natural solicitude."

"Is it solicitude or are you afraid people might
take me seriously if I decided to tell everything I
know?"

"Do you know anything that would help us find
Freddie's kidnaper?" Daniel was suddenly and un-
accustomedly terse. "Because if you do, why hav-
en't you told us—and the authorities?"

"Oh, Pop! That from you! 'Let sleeping dogs lie.; . . . 'Least said, soonest mended.'"

"You might stop to consider what sleeping dogs I advised you to let lie. You never even hinted you might have stumbled on some valuable clue. I supposed you were always referring to the general—situation when you'd say we hadn't told everything. And can you truthfully claim anything would have been gained by admitting Frederick was not a lovable child or easy to live with?'"

"N-no. It wouldn't have helped to admit we didn't care for him when all of us gained by his death."

"Exactly. And I wasn't the only one who advised thinking twice before speaking once."

"No, but you always keep up the fiction that there never was anything wrong," Ariadne said sullenly. "And that we regretted Freddie's—death. I suppose he is dead."

Daniel shrugged. "When you're older you'll learn it saves trouble to keep up polite pretenses. You can be human without being inhumane. You haven't really grieved for the boy—"

"No. If he'd died of some illness I'd have soon forgotten."

"Exactly. Time is a great healer. But you're inclined to think things must be either black or white and never gray. Either we must be deeply grieved that Freddie is gone or glad that he is. Whereas the truth is that while we were shocked by what happened to him we are not really sorry he is dead. And you shouldn't take everything I say too seriously. Remember that Hortense is an ever-present thorn in my flesh."

"And Phil? He hinted that he knows something about you you wouldn't want him to tell."

"Barking dogs don't bite," Daniel said placidly. "Don't worry about Phil: I'm quite capable of handling both him and Hortense."

"Y-yes, I suppose you are. And I don't know anything that it would help to tell. No more than the rest of you do, I suppose. But have you—have you really been worried about me?"

"Haven't I had reason to be? I've seen one daughter cut off in the flower of her youth, you know."

Ariadne sighed. Pop simply couldn't help talking that way. He belonged to a generation that grieved verbally and in time-honored phrases. A generation that might accuse her of not having grieved for Gloria at all because she almost always referred to her matter-of-factly. Neither was there any use in telling Pop that Gloria died young because she'd been overworked and undernourished in her teens.

"But I was a little upset last night," he went on, "when you told me your bracelet had been stolen—"

"Even before Mr. Allan informed us he wasn't going to try to discover who took it?" Daniel nodded. "But why, Father? Of course when he asked those last questions I guessed he thought it might be an imitation—"

"Cochrane had showed his interest in it, you know. And I saw Allan take him outside before we went in to supper."

"Oh. Well, did you take it, Father? When it disappeared last year I thought you might have pawned it—temporarily. That's why I didn't make too much fuss about it. Though I'd never have been so careless if I'd known what it was worth. I think Gloria didn't tell me because she wanted me to wear it just for her."

"I'm sure she did. Well, my dear, if the bracelet you've been wearing for the last year was a copy of the original, the copy must have been made when it was first missing. I'll admit I know a great deal about pawnshops—"

You should, considering how many times you pawned your watch and Mother's engagement ring, Ariadne thought. To back some long shot that's probably still running. . . .

"But I know nothing about precious stones. And I wouldn't know anyone I could trust to copy a bracelet for me so that I could keep or sell the original." Daniel stood up. "That's what I wanted to say to you, my dear. A word to the wise, you know. Straws show which way the wind is blowing. At least drink your coffee and try to go back to sleep."

He meant, of course, that Basil did know something about precious stones. He always said it was very little but that little was a great deal more than most people knew. He'd worked quite a while for Mr. Burris. He must know someone who could copy pieces of jewelry.

Though—Ariadne pressed her fingers hard against her forehead—why shouldn't people have copies made of valuable things? You read of its being done all the time. But Basil would know someone who wouldn't ask questions: that was what Pop had meant.

There was Hortense too. She'd gone to live with Basil after Eve Burris had been sent to the sanitarium and while Basil was still with Mr. Burris. Hortense had always begrudged her that bracelet. But what good could she get out of it if she wouldn't dare wear it? Someone had wanted to get money but by a transaction there'd be no record of. . . .

She muttered fretfully: "My head aches so," and recognized Basil's step in the hall and his staccato knock. She said: "Come in," and before he was well in the room: "Basil, didn't you suspect that bracelet wasn't the same one Gloria gave me?"

She hoped he'd say: "Yes, I did," because there were so many good reasons why he might have thought it best not to tell her if he had. But he said evasively:

"I never looked at it closely, Ariadne. I simply took it for granted."

"I see." Ariadne turned her face into the pillow. "I wish you'd go away. I'm—I'm tired of talking to people!"

"Why, of course. I—I only wanted to ask how you were. I'd—I'd hoped you might have enjoyed yourself last night—"

"I did, beyond all expectations. You have no idea. Fiddling while Rome burns, Pop would call it. Or would he?"

"I'm sorry," Basil said. Not as Pop would, forgiving you for being unreasonable. But seeing through what you said to what was behind it.

"I'm sorry too. I've gotten to the point where I can't even believe—I can't believe anyone. Basil, what special meaning has 'Alouette'?"

"The song is one that—" Basil stopped. "It has unpleasant associations," he finished carefully.

"But none that you've any connection with, Ariadne. Don't worry, my dear. I'll keep Hortense away from you."

When he had closed the door Ariadne got up and took three phenobarbital tablets. They were slow in taking effect but when she did sleep it was soundly and well into the afternoon. She was dressed and had propped her door open when Jonathan slouched up to it, peering at her inquiringly over his glasses.

"I was warned off but I see you're up. Like to come for a walk? Though it's hot as hades."

"Then I'll just sit outside on the lawn. Don't tell me you've been neglecting your fishing?"

"I was out this morning by myself. Basil wasn't up to a five-mile hike after waiting on Phil all night."

"It's a wonder Hortense didn't do that."

"He wouldn't let her. She's been warning me against strangers within the gates," Jonathan said.

"Yes? My impression was the strangers were solely on pleasure bent until we drew their attention to ourselves by our—our antics."

"Perhaps," Jonathan said dubiously. "Apparently Mrs. Cochrane had expected them to be here. But Basil has an idea— It seems farfetched to me but there may be something to it. It concerns our last summer in this vicinity when you weren't with us, so you needn't be bothered about it. I think I'll take a plunge in the pool. You come outside too: I don't like to see you sitting in here all day."

He went on toward the swimming pool with his old bathing suit, a garment sufficiently modest for prewar days, over his arm. Ariadne lay down in the nearest couch-hammock with a magazine she had been trying to read for three days.

But people kept passing up and down the walk; mostly girls her own age and the few available youngish men. She caught snatches of their talk: it seemed Mrs. Cochrane's dance must have furnished them with catch phrases and allusions to last a week. Or they were planning for tonight: a weenie roast, midnight swimming . . .

Ariadne sat up, dug a heel viciously into the lawn and set the hammock swinging. "It's your own fault," she muttered. "If you held your head up and tried to mix with the crowd—"

"Talking to yourself, Spider?" Phil said. "Or just reading aloud? Here's something to amuse you, though you'd better read it to yourself."

He threw a crumpled sheet of violet note paper into her lap. Instinctively she glanced down at it and, seeing the salutation, "My own darling Billy-boy," kept on reading because she couldn't stop, even with the sprawling, slipshod writing dancing crazily before her eyes.

"I know you don't want me to write to you but I just must even if you do keep telling me we must be very very careful. But we have been such a long long time it just seems endless ages to poor little me and it's been more than a year since the kiddie disappeared so couldn't we come right out and tell people about us? We could pretend we've just met and that it's love at first sight, couldn't we, because it really was. Since you worry so much about me maybe being mixed up in something and of course I wouldn't want to be and people do say such unkind things. But then no one ever has to know we ever wanted to get married before and there's no reason why we shouldn't now, is there?

"I'm afraid your baby doll is just a tiny bit too fond of pretty things and you spoil her by always wanting to give them to her. Of course I just love you for it and I'm so sensitive I just couldn't have gone to live with all the others even if you'd want-ed me to. I don't want to share my Billy-boy with anyone else and while I just love kiddies I always say the English have the right idea, keep them out of the way. But we don't need to worry about that or anything, do we? I know you had to go away but do come back soon and write me a little note to say you won't forget me. I'm just a little bit jealous because you know you are so attractive to women, like that nurse you told me about. It's time you began to live your own life, Billy-boy, and we'll be so happy, living just for each other so please come back soon to your own lonesome baby doll. . . ."

"Hot stuff, hunh? Buck up, Spider. You wouldn't believe me if I'd just told you so there it is."

"You—you knew about her?"

"What?" Phil bent down to catch her dry whisper. "Of course I did. Her name's Daisy Something-or-other. One of these luscious blondes. Well, gentlemen apparently keep going back to 'em."

"You mean . . . Not before Gloria . . ."

Phil shrugged. "She was sick six months before she died. What would you expect? None of us did expect the house to be turned into a royal residence for his highness, Frederick II, with Basil William as prime minister. Baby Doll would look after her own skin from the peek I got at her, or she'd have been insisting he do right by our little Nell a lot earlier— Where are you going?"

"I—I don't know. Back to my room—"

"Good Lord, Spider, what's it to you? See here: are you going to marry me?"

"Don't be a fool! You aren't serious. You think you're in love with me because I'm the only girl you ever see. And you're just a boy."

"Don't talk like you were born yesterday. I'm not a—boy. You know what I mean? But it's you I want. I don't know why, when you're nothing but skin and bones," Phil added crudely.

"My money wouldn't make my bones very acceptable!"

"We've got to live. And it would be too bad for you to cut down the profits by taking your share out of the family. Are you too dumb to see it was always planned like that? No, you stay here! You call me a kid and then you act like one yourself."

He put his arm around her shoulders and after a quick glance across the lawn bent his head until his mouth was against her temple. Ariadne shivered and stood quietly while two middle-aged couples in juvenile bathing suits passed along the walk. Then:

"When you do that I feel as if I'd turned over a stone and found something white and squirmy under it," she said.

"Oh, so that's the way it is! You'll get over that. I could make things damn unpleasant for quite a few people you—like. Your father among them. You might care what happens to him. . . . Oh, all right! Run away if you want to. And think it over—"

But she wasn't thinking at all as she ran down the lawn. Ran until she was conscious of two girls staring at her curiously and after that forced herself to walk very slowly. It was so hot that people would think something was wrong if she hurried. And where was she going? Across the drive in front of the hotel and past the swimming pool. How can people even get cool there? she wondered. With so many people in the pool, a bathtub would be more private and the sun wouldn't be shining on that water. . . .

Water. Of course: the river was across the highway if you walked half a mile through the domesticated forest that shielded the hotel from the common tourist. You didn't swim in the river, Ariadne thought, walking on through the trees. It was too deep or too swift and there were no tanned lifeguards with impressive torsos to rescue you if you got into the current. Or were just too tired to swim at all. . . .

CHAPTER 20

Mr. Allan was inclined to growl a little, removing labels from the suit he had just brought back to Green Street. Another look at the sales slip goaded him to definite protest.

"I didn't want a cheap suit, God knows. And I cert'nly couldn't go aroun' in those things." He gestured toward the filthy slacks on the bed. "But neither do I aspire to be one of the ten best-dressed men in America. What is there about this regalia to set me back a month's sal'ry?"

"You paid for the services of the superior gentleman who served you plus his refined admiration of your chassis if not the garments that draped it," Michael said. "And these little imports are very dear."

"I don't like tweeds. They're sloppy."

"These are not sloppy enough. You had better walk over them a few times, though to get the right effect they must be maltreated for a year.

It's just possible you may be called on to pose as one of these hard-ridin', hard-drinkin' fellas from down the Peninsula."

"Me? I never even met one of 'em. Only when there was a rumor the Duke an' Duchess of Windsor might buy an estate in Burlingame, Eleanor said she pitied the dear duke and duchess because it'd probably be ten years before they'd get their pedigree well enough established for the best people to nod to 'em. What've you got in mind?"

"I think we had better talk to Wales first."

"O.K. It's gettin' on to eleven already. If we'd stopped to think, we'd have saved time to go home an' change our clothes before we started down here. Even if they did do a rush job it took 'em quite a while to fix this suit to wear. I hope the girls got our telegram all right."

"Yes, though the way you worded it was something less than tactful. We probably can't see Hogue until after noon. Unfortunately his shop is in the Shreve Building. Not a secluded spot." Michael frowned. "We will have to persuade Mr. Hogue to come here to look at the pretty etchings."

"What etchings? Jeez, I hate to sit here on my tail all day while you guys are out doing things," Smith complained.

"That sunburn of yours will keep you occupied," Rocky said. "You'll have your shirt off again before long." He eyed Smith thoughtfully. "My subconscious is botherin' me again over some detail in that story of yours."

"Listen: I told you the truth, the whole—"

"It's not that. Never mind; it'll come to me."

"You don't have to worry about the manager. She's in the hospital," Michael said. "Her husband works at night, sleeps most of the day and is not curious about the tenants. Neither, as you may have noticed, does he worry too much about the hot water or steam heat. But if it hadn't been for that I wouldn't have risked staying here."

"A hotel would have been riskier," Rocky said. "Especially as we had to bring Smith's clothes to him. They're not a bad fit—"

"Too tight," Mr. Smith said, wriggling his shoulders. "If you won't let me go with you—"

"You stay here and keep out of mischief," Michael said. "Don't answer either the doorbell or the telephone. We'll be back in a few hours. . . . It's as well we have your car and not mine," he added, getting into it. "There aren't any distinguishing marks or signs on it and— Oh, I'm sorry. Do you want to drive?"

Rocky grinned. "I know you're dyin' to have me. No, you can have this city traffic. How'd you get to drive so well?"

"About my only marketable asset when I came here was a familiarity with foreign cars. I drove a wildcat taxi in the Mission for a while and later on was a private chauffeur."

"I can't imagine you standin' to attention and takin' orders."

"I was told several times that my performance in that respect was something less than satisfactory. But eating is a habit that most of us unfortunately acquire early in life."

Michael turned from Hyde into Post, drove a few blocks and then turned again, down toward Market. "Wales' shop is on Stockton but I think we'd better leave the car in a parking lot on O'Farrell. We'll save time and avoid any danger of being tagged for overparking."

"Just as well not to risk anyone noticin' us," Rocky agreed. "And I'm prayin' I won't come face to face with one of the few people I know down here."

They walked up Stockton Street past Union Square, where blasé pigeons strutted over the grass and about the tall Dewey monument. Rocky looked up at the figure atop of it and finally shook his head.

"I never can quite decide if that's Vict'ry in a nightgown with a wreath and trident or just what."

Michael laughed. "It has been described as a floozie with a doughnut in one hand and a pitchfork in the other."

"That'll do me. If they'd left the lady off it'd look less like an old-time tombstone and be a very nice monument to a very smelly war. How much farther?"

"Only a block and a half."

Wales's shop, near the Stockton Street tunnel, was merely a thin wedge serving to hold a circulating library away from a cocktail lounge. In its window were half a dozen trays filled with dusty and discouraged-looking unset stones and cheap silver rings. Michael, seeing Rocky look at these doubtfully, murmured:

"Not his work but a sop to convention. He doesn't expect or want to sell them— Good morning."

"Oh, it's you? I took some things over to your shop yesterday and Fanny said you were out of town—"

"So far as Fanny knows or ever will know—I hope—I am."

"I see. I can take a hint," Wales said. He was a small hump-shouldered man with gray hair rampant over thick black brows. He looked rather helplessly about the small front room. "I'm afraid there aren't chairs enough—"

"We won't sit down. This is Mr. Allan, Mr. Wales. We wanted to know if you knew a man named Hogue, who used to work for Burris?"

"Oh yes. They were tarred with the same brush. Hogue stayed with Burris until he died—"

"But you didn't. Do you mind telling me why?"

"I'm inclined to do my work and not pay much attention to what goes on around me," Wales said. "And on the surface Burris' shop was simply an ordinary, fairly large jewelry shop. But gradually I began to be doubtful about some of his transactions. . . ."

He hesitated, frowning. Then: "I'll tell you why I left him," he went on. "A Mrs. Garwood who had known Burris for years had her jewelry stolen. The insurance company was suspicious but eventually they had to pay up. I suspected the theft was an inside job and that Burris took the things off her hands. Bought them cheap since she had the insurance money besides. And then I'm almost certain he had the pieces broken up and Hogue reset the stones and sold them over the counter. It's been done, you know."

"Hogue's good at that kind of work?" Rocky asked. "He could copy a—well, say a bracelet, so a person who didn't know anything about precious stones wouldn't know it was a fake?"

"Oh, I should think so. He's a clever workman," Wales said grudgingly. "He did that sort of work when I was with Burris. It was always handled very discreetly. Burris was careful: he wouldn't trust just anyone. I'll say for him, too, that I don't think he ever went in for blackmail, though he must have had opportunities. He wasn't that type. He was unscrupulous with regard to some things, but I think he would take what he considered a fair cut and that would end it."

"But you think Hogue might be the type who would go in for blackmail?" Michael suggested.

Wales nodded. "Yes, and I doubt if he would be as cautious as Burris. Or rather, that he's as good a judge of human nature. Burris really knew and understood his wealthier—clients. He was a well-to-do man himself, though he died poor because he thought the stock-market crash of '29 was only temporary. But Hogue never dealt with them and I think he's easily impressed by wealth—"

"When did you leave Burris? And did you know Dumont?"

"Only to speak to. Burris made a job for him. He was a sort of glorified floorwalker. I left Burris early in '31. In fact, just after he and Dumont had broken with each other."

"D'you know why they did?" Rocky said.

"No. I don't think Dumont knew any of the ins and outs of the business. I heard Burris didn't think Dumont's aunt was the right person to have charge of his son. But Burris hadn't done too well with his own daughter. She was a pretty girl," Wales said. "I saw the boy once and he looks like her. She had black hair, too, and was rather delicate-looking."

"Would you give me permission to refer to that insurance swindle if necessary?" Michael said.

"To Hogue, you mean? I've no objections if it will help you to deal with him. I don't like Hogue. And I don't need to warn you to be discreet."

"Hardly. Our wives and our mistresses: may they never meet. I wish that only one of them would come to Gisele's for her clothes. It's sometimes difficult to remember which bill goes to the gentleman's office and which to his home," Michael said. "But generally speaking, the larger one goes to his office and is attended to by a secretary who is also discreet. And just forget that you saw us, please. . . ."

The noon whistles were blowing when they stepped out into the street again. "I think," Michael said, "we'd better walk down to the Fly Trap and have something to eat if you don't mind an early lunch?"

"Hell, no! That burned toast and one egg apiece we rustled for ourselves this mornin' wasn't very sustaining. But is this one of those fool tearooms where they give you dabs of things on doilies and candles on the table?"

Michael chuckled. "Eleanor must share Valerie's weakness for quaint eating places. No, the Fly Trap's décor and its waiters' dress suits must predate the earthquake and they—the waiters—scorn anyone who rushes through his meal and away. We can talk there."

"Yes," Rocky said when they had accepted the Italian waiter's various recommendations, "we can talk, but what about? Of course it bothers me to just leave the kid's body lyin' up there—if you don't mind such subjects at the table? I should have thought more about a number of things before we came rushin' down here."

"Since the boy's lain there for more than a year, I can't think one day more or less matters."

"Oh, I know. Our prejudice in favor of what we call Christian burial is probably silly—"

"Quién sabe? I suppose you could notify your coroner—"

"No. I couldn't count on Lorenzo keepin' still about as big a thing as this. People might want to know where I was—"

"Well," Michael said, smiling, "for future reference, where are we supposed to be today?"

"Lookin' for the kid's body in the woods aroun' Bancross, I reckon. That's what I told Ed Towne we'd be doin', and thank God, Ed's going to be spendin' the day in bed. Look: if that brac'let was pawned and Roche pawned it—"

"Don't you think he did?"

"Whoever took it wouldn't be apt to risk pawning it themselves. Ev'ryone of that bunch is fairly distinctive-lookin'. Whereas Roche was not, and anyway, even if the police found out he pawned the bracelet, who was he? They didn't know. They couldn't even pick him up down here from your description—"

He stopped, staring at the wallpaper's wide border, consisting of nearly life-sized bears and mountain goats poised in space well filled with fruits, cornucopias and assorted curlicues.

"Another twinge from your subconscious?" Michael said.

"Yes, damn it! I almost had it that time. There was something unreas'nable about some part of what Smith told us. Can't you think what it was?"

"No. And the unceasing activity of the past twenty hours has not been conducive to thought. I do think though, and always have, that Roche's habit of humming 'Alouette' was dangerous."

"Any habit can be dang'rous," Rocky said rather inattentively. "Because you yourself never realize you have it. But how many times do you pass someone on the street who's hummin' some popular tune without realizin what he's doing?"

"Very often. And at least one dance band has taken to playing 'Alouette'—lately. But Roche first appears on the scene two years ago. And you can't deny that if it hadn't been for that song—"

He reached hastily for the menu and spread it open, holding it up so that it hid his face. Rocky started to look around, thought better of it and asked:

"What's the matter?"

"There goes a man who knows me. He also knows Sullivan. I should have known better than to come here."

"Well, he didn't stop or speak, so maybe he didn't see you. No use worryin' about it anyway. . . ." Rocky looked approvingly at the immense platter of sautéd Belgian hare, potatoes, ravioli and zucchini that the waiter put before him. "No, this joint isn't even first cousin to a tearoom. Have you got some idea how you're goin' to handle Hogue?"

Michael put down the menu and picked up his fork. "I think so. And we'd better run over our lines now. . . ."

CHAPTER 21

Mr. Hogue had oily black hair, long supple hands and restless eyes. He rubbed the hands together, hurrying from a workbench at the back of the room to a small showcase nearer the door.

There was some really beautiful work under the glass: rings, pendants and bracelets hand-carved and cunningly set with semiprecious stones. They made good the statement lettered on Mr. Hogue's door: INDIVIDUAL DESIGNS IN PERIOD JEWELRY.

Michael abruptly appeared not only embarrassed but definitely fatuous. "Fact is, I'm—uh—that is, a fella recommended you," he said jerkily. "I mean to say, could you—uh—copy a bracelet?"

"A bracelet?" Mr. Hogue said cautiously. "That—uh—depends." It's catching, Rocky thought. "What sort of bracelet did you have in mind?"

"Little thing that set me back plenty," Mr. Dundas said bitterly. "But she wouldn't know the difference. I mean to say, as long as she thought it cost a lot—"

"She?" Hogue said quickly.

"Yes. There's two of 'em and only one bracelet. And my wife—she's one of 'em—is beginning to wonder why I don't remember to get the bracelet from the jeweler's. That's bad—"

Mr. Hogue agreed smoothly that it was bad; very bad indeed. Michael plunged on:

"Can't have a row with my wife. Her father has too much money. But I didn't expect she'd come back from the East so soon. And the other one wanted persuading. Women are like that: won't love a man for himself, but wave a few diamonds in front of 'em and they come through. You ask my friend here. He had a little trouble a couple of years ago, except he isn't married, the lucky stiff."

"Pair of earrings my mother never wore," Rocky said as coached. "Then my brother got married and what did the mater want but to give 'em to his wife. Well, I was playing golf with a fella named Dumont. Knew he used to be in the jewelry business and asked him if he knew of anyone that could make copies of them. And he said—"

"I understand perfectly. But you didn't come to me—"

"Didn't have to. Caught the girl with another man—in the apartment I was paying for. Cleared out, with the earrings."

Mr. Hogue seemed to find this explanation quite believable. "Boys will be boys," he purred. "Now about this bracelet, Mr. . . . uh . . ."

Michael shook his head. "Oh no. I'm too cagey a bird for that, Mr. Hogue. No names necessary. But I haven't the bracelet with me. It takes a little getting, you know. I will, but women are so infernally suspicious. How's about you coming around to my apartment?"

"We-ell . . ."

"I mean to say, I pay for the place but I don't live in the city. Not—not officially." Michael snickered. "That's good, isn't it? But I've got to go around there to get the bracelet, so why not save everybody trouble by you coming by when you go home?"

"Ye-es, I could do that."

"Maybe you could help persuade the little girl it's all open and aboveboard? Here, I'll give you the address."

Michael, Rocky noticed, wrote the address with his right hand, the result being a sprawling childish script. Cagey bird is right, he thought.

"You won't find any name; just a slip saying 'occupied,'" Michael added. "You know how it is: couldn't put my name up and don't want hers up. Well, we'll be expecting you. . . ."

"It's a gift," Rocky said briefly, walking down Post toward Market again.

"Only an imitation of Lord Peter Wimsey imitating one of P. G. Wodehouse's silly-ass Englishmen. You did your part nobly, amigo. You looked every inch the sun-browned Hercules who knows all about horses but finds life away from the paddock a trifle too complex."

"Why not?" Rocky said shortly. "You're good at assignin' roles."

Michael stopped though the traffic lights at Stockton were green. "So your ego has a few prickles too? This is neither the time nor place for an exchange of compliments but you seem to have forgotten that until now I have tagged along at your heels, up hill and down dale. And surely anyone who seems to know as much about people as you do should guess I'm not fond of—"

"Tagging along at anybody's heels?" Rocky finished, smiling.

"No. This happens to be something I'm peculiarly fitted to do and you should be willing to take your turn playing Watson. Or perhaps you agree with Mr. Van Dine that two detectives is one too many?"

"No, I don't. It's true I've got in the habit of tryin' to do ever'thing myself. But I've almost had to. I'm just beginning to get used to working with someone whose mind works right along with mine and— Oh hell! You know what I mean. If this was a movie we'd start shakin' hands."

"Staring steadfastly into each other's eyes. All pals together and let's put this over for the dear old school, boys."

Michael crossed the street against the lights. "Never mind," he said as a policeman tootled at them reprovingly. "San Franciscans do not take traffic signals, strikes, deficits, graft investigations or Los Angeles seriously."

"And earthquakes—only it was a fire. You know, I was surprised Hogue agreed to come to the apartment."

"Wales said he wouldn't be above a little blackmail. He probably thought it a good chance to pick up a little more useful information. We might as well go back there now. We've nothing to do but wait for him. And perhaps catch up on lost sleep."

But that sleep was lost forever. When, Michael having stopped to remove his name from the mailbox outside the front door, they had wearily climbed three flights of stairs, Mr. Smith was waiting for them at the top of the last one.

"The phone rang so long I had to answer and when it said long distance I thought I'd better take it," he told them apologetically. "And I guess I was right because it turned out to be Mrs. Allan, and she says she has something important to tell you and she's going to call again at four."

Eleanor displayed a tendency to wander about the room, repeating bitterly: "'Got to see a man about a dog in the city.' . . . Well," she added finally, "after staying up all hours, I suppose we might as well go to bed whether or not we sleep. Wasn't it nice of them to think of wiring?"

"I think this would be an excellent sedative," Valerie remarked, riffling over the pages of the book they had taken from the library during a stroll about town. "I thought it might be worth reading but it looks unbelievably dull. It's odd how many people who talk entertainingly can't write at all—or vice versa."

"You go to bed now," Sing Toy said severely from the hall. "You wake baby, you talk too loud. Boss will come back. And will not make him pie for long time."

"That's an idea. Give him hash and what he calls wind puddings."

"Can do. Missy go to bed. Car just stop outside," Sing Toy said. "But Missy not bother."

"Oh, I'd better. It must be something fairly important for anyone to come here at this time of the night. I suppose I'll have to do a little artistic lying. . . ."

Valerie followed Eleanor out into the hall. "It couldn't be a message from Michael and Rocky, could it, when that wire came from Oroville? But—"

Eleanor opened the door before the young man on the porch had time to knock. It was the deputy Rocky had sent over to Pluma Blanca that morning. He had a worried frown on his tanned face and Ariadne Holaday on one arm.

"Gosh, I'm glad you're still up. Look, I managed to find out this lady was missing from the hotel. They were looking for her but no one knew it yet. So I sneaked out in my car and found her walking along the road. She said she was coming here, and when I said wasn't she at the inn and didn't she want to go back there she tried to get out of the car. I didn't know what to do so I just— Hey, don't do that!"

"She's only fainted," Eleanor said calmly. "You were right to bring her here, Jack. Can you carry her in? . . . Just put her on the couch. You'd better get back to the inn right away. Rocky hasn't come back from Bancross yet. I'll telephone her father and tell them that a passer-by picked her up."

"Well, if you're sure there's nothing else I can do?" Jack Wolter said. "I'm supposed to keep kind of under cover, but Rocky said not to let anybody get away either."

"I'm sure he won't find any fault with what you did. You run on. . . . Sing Toy! Bring me that bottle of old brandy. Yes, I know it's kept for special occasions but bring it just the same!"

"I went down to the river," Ariadne said when she came to. "But I couldn't help thinking Gloria wouldn't have wanted me to kill myself. She wouldn't ever have done anything like that."

"Of course she wouldn't." Eleanor poured brandy into a small glass. "Drink this. How far did you walk?"

"I don't know. I just lifted one foot after the other and that kept me from thinking. And you were the only person I could think of to come to. I couldn't go back."

"I'll call the inn and tell them you're here—"

"Oh no—please!" Ariadne caught at Eleanor's dress. "They'll come after me and say I'm overwrought and must go back so people won't talk. And I won't go!"

"You don't have to," Eleanor said. "I'm only calling them so they won't look for you." She went out to the telephone and put through a call to Pluma Blanca. In a few minutes Valerie heard her say: "Hello. I must speak to Mr. Dumont. . . . Oh, he is? Well then, Mr. Holaday. It's quite important. . . . Mr. Holaday? This is Mrs. Allan. Your daughter is here with us. . . . Yes. I'll keep her here tonight and let you know how she is in the morning. . . .

"Yes, certainly she's upset and she doesn't want to see any of you. . . . Those are her words, Mr. Holaday, not mine. We're glad to have her here and I'd advise you to tell people she's visiting us. And if you do come here I won't let you see her. Is that clear?"

She came back into the living room. "It's all right. Now you must go to bed—"

"Not yet," Ariadne said. "I've got to talk to somebody. I want to tell you everything. About Gloria and the money . . . and everything . . ."

The low husky monotone went on and on, recalling how Gloria had struggled to keep Ariadne decently dressed and well fed. Because Daniel hadn't been willing to work except in the theater and couldn't get engagements there. And Gloria had married Frederick as much on their account as her own—and told him so. But they'd been very happy and he'd insisted on leaving her everything though Gloria hadn't wanted him to.

Then she'd met Basil and they'd seemed so much in love with each other. He'd said he didn't want her to leave him any of Armstrong's money: that it was his son's. And Gloria herself didn't feel she had the right to leave much of it away from Freddie, though she was afraid of what it would do to

him. "But as it turned out we were all living off
the estate," Ariadne said. "The house had to be
kept up for Freddie, and the allowance or whatever it's called was so generous . . . And Gloria had
left letters of instruction that I suppose weren't
legally binding but saying she wanted us all to have
a home there and—and everything that went with
it. I know she thought Freddie would look after us
after he was of age. She didn't know he wouldn't
be at all like her or Frederick. Because after she
died nothing was the same: Freddie or Basil or
anyone. And finally Freddie was kidnaped. . . ."

She told all of it, holding tightly to Eleanor's
hand. It was a good hand to hold to but she found
herself looking more and more at Valerie, increasingly certain that, however happy Mrs. Dundas
might be now, she remembered what this was like.

There wasn't much she could say about the kidnaping itself. They'd kept people away from her,
and Dr Monroe insisted she'd had a slight relapse.
But there was her meeting with Ted Smith in the
little restaurant; his saying he had been drugged.
. . . And their conversation at the breakfast table
just before they heard of Edith Parnell's death.
And then she had overheard Jonathan telling Basil
that Miss Parnell had wanted to talk to someone
in the house.

She went on to their first night at Pluma Blanca: being certain she heard Basil in the hall after they were all in bed. His denying that; denying he'd ever suspected the bracelet that was stolen was only a copy. Her suspicion that her father might have taken it to pawn; his "word to the wise" this morning. That might have been purely spiteful, though he'd always liked Basil well enough. Phil and Phil's threats and the violet letter that Basil had been reading yesterday . . .

Eleanor, glancing at the crumpled letter, muttered: "So this was the last straw? This and what Philip said about it?"

"I thought Basil really loved Gloria and that he'd tried to love Freddie and take care of him for her sake. If I have to believe that even before she died he was . . . Well, even if he did love Gloria until she died but forgot her so quickly for the kind of woman that wrote that letter—"

"You love him yourself, don't you?" Valerie said.

"Of course. I've never cared for anyone else. When he and Gloria were married I thought he was the kind of big brother any girl would like to have. I know some people call him dull but I am too. Your husbands are both—both fascinating in different ways but they'd tire me out. I thought I could trust Basil and I have! I've made excuses for him even when I've been certain he knows things he's never told. I could even excuse his being willing Phil and I should marry if it wasn't all part of the same plan—"

"He's too old for you, no matter what sort of person he turns out to be," Eleanor said bluntly. "Twenty years, isn't it?"

"That might not matter," Valerie said. "Michael's nine years older than I am. But—but you may just want someone to love, Ariadne. I did once. And that's entirely different from being in love."

"I suppose it is," Ariadne said listlessly. "Perhaps I'll grow out of it. But it was the last straw." She laughed hysterically. "That sounds like Pop. Gloria and I used to call him that and he's still Pop to me. He hasn't changed. He was probably nice to me this morning because he was afraid I might really know something. And very likely Jonathan was sounding me out, too, not really caring at all how I felt. Will I have to repeat all this to Mr. Allan?"

"I'm afraid so. He and Mr. Dundas haven't come in yet," Eleanor said. "And it's so late I think you had better go to bed and not wait for them."

"I want to now. And tomorrow I'll try not to act like something out of *Children of the Abbey*.

You remember? The heroine swoons regularly at the end of every chapter. . . ."

She closed her eyes and lay still. Valerie walked quietly over to the table, picked up the book she had been looking at and brought it over to Eleanor, opened at the copyright page.

"Did you notice this?" she whispered. "Should we—speak to her about it?"

"N-no. No, we'd better wait until we're sure."

CHAPTER 22

"Well," Rocky said, sitting down, "it's as well you did answer the phone. Did you tell Eleanor who you are?"

"She got it out of me. I don't just know how—"

"I could guess."

"And what about my wife?" Michael asked. "It must have been her idea to call here."

Smith grinned. "I did hear someone say, 'I know it was Michael's idea.' And then—maybe I was mistaken—I thought I heard this same voice say, 'He knows the queerest people.'"

"You weren't mistaken. She forgets it was she who had known Edith Parnell." Michael lay down on the chesterfield. "Suppose you mix us some drinks, Smith: strong ones. There's no use in our trying to sleep. We'd only be waked up when Eleanor calls again."

"I napped on the way down last night," Rocky said. "And for a guy that squalled like a catamount about gettin' up at six you seem to be doin' right well."

"I don't object to doing without sleep. Only to being dragged untimely from my bed once I'm in it."

"Oh. You'd never make a railroader. Bein' one was how I got so I could go to sleep any time and wake up quick."

"Then why don't you?" Michael said discouragingly.

Mr. Smith, returning with the drinks, heard that and decided he would not ask questions after all. Neither one of 'em acted like they wanted to talk, he thought resentfully. He sat down beside his own glass, reached for a bottle of lotion and attended to his sunburn. After an hour of what he dubbed "silent prayer" the telephone rang.

"She's callin early. She would." Rocky got up and started for the bedroom when Michael did not move. "If it's Eleanor, all right. But if it's Valerie, you can deal with her. Because I'm not going to . . . Hello! . . . Oh, hello honey," said Mr. Allan so ingratiatingly that Michael snorted derisively. "We were goin' to call you but . . . What! She did? . . . Wait a minute.

"Come here and listen to this," he said to Michael. "It seems Ariadne Holaday turned up at our house last night. . . . Eleanor! What did she say? I mean, did she—"

"You mean, is she talking," Eleanor said. "She's told us all she knows and it serves you right for not being here—"

"I know! But does she know who hired Roche?"

"Of course not. We've told her about him but she's no wiser than before. And you know our small-town operators," Eleanor said with complete disregard for Flo Hardy's feelings if that young woman was listening in. "I don't think there's anything that won't keep if you're coming back soon."

"Early in the mornin', honey."

"You'd better. Is there anything you want to ask?"

"I don't think so. I guess that's all—"

"Oh no, it isn't. Valerie wants to talk to Michael."

Rocky moved politely away from the telephone but it was his turn to grin, for Michael looked distinctly harassed, listening to Valerie. When he was given an opportunity to speak he answered her in Spanish but so slowly that Rocky was able to translate roughly. His grin widened. Eleanor, he thought, usually hit it about right. Valerie was undoubtedly Michael's "soft streak." But it wouldn't do to say so. When Michael put down the telephone he remarked perfunctorily:

"I hope she wasn't too upset? But they've had some excitement of their own so we're going to get off easy."

Michael walked over to the windows. "I wonder what happened to drive the girl to—" He broke off, looking down at the sidewalk. "Eleanor isn't the only one who calls early. Mr. Hogue is just getting out of his car."

Mr. Hogue considered the apartment house distinctly promising. It sat high on a hill above the sustaining wall that kept its small front plot of shrubbery from sliding down into Green Street. That meant there would be a marine view, and even a three-cornered glimpse of the bay, as Mr. Hogue very well knew, was a potent lever where rents were concerned.

He approved, too, of the manner in which apartment 6 was furnished. You didn't buy old rosewood and mahogany for a song, he thought, and the carved Chinese chest and mounted jade screens hadn't come from stores that catered to tourist trade. And his host was wearing a brocaded dressing gown; the sort of garment Mr. Hogue considered a young man should wear during a quiet evening in what he labeled "a little love nest." Mr. Hogue rubbed his hands together and began genially:

"Well, I trust you had no difficulties with the little lady? If I might see the bracelet . . ."

"There isn't a bracelet," Michael said.

Mr. Hogue blinked. This was not the voice he had heard in the early afternoon. And now that the fellow wasn't smiling foolishly—or at all—he didn't even look the same. It was very disturbing. And more so to have the tall blond man emerge suddenly from the bedroom, turn the latch on the front door and set his shoulders against it. Mr. Hogue wet his lips and turned instinctively toward the windows.

"It's a sheer drop," Michael said solicitously. "And the other apartment on this floor is vacant and the tenants of the one below are vacationing. May I present Mr. Allan? And Mr. Smith?'"

"I'm mighty glad to meet you," said Mr. Allan with flattering emphasis. Mr. Smith, coming in from the bedroom and appearing to Mr. Hogue's demoralized gaze not only a sunburned "hairy brute" but also distressingly muscular, said briefly:

"This the guy?"

"Mr. Allan is an officer of the law," Michael continued. "Really a charming person when you know him. But rather like Abdullah Boul Boul Ameer. You know Abdullah, of course?"

"I . . . uh . . ." said Mr. Hogue.

"He don't know Abdullah," Rocky said sadly. "Somethin' ought to be done about education in this country."

"'This son of the desert in battle aroused, Could spit twenty men on his spear. . . .' Except that Mr. Allan gets along very nicely without a spear."

"See my head?" said Mr. Smith. He allowed it to wobble alarmingly. "See! Just from him slapping me twice."

"But when he isn't crossed he's gentle as a lamb," Michael assured the shrinking Mr. Hogue. "He wants you to tell him something. And then he'd like it so much if you didn't run to the city police to tell them without first having his permission to do so. I am a sensitive sort of person, Mr. Hogue, and I will probably have to retire to the bedroom and put cotton in my ears if you exasperate Mr. Allan."

Rocky rolled his sleeves suggestively higher over his bronzed arms. "Let's get on with it. I want to describe a bracelet to you and you listen close. It was wider 'n most di'mond-and-sapphire bracelets would be and made in four pieces kind of linked together. Each piece had one large diamond in the center with some fairly big sapphires aroun' that. Then what space was left was filled up with a lot of smaller diamonds an' sapphires. That right, Smith? You said you saw it once or twice."

"There was everything on it but the kitchen stove."

"So you oughtn't to forget a thing like that," Rocky said kindly. "Is your mem'ry beginnin' to function?"

Hogue wet his lips. "I . . . uh . . ." he remarked inadequately.

"Mr. Hogue is a man of few words," Michael said. "Who hired you to make a copy of the bracelet Mr. Allan has described?"

"There are dozens of bracelets in the world, you know. Why should you expect me to recognize any one of them from that description? You're making a mistake—"

"No, you are." Rocky stepped away from the door. "Had we better gag him first?"

Mr. Hogue squeaked and scuttled into a corner. "No, you don't! I didn't do anything illegal. I did copy a bracelet like the one you described. But if someone brings it to me and says it's hers—"

"Hers?" Rocky said sharply.

"Hortense Dumont. You seem to know the name. She asked me to copy a bracelet, and why should I refuse?"

"I don't know. I didn't ask you, so why bring it up? Was it because you wondered how she came by it?"

"Yes," Hogue said sullenly. "I knew she had only a very small income of her own. She said Mrs. Dumont had given her the bracelet. Well, Mrs. Dumont had money to burn and I always understood, from what people said, that she was very generous. The bracelet was an atrocious thing and she might not have cared for it. But I did get in touch with Dumont. He said it was all right; that he'd recommended me to Miss Dumont."

"Oh. Did that satisfy you?"

"Why not? He didn't appear at all—upset, if that's what you mean. Though I talked to him over the telephone."

"Yeah? Well, did Miss Dumont come back for the copy?"

"Oh yes. She seemed in rather a hurry for it. She had to come back a second time late in the afternoon to get it. That was around Easter a year ago—in '37, that is. It's on my books if you want to know the exact date."

"That's near enough for now." Rocky looked toward Michael. "That about covers it, I reckon?"

"Yes, except Miss Dumont didn't happen to buy her pearls through Burris, Mr. Hogue?"

"Pearls? What— Oh yes, she did. It seems that an aunt on her mother's side left her around ten thousand dollars and she spent a good part of it for those pearls. Of course Burris made her a price on them because Dumont was still with him then—"

"And she probably used what was left to pay you for your work," Michael said. "Because I don't imagine it comes cheap."

"There's no reason why it should," Hogue said with a certain professional pride that approached dignity. "And I must protest against your—your procedure. I could have you persecuted for attempted intimidation! And I'm not—"

"And you aren't at all certain you won't? I don't think you will, Mr. Hogue. Do you remember Mr. Wales? Because we were talking to him this morning and he told us so many interesting things. 'Why the sea is boiling hot . . . And whether pigs have wings.'"

"And what becomes of jew'lry that's supposed to be stolen but somehow turns up in a high-class shop," Rocky said affably. "Nice guy, Wales."

"And a very good friend of mine," Michael assured Mr. Hogue, whose lips appeared in need of wetting again. "He believes in attending to his own business but he might break that rule if he were sufficiently annoyed. And anything that annoys me is apt to have the same effect on him. He has an excellent memory too. He even remembers the name Garwood. Need I say any more?"

"No. Though there's nothing to that—"

"Oh, of course not. I'm sure we understand each other. And that you understand that if the police come asking you the same questions we have, you won't remember that you ever answered them before?"

Mr. Hogue nodded unhappily. "If that's all—"

"I'd kind of like to know if maybe you didn't think it might be just as well to be obligin' toward Basil Dumont?" Rocky said. "And why did he an' Burris split up?"

"If you mean what I think you mean—I never supposed Dumont was ever in Burris' confidence. I couldn't be certain about that though," Hogue said with a slight approach to candor. "Burris said they didn't agree about the way Dumont was raising the grandson, Philip. And I heard that he accused Dumont of wanting to marry again before poor Miss Eve was dead. But I didn't think Dumont knew Mrs. Armstrong, as she was then, until after Miss Eve killed herself."

"Oh. Well, I guess that's all. Let me hold the door open for you, Mr. Hogue. . . ."

"It would have been funny if Hogue hadn't been the right guy after you put on that act for him," Smith said reflectively.

"He almost had to be the right person. I mean, he's the only one Cochrane mentioned as bein' an expert at that kind of work. And there was his connection with Dumont, through Dumont's first father-in-law—"

"Yes, but it seems this Wales Mr. Dundas spoke about must have helped you out a lot when it came to handling Hogue. It beats me how you always know a fellow who knows something about someone else or who can tell you someone who does. Just plain lucky."

"Not at all," Michael said. "I've lived here more than eleven years, progressing upward from park benches and flophouses. I've known thieves, whores, bartenders, fake spiritualists, fences, pawnbrokers, con men, pimps, touts, jockeys, bail-bond brokers, shysters, torch singers—"

"Je-eez!" said Mr. Smith reverently.

"And a few of our best people as only their chauffeurs can know them. And still more as only a couturier, a personal maid or a hairdresser can know them."

"Or a masseuse," Rocky said. "And what's the common denominator?"

"That almost everyone has his price and self-preservation is the strongest human instinct. 'There's no striving against the stream; and the weakest still goes to the wall.'" Michael turned abruptly to Smith. "You might mix us another round of drinks. . . . No: on second thought, just bring the bottle and some whisky glasses. Both bottles."

CHAPTER 23

Michael refilled his own glass and Rocky's but frowned at the one Smith pushed toward him.

"One of us should stay sober," he decided. "And I think it had better be you. What do you think, Mr. Allan?"

"Right as usual, Mr. Dundas. From a moral as well as a practical standpoint," Mr. Allan said benevolently. "We wouldn't want anyone as young as him learnin' bad habits."

Mr. Smith glared at them. "I'm twenty-seven," he said, retired to the chesterfield and sought solace in his bottle of sunburn lotion. Presently he observed sulkily: "I don't see why you guys sit around and—and brood. All you've got to do is go back and arrest Miss Dumont. Or Basil Dumont."

"Since you suggest an alternative, you must see there's still a few gaps that need pluggin'," Rocky said. "Miss Dumont had the bracelet, all right, but—"

"But she may have been acting for Dumont? Sure, I see that. She'd help him any way he wanted her to."

"Miss Parnell certainly didn't bleach her hair to captivate Miss Dumont," Michael murmured.

"That's right," Rocky said. "And you heard Michael ask Hogue about her pearls?"

"Y-yes, but . . . Well," Smith said, "she could have pawned them but maybe she didn't want to?"

"That goes without saying. Did you ever read a story by Hergesheimer called, I think, *Blue Glass?*" Michael said.

"I don't think so."

"Well, I have," Rocky said. "And I see what you've been drivin' at in regard to those pearls. You see, I don't know all about women—like you do."

"Them's fightin' words, pardner," Michael said absently. He emptied one whisky bottle and broke the cap on another.

"Hey!" Smith protested. "You're going to be tighter than ticks. Those are imperial quart bottles."

"Impossible, Mr. Smith. At one time and another, singly or combined, all of my beloved fraternity brothers tried to put me under the table—and failed."

"I didn't know you'd gone to college. What fraternity?"

"Deke. Grandfather had money. I went two years but it didn't take. Unfortunately I was an adult when I entered."

Smith blinked. "If the guys in your chapter were like the Dekes I know you had pretty good training handling booze."

"Of course I don't know about Mr. Allan—"

"I cut my teeth on co'n liquor an' come of a long line of Southern gentlemen that always went to bed with their boots on. Fill'er up."

Smith groaned and applied a fresh coat of sunburn lotion. "Before you get too pie-eyed—you've got a good case against Dumont. I did tell him about Miss Parnell. He did at least know that bracelet was a copy. And he did ask her not to tell anyone about that sleeping medicine being missing. And—"

"That reminds me," Michael said. "Why has he never been more than a runner-up in golf tournaments?"

"He's got the strokes but he's like one of these guys that kicks 'em sixty yards warming up before a game and then they block it on him if he has to kick from behind his own goal line in a game. You know what I mean?"

"Loses his nerve when the chips are down? Another thing: what caused you to tumble to the fact that Ariadne Holaday didn't care for you?"

"I never really had much hope but I finally realized it's Dumont she really cares for."

"I wondered about that, but he's twice her age," Rocky said. "What about him? And Philip Dumont?"

"She wouldn't marry Phil and I don't know how Dumont feels about her. Of course he'd double his profit if he married her. Or if Phil did, have him off his hands."

"An Miss Dumont wouldn't object to that?"

"She don't like Ariadne but she'd pry out her front teeth if Phil wanted them."

"And what is his attitude toward his father?" Michael said.

Smith frowned. "It's hard to tell. I do think he's jealous of him. Not just because of Ariadne, but because of Dumont's looks and the way people usually like him."

"And would Holaday oppose Ariadne's marriage to either Dumont, do you think?"

"He might talk against it but I don't think he'd really care much. I mean, so long as he's O.K. he don't really care what happens to anyone else. He's a self-centered old bastard. He knows he'd never get his hands on Ariadne's share. She knows him too well. She's got to marry someone and he's always gotten along well with Dumont. He just kind of laughs at Phil. He always can get his goat. I'll admit it used to tickle me to see him put Miss Dumont in her place."

"I reckon he needed to do that pretty often," Rocky said.

He poured himself another drink. And that, Smith thought, seemed to be that. He looked thirstily at the whisky and wondered what Dundas would say if he made some coffee. Just to have ready in case it was needed. And a bite to eat. . . .

"Well," Rocky said suddenly, "I admit I'm licked. We've figured out ever'thing that can be reasoned out. When you keep tryin' diff'rent roads and just come to a large mountain at the end of 'em all, about all you can do is jump over or tunnel under—"

"But you can't lay a trap for five people and expect to catch the right one in it," Michael said.

"Hell, no! There's no use concentratin' on who killed Freddie Armstrong. Maybe Roche attended to that pers'nally too. I'd hoped we could get our man through Roche's death. But nothing about that has helped us."

"And if he killed Miss Parnell her death don't help you any," Smith contributed. "The police down here didn't get anywhere with it. Of course they didn't know about Roche, and even when Mr. Dundas tried to describe him—"

"Got it!" Rocky cried. "Roche—Miss Parnell! Look: you described him to her the best you could, includin' his habit of hummin' 'Alouette.' And the song was familiar to her and you told her about him livin' in Bancross. But hell, it's not reas'nable she should have been so certain right away that she'd seen him, just from your description—which wouldn't help—and the fact he was humming that song on a street corner."

Smith's jaw dropped. "Jeez, I—I forgot about that. Well, I was feeling so woozy last night I—"

"Never mind that! Speak your piece!"

"Well, I said to her, "How can you be so sure it was Roche you saw?' And then she mumbled something about him looking like someone whose picture she'd seen once. Then she said 'just *a* picture' she'd seen. But that isn't reasonable either, only I was so glad to have her say she had seen him— Hey! Are you passing out already? I thought you—"

"I am not," Michael said without removing his head from his hands. "I'm overcome with a rush of ideas to the brain."

"Let's see if I can help," Rocky said. "Phil Dumont took some pictures when they were at Bancross. He may have taken Roche's. But Ed Towne told us he claimed that film was stolen the day before they left. So Miss Parnell never saw one of those pictures unless they turned up later—"

"I'm sure they didn't because Phil still complained about losing them after we were back here. But he did have a whole morning the day we went back to Pluma Blanca from Bancross because we didn't leave till after lunch. I don't know what he did to occupy himself then because Freddie kept me busy. Phil was well by then: you know he'd been sick most of the time."

"Yes, I was thinkin' that would explain quite a lot that needs explainin'."

Michael sat erect. "Did anyone besides Philip have any photograph albums?"

"I never saw any. Miss Dumont had a whole stack of regular photographs of Phil and Dumont—"

"Did you ever see her showing those to Miss Parnell?"

"No, but I guess she might have. She even showed them to me. But look," Smith said, "I hate to discourage you but Phil got a new expensive camera before Freddie was kidnaped and he hadn't any use for his old snapshots. He said they were just 'kid stuff'—"

"So I've been told. By Ariadne, who also told me that Edith Parnell was the sort of person one shows the family album to. And if I had detected the weakness in Miss Parnell's account of how she recognized Roche, as Mr. Allan did—"

"Don't call me Mr. Allan! And you're doin' all right."

"Pues bien, amigo. Ariadne said Phil had gotten rid of his boyish efforts. But did she mean he had actually destroyed them? I took for granted she did. But she did also imply that Miss Dumont is inclined to be a hoarder."

"That's no lie! The whole third floor—what was meant for servants' rooms, only old Armstrong didn't want them there—is filled with stuff she's saved. And gosh, she wouldn't throw away anything belonging to Phil even if she never really looked at it again—"

"All right, there it is," Rocky said.

He reached for the whisky bottle. Smith wanted to ask: "There what is?" then decided philosophically that he might as well save his breath. It was exasperating, the way they seemed to understand each other without talking. Dundas had himself another drink too before either of them said anything.

Then: "We could get a warrant an' search the house," Rocky remarked. "But we'd have such a hell of a lot of explainin' to do first. And maybe we wouldn't find anything after we'd tipped off our hand that way."

"Just what I was thinking. But I am not an officer of the law. You're drunk, *amigo*."

"I never," said Mr. Allan with some dignity, "felt better in my life. How about you?"

"I think," said Mr. Dundas thoughtfully, "that if a man-eating tiger walked up to me I would try to pet the nice kitty. Whose idea was this?"

"It's your liquor, so it must 've been your idea. But I can't just recall why it seemed such a good one."

"Because you thought that I thought that you thought you could drink me under the table. And I thought that you thought that I thought that I could—"

"You're higher'n the Empire State Building," Rocky said, grinning.

Michael shook his head. "No. Perfect muscular control," he insisted, rose and turned a back somersault. "See? You try it."

"I am not an acrobat," Rocky said aloofly. "But I do know one that—"

"Oh, Lord!" said Mr. Smith. "Say, I'm going to make some coffee—"

"Mr. Smith's disapproving attitude hurts me." Michael regarded him fixedly and then turned to

Rocky. "But my frank and manly nature compels me to admit we are both a few steps along the road to oblivion."

"Well, as long as you admit it, I reckon I'd been just as well off without that last slug. I think," Rocky said, getting up, "that we'd better take steps. While Smith makes that coffee . . ."

Smith was just reflecting that cold water, food and black coffee had worked wonders when a sudden question from Michael made him gulp and stare at him doubtfully.

"W-what was that?"

"Could you get into the Armstrong house without being seen if you had a good set of picklocks?"

"Look: are you sure you're—"

"We're sober—enough," Rocky said. "Tell him."

"I suppose I got to. Your picklocks wouldn't do any good. The doors all have night latches and Otto—that's the gardener who acts as caretaker—would be careful to see they're on while the family's away. But I guess—

"Well, you know there's an alley in from Laguna that brings you in at the servants' quarters. There's a covered passage from them to the kitchen but there's an outside door from the kitchen to the back yard too. And there's a cellar underneath because the ground slopes and there's one little window in the cellar, right near the ground."

He looked speculatively at Rocky's shoulders. "You couldn't do it but Mr. Dundas might manage. They always let the maids go on vacation and Otto and his wife go to bed early. Well, there's just one pane of glass in that window. But it mightn't be locked because Freddie broke the lock that May, hammering it loose so he could crawl in and out. They might never have noticed it and I forgot to tell 'em."

Rocky looked at Michael. "Can do?"

"As old Hymie Rose says: und vy not?"

"Look: I had to tell you what you asked. But you guys are nuts," Smith protested. "Taking that kind of risk just to find out if there's a picture of Roche in Phil's albums—if the albums are still there. Besides, what's a picture of Roche—"

"Mr. Smith, there are times when I suspect your muscles developed at the expense of your brain. Why would Edith Parnell take more than a passing glance at a picture of Roche?"

"I don't know. But you just said she must have seen a picture of him or she wouldn't—"

"Never mind," Rocky said solicitously. "You just take it easy and don't worry."

"And tell me something more. How did you know Roche was in the habit of humming 'Alouette' if Freddie Armstrong kept you so busy? Roche didn't help you amuse the boy, did he?"

"Oh gosh, no!" Smith said hastily. "We'd just stop to watch him mining once or twice when we were walking along that road. No; I forgot to tell you that Dumont took charge of the kid one morning so I could go fishing. And since it was pretty well fished out near Bancross he had Roche take me where I'd be sure to get some fish. Well, I can't say I got acquainted with Roche that morning, though we were together seven hours. He just slouched along and didn't talk even when we were only walking. But that was when I noticed how he kept humming all the time. And I kind of laughed about that to Dumont and he told me the name of the song. And afterwards I heard Ariadne singing it—"

"Satisfied?" Rocky said, grinning at Michael. "That simplifies things, doesn't it? See here, Smith—maybe you'd better draw me a diagram of the layout back of the Armstrong house."

CHAPTER 24

An alley cat, straying through the fog across damp grass and round plots of newly planted pansies, discovered four feet and trousered legs in a dark angle around the corner of the house. And, rubbing against the larger pair of legs with a rusty but affectionate purr, found herself speedily shunted back to the graveled path.

"I'd hate," someone murmured, "to kick a cat. But keep the beast away from me till I see—"

"Is it locked?"

"Just stuck, I think. I don't want to— Oof ! It got away from me. But it's up. Now it's your turn."

"You'd better hold my coat. It's going to be a tight squeeze. Don't be so damned helpful!" Michael protested. "That shove of yours took two inches off my right shoulder."

"Try contractin' your muscles."

"'Oh, that this too, too solid flesh would melt'! Dios! There goes more skin. . . ."

"Are you in?" Rocky whispered anxiously, looking nervously back toward the servants' quarters before he moved through the misty darkness
closer to the window.

"'Observe with what an airy flop I plant myself
upon the top.' Give me my coat." Michael thrust
a hand out the window. "I'll unlock the kitchen
door for you."

Ted Smith lay across the bed with the window
shades pulled down and tried to obey Rocky's parting injunction to "get some sleep because you'll
have to do part of the driving." But it was no use:
he couldn't even nap. He lighted another cigarette
and tried not to look at the clock.

They were crazy, those guys, he thought irrita-
bly. Crazy like a quarterback calling for passes behind his own goal line. And Allan reminded him
in some ways of the big fullback he'd played with
at his second college, the one that used to sleep
in the dressing rooms right up to game time. That
was what Allan had done: laid down and slept until nine o'clock and then bounced up ready for
action.

But Dundas had gone out and parked the car
several blocks away from the apartment house.
When he came back he said he preferred not to
sleep at all if he had to get up in three hours.

He made another pot of coffee and then produced several pieces of brilliant velvet that he wove and twisted into what even Smith recognized as a peaked turban.

He put out his cigarette, half smoked, and looked at the clock again. Nearly eleven. Hell, they ought to be back by now. It shouldn't take them all night to do what they had in mind.

The telephone rang. Smith started so violently that the bed springs creaked. He eyed the telephone doubtfully, but when it had rung four times he picked it up. It was probably Mrs. Allan again and he didn't dare not answer.

But it was a man's voice that replied to his "H-hello" with: "That you, Michael?" The voice was one Smith felt he should know. He gulped and said cautiously: "N-no . . ."

"Well, who is it? Where is he? This is Inspector James Sullivan."

For an instant Smith was convinced he had permanently swallowed his Adam's apple. And with Sullivan barking at him, "I said, who is this?" he lost his head and stammered:

"I'm j-just a friend of his. He's letting me use his apartment for a night while he's away."

"He didn't mention anything like that to me," Sullivan said. "But I suppose you wouldn't answer the phone if you weren't— You're sure he's not in town? I was just talking to a fellow who said he saw him in the Fly Trap today."

"It must have been two other guys," Smith said feebly. "I'm from Los Angeles myself. I'm just in town overnight—"

"Yes? I'd like to talk to you. Stick around, will you? It won't take me ten minutes to drive over."

Smith set the telephone back on its table, rubbed his sweating hands together and then pressed them to his temples. If I stay here, Sullivan will pull me in again, he thought. But if I clear out, Allan and Dundas will think I've double-crossed them. And whichever I do, they may get back here just in time to run into Sullivan.

The bedroom was furnished with a heavy, tall-headed walnut bed, a wide bureau with a small mirror, one or two high-backed, forbidding chairs. The wallpaper was thick and dark, very expensive and very ugly. There were stiff lace curtains at the windows, elaborate glass lighting fixtures, Landseers and indistinct historical etchings on the walls, while on the carpet the last rose of summer bloomed defiantly but by no means alone.

"I guess this was Frederick Armstrong's idea of luxury. It would drive me nuts," Rocky said. "Look: even if you hadn't any gloves to fit me, why worry about my fingerprints? They aren't on record and you could work faster without gloves—"

"My prints are on record. And yours will be too if you're careless."

Michael opened the bottom drawer of a massive chiffonier, glanced into it and shrugged expressively. "I don't think there is anything of interest here either and this is the last one."

"I don't see how we could've overlooked anything up on the third floor. We were there long enough," Rocky said gloomily. "It beats me why anybody wants to hang onto all the old furniture and clothes that have wore out durin' the last ten years. Those rooms up there were as bad as old Rose's junk shop but I didn't think we missed anything."

"We didn't." Michael closed the drawer and stood erect. "Well, that leaves the closet."

"There's not apt to be anything in— I'll be damned," Rocky said, staring into the closet. "I haven't seen one like that for years. Maybe . . . Well, I've got my fingers crossed."

The closet was the usual shallow niche considered by the old-fashioned architect ample accommodation for any wardrobe. And to make quite certain no one would accuse him of wastefulness, he had added a covered, built-in box to take up as much floor space as possible.

"To stow your shoes and hats away so you can't possibly get at 'em in a hurry," Rocky said.

"And for the better propagation of moths," Michael added, removing three venerable felt hats from the box. Under those was three quarters of a crocheted afghan with the yarns needed for its completion. They spilled onto the floor, greens, reds, yellows and browns, as Michael tossed the afghan aside and pounced on three leather albums lying beside a stack of photographs.

"Damn it, fingerprints or no fingerprints—"

"Tut-tut! Put your hands behind you and Papa will show you the pretty pictures," Michael said. "Mustn't touch. No, it's not this one. These snaps were taken in '34. . . ."

"Try the bottom one. You always find what you're looking for the last place you look."

The pages headed "Bancross, July 1936" were in the middle of the book. The eight snapshots had neat captions in white ink: "Woodland Scene", "Forest Primeval", "Bancross Bridge", "Rustic Cabin" . . .

"As Ariadne told me, he always had a leaning toward the 'quaint,'" Michael said finally.

"And I reckon that spelled quaintness to him. Probably he took it more for the background than anything else. But the figures are clear and she— Edith Parnell—must have looked mostly at them.

The likenesses are damn good; one of those lucky shots. I don't suppose it was Roche she was interested in—then."

"No. As you say, it's a very good likeness. And from what Ariadne said, I imagine she was too polite merely to glance at a page and go on to the next. Besides, she probably 'liked to look at pictures.'"

"Her misfortune—indirectly. I like lookin' at this one myself. Do you think Phil Dumont had it enlarged? They're all the same size in this book but consider'bly larger than the ones in the first album. That's one reason she got such a good idea what Roche looked like."

"I think these are what are called flash or jumbo prints," Michael said. "If your camera takes small pictures you can have them printed on larger paper at a little extra cost."

"Oh. Well, we can't take this with us, though I'd like to. We'll have to let the city police find it for us. Let's get out of here."

He opened the door into the hall and looked out while Michael was putting the albums, the afghan and old hats back into the closet.

"All clear," he reported. "Do you think we'd better go out the same way as we came in?"

"I suppose I won't miss another patch or two of skin, and we don't want anyone even to suspect

the house has been entered. You go out the kitch-
en door and I'll lock it after you. . . ."

Rocky had time to repulse the alley cat again,
relent, stoop and rub its head and then murmur
anxiously: "Don't purr so loud," before Michael's
shoulders appeared in the cellar window. Rocky
hauled him out by main force and suspected that
what Michael said in Spanish had better not be
translated. Not unless he was prepared to ignore
several slurs cast on his ancestry with the detail
peculiar to Latin races when dealing with that
subject.

"Did you understand what I said a while ago?"
Michael asked when they were safely away from
both California and Laguna streets.

"Me? *No hablo español,*" Rocky said cheerfully.

"Then I needn't apologize. But goddamn it, my
shoulders are sore! My sunburn is not worthy of
being even mentioned in the same breath with Mr.
Smith's—"

"But you got cooked enough to get tender? It's
surprisin' how much you can burn in just an hour
or two, but there's no use tellin' some people.
I admit I wanted to get away from that place,"
Rocky added soberly. "It may be what you'd call
luxurious, even if it is old-fashioned, but it just
depressed me. Say, there's a taxi. Could we—"

"I don't see why not."

Rocky put two fingers to his lips and produced a piercing whistle. "But maybe we'd better get out a block or two away from your place."

They left the cab at Larkin, saw it out of sight and started up Green. A black car with a frond of antenna vibrating over its top passed them and proceeded slowly along Green. Michael hastily dropped a little back of Rocky, watching the car over his shoulder.

"Prowl car?" Rocky said. "Well, it's in no hurry—"

"They often cruise past the apartment at about this time of night. The trouble is that I know too many cops. If those were the regulars in this territory, they know me. But as I was on the inside of the street, I don't think they saw me."

"I hope not," Rocky said rather pessimistically. "But anyone who knows you could pick you out in a crowd just by the way you walk."

"And you are not one of these small mouselike creatures who escape notice," Michael retorted.

"Yes, but they don't know me." They stopped at Hyde while a cable car clanked by. "Well, they didn't stop so I guess it's all— Say, there wasn't any car parked in front of the apartment when we left."

"No," Michael said grimly. "And if that isn't Sullivan's own private and personal roadster—"

"Sure?"

"Reasonably. A fire hydrant developed murderous tendencies several weeks ago and attacked his back bumper and fender. We'd better not go any farther."

Michael stepped into the entrance to the apartment house two doors away from his own. "He could see us if he happens to have let himself in and be looking down."

Rocky peered cautiously up toward the windows in question. "No lights. The thing is, where's Smith? If Sullivan has him, even with the best intentions in the world Smith couldn't explain why he was in your place."

"Hardly. If Smith had any warning Sullivan was coming here, would he have sense enough to go to your car and wait?"

"He couldn't get in it. I've got the keys. We could go up there, but I don't like to run out on Smith."

"Nor I. His recent activities may have been rather unfortunate but there are other things he might have done that seem never to have occurred to him. He might, for instance, have blackmailed the Dumont-Holaday menage."

"I know. He's a damn fool but he's got guts."

"Nevertheless, I'd rather take castor oil than interview Sullivan. And I suggest you get to the car and out of the city as fast as you can."

"I thought you would. But I reckon I'll come with you. Sullivan may ask some mighty embarrassin' questions."

"I was afraid you'd think of that. Well, let's get it over." Michael stepped back into the street.

Rocky sighed and followed him.

"I haven't felt like this since I was about sixteen an' faced with explainin' to my dad and the principal why I'd thought it'd be funny to sneak a mule into the science room at the high school. It was a real army mule and— Hey! Wait!"

A door onto the street, marked SERVICE ENTRANCE, swung open. Mr. Smith passed a sleeve over his damp pink face.

"Jeez, I thought you'd slipped past me. I didn't dare stay out in the street—"

"Never mind that," Michael snapped. "Hug the inside of the street until we get back down to Hyde. We'll go over to Vallejo and up to Leavenworth and the car that way."

They were on the Bay Bridge before Rocky asked: "How'd you get away from Sullivan?"

"He called up." Smith repeated his conversation with Sullivan. "I put the place in the best order I could and ducked out. He almost caught me: I had to hide in the hall downstairs while he went up. I couldn't just hang around the street, so when I found that service entrance to the next apartment house open I went in there. I figured you'd come by there, and I guess it wasn't so long I was waiting and watching but it seemed hours. I don't know what Sullivan did—"

"He probably went in to see if the silver is missing. At least that's the excuse he'd give if I were in a position to suggest that a search warrant is customary even between friends."

"You aren't," Rocky said, grinning. "You know, we won't have to talk to Ariadne about this last angle. She might tell us for certain that Miss Dumont did entertain Miss Parnell showing her pictures but that can wait."

"I should think so. I was thinking too: that most amateur photographers make nuisances of themselves displaying the fruits of their labors to all and sundry—"

"Phil's touchy," Smith said. "Ariadne said just what you have once—only in different words—and he didn't like it. After that he kind of took the attitude he couldn't be bothered showing his snaps to people that didn't know anything about photography."

"Oh." Rocky stared at the arched ceiling of the tunnel as they passed through Yerba Buena Island. "No, we won't have to bother her. It can be worked all right without that."

"Yes, though there's one danger you can't guard against," Michael said. "If your plan is what I suppose it is."

"There's only one way to work it that I see if we want the thing solved beyond any doubt. And I know what you mean. In spite of what psychologists claim sometimes—and anyway, I'm not a psychologist—you can't be certain how a person will react to a certain situation. We'll have to risk it."

"What person? What situation?" Smith demanded. "Look: I think I've got a right to be told a few things."

Rocky gazed dreamily at the sulphur-yellow lights of the bridge as they approached Oakland. "I'd like," he said pensively, "to come over this just once when it wasn't foggy."

CHAPTER 25

Ariadne, coming to the end of her story, looked questioningly from one to the other of the extremely dirty, red-eyed men at the breakfast table.

"I'm afraid that doesn't help you any. But I'd never heard this Roche mentioned except as 'a guide'—"

"Never mind. You helped without knowin' it. And all you've told us is—useful," Rocky said. "But I'm goin' to have to ask you to do somethin' you won't want to."

"Go back to Pluma Blanca?"

"Back to your folks. They'll have something more important than you to think about then. I'm positive I know where the boy's body is and I'm goin' down to Bancross with the cor'ner in a few minutes."

"Oh, I see. Then you'll tell them and— Yes, I would be expected to break short my 'visit' here then."

"That's a good girl. And I'd be very much obliged if you wouldn't tell anyone we've been down to the city. I'm telling the cor'ner and ev'ryone else that we spent yesterday combing the woods aroun' Bancross."

"The invisible men," Eleanor said. "But with Ed confined to his bed, I doubt if anyone else would be certain whether you were there or not. But if Flo Hardy did listen in when I called you last night—"

"I'll have Flo's job if she talks. And a little chat with her this mornin' to tell her so. As for you"— Rocky turned to Ted Smith—"you're goin' to jail."

"If you say so. I guess you know what you're doing."

"Oh, we'll make you very comfortable and you won't be there long," Rocky assured him. "And if I bring in someone to identify you, just snarl and say you ain't talking." He got up. "I'll have to shave and get going."

"Are you going with him, Michael?" Eleanor asked.

"Not me, señora. I'm one of these carpet knights that abandon themselves to sleep and lazy ease."

"There," Rocky said, "sits the world's most accomplished liar. A guy that always looks at ever'thing 'sensibly.' He's not a man of action: he just likes to set and think. Phooey! He did most of the drivin' last night—"

"After I nearly ditched them trying to make speed," Smith said apologetically. "I don't see how Mr. Allan slept as much as he did, the way we burned up the roads."

"I'm so glad someone slept," Eleanor said sweetly. She put down her coffee cup and rose. "I'll get you some clean towels and you'd better tuck your husband into bed, Valerie."

Michael, having removed his shoes, watched Valerie pulling down window shades and said thoughtfully: "You're being very long-suffering, aren't you? I suppose you know it makes me feel a first-class louse?"

"I am not! Only—only you might kiss me. That polite peck on the forehead when you arrived doesn't count."

"You can't win." Michael rose and took her in his arms. "I'm filthy and I've a fine crop of bristles on my chin but do I get any credit for my remarkable self-control?"

"Just so you're back I don't care if you have a beard like an old-style Russian communist! I knew better than Eleanor that you might be engaged in anything from bribery to burglary. Rocky's being a sheriff might not keep you out of jail."

"'Lovers are commonly industrious to make themselves uneasy.'"

"And men must work and women must weep, I suppose? How much sleep have you had since Wednesday morning?"

"About five hours. What day is this? Friday?"

"Um-hum. Michael . . ."

"Yes, dear?"

"Remember that letter Ariadne showed us? It's written to 'Billy-boy' of course, but—"

"Anyone who allows a woman who refers to herself as Baby Doll to call him Billy-boy should be painlessly exterminated," Michael said, kissing her throat.

"On second thought, I won't tell you," Valerie decided. "You aren't interested. Go to sleep, darling. That was very satisfactory."

"As far as it went. The spirit is willing but the flesh . . ."

Michael threw himself on the bed and was asleep before Valerie had finished darkening the room. He woke late in the afternoon and then only because Rocky was bouncing gently up and down on the foot of the bed. Valerie, standing at its side, was saying:

"I warn you: he will be very unco-operative if you don't let him wake of his own accord."

"Sorry, lady, but it can't be helped. I got to talk to him."

"Age cannot wither nor custom stale his inexhaustible energy." Michael rolled over on his back. "Giddy-ap, giddy-ap, giddy-ap! Hi-yo, Silver!"

"Delirious," Rocky said pityingly. "You'd better bring that coffee in here, Valerie. It might cure him."

"And how," Michael inquired, "are all the little Dumonts and Holadays?"

"Bein' treated for shock and bruises. I just took Ariadne over there—"

"'Over' there?"

"They're stayin' here tonight. I hope they don't think I put it in their heads. Dumont suggested it'd save trouble to come here till the formalities are over. People here will talk but not bother 'em, whereas they've got too many acquaintances at Pluma Blanca. The manager here was perfectly willin' to clear ever'body out of one of the new guest houses since they were willing to pay for the whole thing."

"You wouldn't have had anything to do with that? I suppose you are being very helpful?"

"Not to mention sympathetic. I hope it goes over. I said I was a little preoccupied the night of Suzy's dance, wonderin' why Roche had killed himself. And so it kind of exasperated me to be bothered about Ariadne's bracelet bein' stolen, I said. But then the next day we found the ransom money where Roche had hid it, under the cabin floor—"

"Oh yes. I remember that as if it were only yesterday. In fact, I'm the fellow who helped you tear up the floor. And then you understood why Roche might have killed himself."

"Yeah. So we hunted for the boy's body but we spared them the suspense of waitin' while we did it. An' we found it too late last night to get the cor'ner there. And we also picked up Ted Smith and I haven't made up my mind if he killed Roche or Roche killed himself. I took Dumont to identify him."

"Did he snarl?"

"Rin-tin-tin couldn't have done better," Rocky said. "And Dumont identified the kid's body as well as anyone could. He'd broken his leg once and that matches."

"So the stage is set?"

"Well—yes an' no. While it took some managin', I did succeed in— Here's your coffee."

"Don't let me interrupt you." Valerie put down her tray and poured the coffee. "I hope I'm not in your way?"

"Yes, dear, you are. Be a good girl and go away."

Valerie put down the coffeepot with more force than was really necessary. She very honorably closed the door and then sat down in a chair near it. Now, she thought, it was strictly up to Rocky and Michael—to speak so low that no one could hear them.

And for some time they did. But presently Rocky raised his voice. "So that's how it is. And it's so simple it may not work—or it may, just because it is simple. The only thing is, he may lose his nerve and that's dang'rous. And there's the question of method. But if you—"

It was evident that Michael interrupted him, though Valerie heard no more than: ". . . too dangerous. And you can't be certain he isn't—"

"Just laughin' up his sleeve? But how would it be if I—"

"Even in the dark that wouldn't work. You're too . . ."

Michael lowered his voice again. "You look," Eleanor said, coming into the room, "as if you were turning over in your mind words no lady would utter." She nodded toward the bedroom door. "Council of war?"

"I think so. And that Michael is preparing to stick his neck out like a turkey awaiting the ax."

"Rocky shouldn't ask him to do that."

"Michael probably volunteered because it's something Rocky can't do himself."

"But he gets paid for that sort of thing. Aren't you going to register a protest?"

"I only married him: I don't own him. Of course I do think men are ridiculous. Thank heaven I'm a poor weak woman and don't have to show off. Michael is really quite sensible about what he calls 'heroic gestures' most of the time, but now and then his masculine vanity rears its head and away he goes. Besides, Rocky is a bad influence on him."

"I was thinking it's just the other way around. Though I will admit Rocky has never had any great fondness for tying himself up in official red tape—"

"Speakin' of me?" Rocky opened the door and went on with what he was saying to Michael. "Of course Sullivan wanted to know what it's all about. But he was reas'nable."

"He almost had to be. Roche was killed in this county. I can identify Roche as Roland," Michael said. "And I'm here."

"And we're all happy? Except Inspector Sullivan," Valerie said. "What about reporters?"

"I argued our local editor out of telegraphin' his suspicions to the city papers, though it was one hell of a job. Of course there's a lot of speculation aroun' town but nobody is sure we have the kid's body here. I'm keepin' my fingers crossed. Dumont and the rest of 'em will be glad to avoid the press as long as possible and our editor will keep quiet because I promised him a real scoop."

"You have a good many of the characteristics of a successful dictator, *amigo*," Michael observed from the bedroom. "Valerie, will you find some iodine for me? I've lost at least six square inches of skin—"

"Smith took his sunburn lotion to jail with him," Rocky said. "He's goin' to shed his skin like a snake. And I'm going to take a shower and maybe get a little sleep."

Eleanor followed him into their bedroom. "What time is your little party scheduled for?"

"Sometime late tonight. We'll have supper same as usual and pretend we've gone to bed, just in case."

"Rocky, do you think you should ask Michael—"

"I didn't, honey. Don't worry, I'm not going to let anything happen to him. You know, he's a swell guy. Damned exasperatin' at times—"

"But he doesn't mean to be?" Eleanor suggested, smiling at his back.

"Hell, no! He does mean to be. That's what you've got to get used to. The thing is, he can take it as well as dish it out." He pulled off his wilted shirt. "And I can feel you grinnin' even if you are behind me. Come aroun' where I can see you—an' kiss you. Or are we just parents and getting too old for that kind of foolishness?"

"In your own words, Mr. Allan—hell, no! Besides, if it wasn't for that 'kind of foolishness' we wouldn't be parents."

Hortense complained, but halfheartedly, of the food and service they were given at dinner. "This isn't Pluma Blanca," Basil said briefly. "They served us here as a special favor."

"Oh, I know that," Hortense said hastily. "And I could have done without anything to eat—"

"I noticed you cleaned your plate," Phil said. "Oh sure: you have to keep up your strength. Don't worry, you will."

Hortense pretended not to have heard him. Jonathan, uncoiling out of his chair, said he was going to take a short walk.

"I want some fresh air—and magazines."

"You're sure there are no reporters in town?" Hortense said. "When that plane came in this afternoon, I thought—"

"There are usually one or two barnstormers here over the week end."

"Anyway, Allan's not going to let the G-men in on this till he has to," Phil said scornfully. "He wants to put Smith through a third degree first and grab all the credit himself. Just a typical back-woods cop."

He looked challengingly at Ariadne, though so far they had said nothing to each other. But she didn't have to hesitate over her answer; it was safe simply to say what she thought.

"I think he is inclined to want to do things for himself. Perhaps he feels he's entitled to. He did—did find Freddie and pick up Ted Smith."

"I always told you he had something to do with it," Hortense began. "But you wouldn't listen—"

"It's so easy to be wise after the event, my dear Hortense," Daniel said patronizingly. "Most of us at least questioned his innocence but it was obvious he must have had an outside accomplice. I can't recall you suggesting Roche might be that man."

"Me? Why, I never even saw Roche. I mean," Hortense said as Jonathan lifted a doubting eyebrow, "not to know who he was. Why should I—"

"Why must we talk about it?" Basil said. "I think I'll walk with you, Jonathan." . . .

"Poor Basil had a great deal to worry him, yesterday as well as today." Hortense looked at

Ariadne, hesitated and then spoke directly to her for the first time. "I took some of your sleeping tablets for myself and Phil. Neither of us slept last night and we simply must have some rest tonight. With all we have to face—"

"And just what have 'we' to face?" Daniel asked. "You were in no way related to Freddie, Hortense. So it's hardly suitable, is it, that you should take over the role of chief mourner? I confess I don't see why you didn't go back to the city as Basil suggested."

"She didn't want to miss anything," Phil said. Now and then he would side with Daniel against Hortense; just often enough to make her uneasy lest he should go over to the enemy. She smiled reproachfully.

"It wasn't that. I couldn't leave my menfolks to shift for themselves. And you will go to bed early, lover? I gave you the tablets, so do take them and get a good rest."

"All right, but stop talking about it," Phil snapped. He picked up an old magazine and glanced through it, yawning. Presently Jonathan and Basil came back with a dozen new ones and a large box of candy.

"The dessert wasn't very satisfying," Jonathan said apologetically. "And my well-known sweet tooth is declaring itself again." He passed the box around.

"I'd rather have a magazine," Ariadne said. "And go to bed."

"Help yourself. And take a handful of candy with you. No? Well, good night, Spider. I'm turning in early myself."

CHAPTER 26

It hadn't been so bad after all. It was rather a relief than not that Phil and Hortense hadn't talked
to her. Her father had kissed her and let her off
with a mild: "You shouldn't have frightened us so,
daughter."

Jonathan had been—just Jonathan, cheerfully
detached and tolerant and not really too much interested in what had been or was happening. And
Basil—Basil had asked if she was "feeling better
now" and said he hoped Mr. Allan's news hadn't
been too much of a shock to her.

Ariadne shivered and got into bed. She could
hear Hortense fussing about in the bathroom next
door. This guest house was a low one-story log
building, not large but still too large for them
with its ten bedrooms and six bathrooms. They
had taken the middle rooms on each side of the
hall and a bathroom apiece.

Hortense was making full use of hers now. She could never travel without a large sewing kit, packages of crackers and cookies, malted milk, a small electric plate and an iron and at least one box of soap flakes.

"Hortense's suitcase," Jonathan had said once, "is her home away from home." So now she was washing stockings, handkerchiefs—probably even a slip and nightgown—turning the water on, turning it off, turning it on again. . . .

Ariadne buried her face in the pillow and pulled its ends over her ears. Being half smothered was better than listening to Hortense. Now she would be pasting handkerchiefs on the windowpanes, hanging stockings carefully over the towel racks. And then very likely tiptoeing to Phil's door, asking if there was anything "lover" wanted, telling him not to read in bed.

When she finally turned over on her back Ariadne's face was hot and damp. She kicked off the covers. It was quiet now: too quiet. A dog barked at a passing car but even that sound was not repeated. Brookdale went early to bed and the hotel and its two guest houses were at the edge of the town, well away from the road.

At Pluma Blanca you at least heard cars being driven in and out of the grounds, footsteps on the walk in front of the half circle of chalets and the night wind in the trees. There was no wind tonight and the room, though both windows were open, was hot and stuffy.

Ariadne got up, crept over to the windows in the dark and leaned out, elbows planted on the sill. It was cool enough outside; there was even a little breeze. Were you really closer to the sky in the mountains, she wondered, that it seemed so near and the stars so bright? There was the Little Dipper in that gap between the black columns that were pine trees. . . .

Some slight sound toward the back of the house made her turn her head sharply. A shadow detached itself from other shadows thick along the side of the house, hesitated and then moved around its corner. Ariadne stood erect, took two steps toward the door and stopped.

Let Phil go, she thought. Basil should know he might slip out to buy liquor. And she must get used to not caring or feeling responsible for what any of these people did.

She turned toward the bathroom. She would have to take something—whatever Hortense had left—if she was going to sleep. She had put the box in the drug cabinet, hoping to get along without a sedative tonight. But it was no use. If she laid awake she wouldn't be able to keep from thinking of Gloria.

She turned on the light over the washbowl and filled a glass with water. She wouldn't wake anyone, moving about in here. There was only a vacant room on the other side of this bathroom. With a connecting door . . . She wondered suddenly if the door was locked, put down her glass and went over to it.

It was not locked. She opened it, looking into the vacant room. By the light behind her she could see its front windows. Why, she thought, didn't I take this instead of a side room? There are south windows here and that breeze was from the south. If the bed is made up I can move. Away from Hortense too, and what she'll say when she misses Phil or when he comes back.

She moved toward the bed at the side of the room. The door behind her swung shut and she whirled about nervously. There was no light in the room now but there was sound. The sound of someone's cautious breathing in the corner by the door. . . .

She thought her scream would surely be heard as far as the hotel. It was unbelievable that, wanting to scream so much, she'd managed no more than the sort of low choked cry whose echo she had caught sometimes, waking from a nightmare. She didn't wake this time; she was awake.

There was a hand over her mouth and an arm pulling her back, away from the bathroom door.

The arm was brocaded silk; a dressing gown like her father's. But it smelled of pipe smoke and the hand over her mouth was large and muscular. Her father's hands were small and soft and this man was tall. As tall as Basil . . .

She was standing in a swift dark stream. It swept her off her feet and she went under its black waters, not struggling, almost gratefully.

Rocky's final words: "Just take it easy and don't forget to yell," were undoubtedly excellent advice, Michael thought. Unfortunately patience was a virtue he'd never cared to acquire. And Rocky had not bothered to say: "Keep cool." That omission might have been purely tactful or even complimentary—or simply due to a singular lack of imagination. He would probably boast that he "hadn't a nerve in his body."

Michael smiled derisively into the darkness but the derision was for himself. He was perfectly aware that Rocky was neither unimaginative nor insensitive. And whatever the outcome of this thing, the final responsibility was his. He must wait too and not fail in alertness.

"At least," Michael thought candidly, "I sincerely hope he doesn't. It would be sad if he arrived just in time to exchange a last line. I don't envy him his assignment except that he can literally keep cool outside. This place is damned stuffy."

Stuffy or not, he must stay in it for only God—
and one other—knew how long. And there was
what Rocky had called "the question of method"
to consider. If not precisely a pleasant subject for
thought, it was at least a timely one and he would
like very much to know what to expect.

"Not a gun," Rocky had said. "At least I don't
think anyone would risk keepin' Roche's. And if
they didn't there'd be some difficulty getting one
now. The trouble is, if it's another suicide, that'll
take some figurin' out."

He'd been thinking of Roche's supposed suicide.
But what was it Sullivan had said? "She was in a
sanitarium but they didn't watch her well enough.
She got hold of a razor and cut her throat."

Michael grimaced. A nice time to remember
that. Now if someone here had an old-fashioned
razor . . . Without reason, he expected that someone did. He also thought it a thoroughly unpleasant weapon to contend with in the dark. Perhaps
refusing to face a firing squad blindfold was not
simply a traditionally heroic gesture after all.

He stretched cautiously and considered what he
knew of the gentle art of throat-cutting. If you
were righthanded you cut your own throat from
left to right. Elementary, my dear Watson. But
a right-handed man, facing you, couldn't follow

that natural instinct. He would have to do the unnatural thing and . . .

Someone had just tried the hall door and found it locked. Rocky had insisted it wouldn't "look right" not to lock it. He was probably right but Michael would infinitely have preferred that the door be open. He decided that he, at least, would be accommodating, turned over on his back and unfastened another button on Philip Dumont's pajama jacket.

There, he thought, was a throat anyone should be proud to cut. His hair, falling over his forehead, was a minor annoyance becoming increasingly greater. But it had better be that way and his face turned just a little into the pillow . . .

He waited. Waited until there was the faintest sound of a foot scraping the side of the house and across the window sill. A floor board squeaked complainingly and then another, closer to the bed. A hand touched his shoulder, very lightly. Too gently to waken any but the lightest sleeper and certainly not one presumably under the influence of a fairly strong sedative.

Still, it was better not to overdo it. Michael stirred, sighed briefly and lay still again. The hand that had been instantly withdrawn just touched his throat and was gone again. . . .

"Wouldn't you," Michael said softly, "do a much better job if you had a little light on your subject?" And flung himself toward the farther edge of the bed.

He meant to land feet first on the floor, shout to Rocky and cover the door himself. The plan made no allowance for a hotel maid's habit of tucking sheets very firmly under the mattress. Before he got free of the covers the man had hurled himself across the bed.

A thin sharp edge of steel grazed Michael's cheek and drew blood. His left hand found and held the other man's wrist. He twisted it viciously, threw up his elbow and felt it smash against flesh and bone. The man groaned, panting, clawing at Michael's face with his left hand.

Michael set his teeth, jerked his head back and his body over the edge of the bed. He still held the man's right wrist when they crashed to the floor. Somewhere, someone was screaming and hammering on a door. A blanket, settling perversely over his head, deadened the sound but his feet were finally free. He flung away the wrist he held and kicked out savagely.

There were two people screaming then and Rocky was saying: "For God's sake, shut up! Michael—"

"Present," Michael said, emerging from the blanket. The lights hurt his eyes. He blinked at the long razor lying on the floor. It had a bone handle with three silver initials—B.W.D. But Rocky was speaking again:

"You cert'nly get aroun', Mr. Armstrong."

"Yes," Jonathan Armstrong said coolly, "and I'm afraid I've bungled things. But you didn't take me into your confidence and I thought Ariadne was the person who should be watched. It seems I only wasted my time and frightened her into fits. She needs a doctor too."

He stared with an impersonal sort of distaste at the man crouched on the bed, moaning over the slashed wrist Rocky was bandaging.

"So it's you we have to thank for all this, Daniel? I hope," Jonathan said pleasantly, "that you bleed to death."

CHAPTER 27

"You might have told me," Hortense Dumont said weakly.

"You! You'd have managed to give the whole thing away," Phil said rudely but he let her cling to his hand as he stood by her bed.

She had stopped screaming and fainted when she was unable to get through to his room. "I never," Rocky remarked to Michael, "met up with so many faintin' females in my life." The ten minutes before Dr. Bradley arrived had been strenuous ones. Ariadne, regaining consciousness in the vacant room where Jonathan had left her when he heard the disturbance down the hall, was dangerously hysterical.

The doctor had produced his hypodermic, ignoring Daniel, whimpering that he was bleeding to death. He looked at Hortense when he had finished with Ariadne, told Basil to "throw water on her." Then nodded as Rocky murmured briefly in his good ear and shut himself into Phil's room with his patient.

"You didn't remember that picture," Phil went on. "You didn't know Roche either. You stuck around the hotel with me while I was sick. I knew Roche was a guide Dad and Jonathan went fishing with but I didn't know he had that habit of humming 'Alouette.' Even if Sullivan had asked me about Roche, you say he was calling him Roland then and what he said about him wouldn't have meant anything to me."

"It did to you two," Rocky charged, looking at Basil and Jonathan.

"Oh yes," Jonathan said calmly. "We began to wonder if Roche was the Roland Sullivan was looking for. We thought we would nose around if we were allowed to come up here though we had no hope that if Roche were mixed up in the kidnaping he would still be in Bancross. I didn't want to speak too soon. I thought it was Daniel who had been responsible for the suggestion that we come up here—"

"And I thought it was you who was," Basil said.

"I may have put the idea into your head when Daniel had planted it in mine. And frankly, it occurred to me that if Roche was the kidnaper, Basil and I could be proved to have known him better than anyone else. He must have had an accomplice and if it wasn't Ted Smith . . ." Jonathan shrugged expressively. "But tell us about this snapshot, Phil."

"Well, after the first two rolls I'd taken disappeared, I went out and snapped another roll the last morning we were at Bancross. I came through the brush back of that cabin and there was Daniel and this fellow I thought was just a prospector or guide sitting by that spring, talking. Roche was sort of dressed up that morning though. I'd only seen him once to remember before, when he was working on his claim or whatever you call it. I snapped him then and I suppose he told Daniel to steal the film on that account.

"Well, they were sitting there and it looked like a good shot so I snapped it. Got a big pine and the cabin and the two of them. I was pretty close but they didn't see me. Then I had jumbo prints made, so of course that made their faces and figures larger."

"And you showed Miss Parnell his photograph albums, Miss Dumont?" Rocky said.

"She seemed so interested. You see, Phil said he had too many things in his room and he was going to clear away his old pictures when he got his new camera. But I wouldn't let him throw away those nice pictures—"

"That you never really looked at."

"But I'm so busy, lover. And I—well, I do need glasses," Hortense admitted. "I can't even read comfortably any more. I did look at those pictures once but how would I remember all of them?"

"You wouldn't. I did mention I'd taken another roll before we left Bancross. That was just before we came up here. But I did say I'd gotten rid of all my old pictures. Lucky for me I did, I guess. And that Daniel never knew I'd taken that one of him and Roche. You see, we've never been on good enough terms for him to do anything more than just make fun of my hobbies. So I'd never go out of my way to show him my snaps."

"Of course I did think Miss Parnell liked Daniel," Hortense said. "But she—she liked Basil too. And she did look at some of those pictures a long time."

"We figured she must have. We'll leave you to rest now," Rocky said politely. "Can we go in your room, Armstrong?"

"Oh, but why can't you talk in here? I'd like to—"

"Would you like us to, Hortense?" Basil said. "You know what I mean, I think. If you'll think—"

"About the— I—I didn't know." Hortense looked away. "I'll—I'll leave it to you, Basil. You—you say— say whatever you think you should."

"You see," Rocky explained when they were in Jonathan's room, "that bracelet comes into this. I managed to talk to Phil alone this afternoon. I told him we figured there must be a snapshot of Roche in existence and that the city police were looking for it in your house in the city—"

"So then of course I remembered," Phil said. "Then he told me even more about Roche than he'd already told all of us. And we knew Roche was the kidnaper and Mr. Allan said if Daniel considered that picture—after I'd described it to him—important, that would show he'd hired Roche. And—and that it wasn't you, Dad.

"Even if you don't get along with him any too well it—it's no fun thinking maybe your father's a murderer." Phil flushed painfully, not looking at Basil now. "I knew Hortense had taken Ariadne's bracelet because I heard Dad talking to that guy Hogue on the phone. I know how Hortense is about jewelry. And of course Dad would cover up for her. I—I thought you'd made her put back the real bracelet. That is, until what happened at the inn the other night. I couldn't figure what connection it had with the kidnaping, but if there was any, you and Hortense must be in it up to your eyes and you'd certainly know an imitation when you saw one."

"I see. And what," Basil said grimly, "about Ariadne?"

Phil winced. "I've got it coming for what I did with that letter. I knew it wasn't yours though you had it. I knew about Jonathan's girlfriend."

"Jonathan's?" Michael said. He grinned. "Are you 'Billy-boy'?"

"With shame, I confess I am. My name is Jonathan Willis but it never appears in full except on the copyright page of my books."

"Next time I'll listen to what Valerie wants to tell me."

"Yes, Mrs. Dundas spotted that on a book of yours she got from the library," Rocky said. "Makin' Billy-boy out of Willis is kind of farfetched but it could be done."

"It was. You see, I've known some ladies but no—uh —tarts. I've sometimes thought of writing fiction and I thought some gaps in my education should be filled. Daisy was very educative," Jonathan said thoughtfully. "And difficult to get rid of—after Freddie was kidnaped. Until I stood to inherit a great deal of money, she was willing enough to call it quits. Fortunately she was also shrewd and cautious and vain enough to believe people might think I did it all for her if they knew about our little affair.

"I'll buy her off now. She was an experience and I hardly think she put up with me because she liked to look at me. As to that reference to 'that nurse' which no doubt intrigued you . . ." Jonathan grinned sheepishly. "The fact is, Daisy boasted so much of her conquests, past and present, that I decided to play too.

"Edith Parnell was in the house and popped into my head. So I manufactured a good-looking, fairly young nurse who 'seemed to like to talk to me.'" He looked at Phil. "I suppose you trailed me once or twice? Basil has known about Daisy for some time. He answered the telephone once or twice and turned her away with soft answers."

"That was what you meant when Ariadne heard you tell Mr. Dumont you'd suppressed other calls besides the one Miss Parnell made to the house?"

"That was it, Mr. Allan. I didn't know Ariadne knew that though. But because she'd been with you and might have told you all she knew, I thought she might be in danger tonight. Considering her state of mind lately, a faked suicide might work in her case. So I went on guard in the vacant room next to her bathroom. It was unfortunate she happened to come in there. I hoped she'd go out without knowing I was there. And when she discovered that I was, she fainted before I could explain. And about that time all hell seemed to be breaking loose in Phil's room. Well, I knew his door was locked—"

"So you ran outside in time to scramble through the window right on my heels," Rocky finished. "That clears the record so far's you're concerned. Mr. Dumont—"

"Probably you don't want a—a psychological explanation from me but it's really necessary," Basil said. "I once came across the phrase 'a man of remarkable hesitations' in some historical work—"

"Harold Lamb speaking of Hugh of Vermandois," Jonathan murmured. "Hugh the Great of France."

"It describes me too. When I do act promptly it's usually because I lose my temper. That doesn't give me self-confidence. And I do prefer to think well of people. From what you've told us, Ted Smith pretty well covered the mistakes I made immediately after Freddie was kidnaped. I knew we should tell the whole truth but I did think it was a bona fide kidnaping.

"And when I began to suspect it wasn't I did what's always easy for me: let things go. I promised myself I'd speak if I ever learned anything definite. But then when Smith came to me and told me about Roche and what Miss Parnell had said, I still did nothing. Except to talk things over with Jonathan.

"But I hadn't connected that bracelet with the kidnaping. I'm so stupid it never occurred to me it could have been used to provide Roche with money. Did you—have you had the city police investigating that too?"

"They're tryin' to find out if Roche pawned it. I haven't spoken to them about the copy yet. Cochrane mentioned this same fellow Phil just spoke of—Hogue —but I thought before we put the police on him I'd see what you said about it."

"Hortense did take the bracelet and have him copy it. And he telephoned to ask me about it. I protected her—and hinted to Hogue that he'd better not talk about it. I was never in Burris' confidence but Hogue couldn't be sure of that and I did know my father-in-law's reputation and that Hogue was his right-hand man," Basil said. "I should have told him not to make the copy, shouldn't I? But then, if I had he would have been certain the bracelet wasn't Hortense's and—well, I didn't think about that until afterward. And then I couldn't decide . . .

"Well, what I did was to tell Hortense she could keep the copy if she liked but she must return the original to Ariadne's room. But neither of us was able to do that safely the night Hortense brought the bracelets back to the house. The next morning only the copy was in her room. I did think Daniel might have taken it and that Ariadne was afraid he had. But she didn't question the copy and I didn't want to upset her.

"I watched Daniel but he hadn't more money than usual. So I let it slide. I suppose you can't understand why Hortense was so—foolish. But she took most of the only large sum of money she ever had to buy her pearls and used what was left to pay Hogue—"

"Mr. Dundas had her pretty well figured out. He noticed those pearls and asked Cochrane about them."

"She's always loved jewels. You might almost call it a—mania. She resented Ariadne's having that bracelet when she didn't even know the stones in it were good ones—or care for them. Hortense expected to have them reset in time. She'd heard me speak of—of such things being done. She didn't seem to realize the danger—or she wanted them too much to care. I should have told Ariadne the truth. She'd have been decent about it. But there was so much friction in our household after Gloria died that I—"

"You let it slide," Michael said unsympathetically.

"I don't blame you for feeling like that, Mr. Dundas. But I imagine you never have the least difficulty in making up your mind so you don't know what it is not to be able to come to a decision. Well, it was Hortense who finally took the copy of the bracelet because she became frightened when Cochrane appeared interested in it—"

"She took it after Ariadne was dressed for the dance that night and while she was waitin' on the porch for the rest of you to be ready, didn't she?"

"Why yes. She saw that Ariadne wasn't wearing the bracelet and she was able to get into her room then and— But how did you know that, Mr. Allan?"

"Ariadne told us that the bracelet was in her bureau drawer when she left her room but that she had to wait for the rest of us on the porch," Jonathan said.

"Yes, and you all had pretty good alibis for the time after you arrived at the hotel," Rocky said. "Except you, Mr. Armstrong. You did go back to get your pipe—and had it—when my wife and I came over to your chalet with Phil and Ariadne and Mr. Dumont. So you could've taken the bracelet before we got there."

"I suppose," Basil said, paying no attention to Jonathan's rueful gesture, "that Ariadne told you she thought she heard me leave the chalet Sunday night? I don't know why I told her she hadn't heard me. The only reason I lied was because I didn't want to say I hadn't been able to sleep and had gone out for a walk. Not a good reason, of course. That was about midnight and there were still people strolling about the grounds."

"So you missed Daniel? I take for granted he must have found some means to transport himself to Bancross," Jonathan said cheerfully. "But tell me about this trap you set for him."

"Mr. Allan asked if I'd go to him and say that since we knew about Roche I remembered taking their picture together and still had it. But that I'd destroy it if—if he'd make Ariadne marry me." Phil hesitated. "It was the kind of thing he'd expect from me. Oh yes, it was! And I'm not sorry Freddie's dead. . . .

"Except that the way it happened has messed things up for us—permanently. I see that now. I was mad clear through the morning after the dance because Dad slugged me and Ariadne acted like she did. That's why I swiped that letter and let her think it had been written to Dad. Well, after I was over being mad and she'd run away, I was—I wished I hadn't.

"So when Mr. Allan put this proposition up to me I—I wanted to make up for it. Maybe that's a

queer way to make amends: to help prove her father's a murderer. But she hasn't so many illusions
about him and she'd rather it was him than Dad.
So—"

"So you agreed to go through with it," Rocky
said.

He could have told Basil a great deal more than
Phil had. "When I was a kid I thought Dad was a
swell guy," Phil had told him. "Big and strong—I
was sickly—and damn good to me. I was just jealous when he married Gloria, and that was mainly
Hortense's fault because Gloria was O.K. And I
know all about my—my mother and that isn't—
fun to think about. So sometimes I think: a quick
life and a merry one. But even when I'd get mad
at Ariadne liking Dad better than me, there was
more to it than that. I did wonder if he either intended to marry her and her money himself or see
that I did—"

By that time, to his own disgust and Rocky's
secret embarrassment, Phil had been nervously on the point of tears. Which, of course, was
why he was looking at him so uneasily now, Rocky
thought. He said:

"He wanted to go all the way through with it
but that was too risky and he's too valuable. He
can swear he saw Holaday and Roche talkin' together—"

"And you were afraid I couldn't stick it out," Phil said disagreeably. "I'll bet you were afraid I might double-cross you too. But I don't think I could have stuck it. Mr. Dundas was the only one near enough my size to take my place and we've both got dark hair. We wanted Daniel to think I'd be sleeping soundly and Hortense tended to that very nicely without knowing she was.

"When we talked about what Daniel might do to me, I never thought of what he did decide on," Phil said, shivering. "I don't know why. If you'd found me with my throat—found me like he meant you should, you'd have thought I did it. And maybe for no reason connected with the kidnaping."

"I figured he'd figure it out like that," Rocky said. "Except that I didn't think of a razor because I'd forgotten that— Well, Michael didn't think of it either."

"Oh, didn't I? I not only did but I had the rare privilege of continuing to think of it for some time. How did he cut himself? I didn't do that: I only kicked him. In the stomach, I think—I hope."

"Which apparently tangled him up with the razor. Well, there's still a lot of details to be cleared up—"

"As I was thinking," Jonathan said. "You have that snapshot—or have you?"

"They sent us a copy by plane this afternoon."

"Oh. But did Daniel admit anything to you, Phil?"

"He did not! He said: 'Don't be silly, my boy. Of course I chatted with Roche at various times. But it might be as well if the authorities never saw that picture. And I've always hoped that Ariadne would marry you.'"

"They never leave well enough alone," Rocky remarked. "He should've stuck to his bluff."

"But if he won't confess, where are you?" Jonathan said.

"It would save trouble if he would. I think he will."

"Nonsense!"

"Five will get you ten he does," Michael said.

"I won't take that bet," Jonathan decided. "Why do you—"

Dr. Bradley thrust his graying bullethead and scraggy mustache in at the door. "Hey, Rocky! Maybe you want to talk to this guy now? He thinks he's dying."

"I hope you didn't disillusion him?" Rocky said blandly. "Come on, Michael. . . ."

"Oh?" Jonathan said again. He took off his glasses and sat down on the bed. "Well, well," he said mildly, produced a large clean handkerchief, blew on the glasses and settled himself to polishing them.

CHAPTER 28

"But until you saw that snapshot of Mr. Holaday and Roche you had no idea who had hired him?" Eleanor persisted.

"We-ell . . ."

"We hate to admit it but we didn't," Michael said. "I did think it wasn't Miss Dumont. Roche was too wise to work with or for a woman. It wasn't likely that Miss Parnell would fight so against believing Miss Dumont was responsible for the kidnaping. A man was indicated in that connection, always remembering her attempts at self-adornment after she left the Armstrong house as a nurse."

"An' Miss Dumont wouldn't have been fool enough to pay Roche off with that bracelet when it could be proved she'd had it copied. If she acted for Dumont the same objection applies," Rocky said. "He had a part in that transaction an' Hogue could testify to that."

"Well, I knew all that," Smith admitted. "But you didn't play fair and tell me about the snapshot."

"Michael told you Miss Parnell wouldn't be apt to study just Roche's face if there wasn't someone else in the picture that she knew, to make her look at it carefully. Or at least that's what he meant even if he didn't explain it in words of one syllable. And if we'd told you we'd found a snapshot showin' one of those men talkin' earnestly to Roche and that it clinched things so far's we were concerned, would you have known who the man was?"

"Of course not."

"But why not? If it had been either Dumont or Armstrong in the picture, would they have had any particular explainin' to do? Roche took them fishing; either of them might have been just arrangin' other trips. But Holaday didn't fish or hunt or even walk much. So why did he want to talk to Roche alone just before they left Bancross?"

"Another thing," Michael said. "Roche had that one dangerously distinctive habit of humming 'Alouette.' Armstrong and Dumont, tramping the woods with him, must have noticed that. Smith did, when he went fishing with him. Well, either of those two might have considered that a dangerous habit if either of them was thinking of employing Roche. Especially Dumont, who knew the song himself and was of French-Canadian descent. That might conceivably suggest a connection between him and Roche to some people.

"But Holaday didn't go on long hikes with Roche. If he met him at all it was because he stopped to talk to him on that road or at his cabin. And if they talked, Roche wasn't humming 'Alouette' very often. At least, that's what I thought. There is," Michael admitted, grinning, "a much simpler explanation which you will find at the end of Holaday's statement. And that is that he can't carry a tune and 'America' is the only song he recognizes when he hears it. That was a great hindrance to his career in vaudeville."

"And it's too involved for me anyway," Valerie said. "Besides, when you had that picture, why did you have to stage this show tonight?" She looked at the strip of adhesive across Michael's cheek where Dumont's razor had grazed it.

"He might have managed to explain away that picture, being a very plausible cuss. It was better to gamble he couldn't resist tryin' to remove Phil," Rocky said, "and that Phil would play ball with us. Explaining why he tried to kill him wouldn't be so easy, and it always makes 'em panicky for a while after they get caught. And if Michael had yelled like I told him to—"

"I had no chance to yell."

"And you're too stiff-necked to want to. I told you to shout when he got to the bed—"

"Gratitude is not in you. Didn't you want to catch him in attempted murder? Well then! And it's as well you were not doubling for Phil Dumont. You'd have tried for a gentlemanly and sportsmanlike right to the jaw and found yourself tangled up with a razor—"

"Let's forget that razor," Valerie begged.

She picked up the copy of Daniel Holaday's statement that Rocky had brought home. The courthouse stenographer had been torn from her bed at the hotel to take it down. Being a prim, fortyish person, she considered a house coat over a nightgown, curlers and a thin frosting of cold cream improper attire for any occasion. She was too demoralized to revise the statement when she typed it, though usually she would have turned Rocky's questions into the most formal and official English. Valerie smiled over the first one:

Q. Well, since you want to get it off your chest, shall we start at the beginning? How did you and Roche happen to get together on this business, Mr. Holaday?

A. I walked out that road twice with Smith and Freddie. We saw Roche and talked to him. Freddie was impertinent to him and he didn't like it. He knew our situation with regard to him and . . . Well, one evening I walked out there alone and Roche and I talked. He said he supposed Basil was afraid the boy might be kidnaped and that a kidnaping could be managed only with the aid of someone in the house. He said the reason most kidnapers were caught was because they were forced to spend the ransom money too quickly. If one didn't and was someone no one would ever connect with the family or the child and was able to take the body so far away from his home that no one would ever think of looking there for it—

Q. I get you. But he wanted a down payment, didn't he?

A. Enough money to live on comfortably for a year or more and then take him a long way off. To South America or Mexico. He was a Canadian but that's all he ever told me about himself. He insisted I take the films Philip had snapped while we were there. He was certain Philip had taken one of him and he said it wasn't safe for him to have it.

Q. And did he insist his down payment had to be managed so it wouldn't be traced back to you?

A. I knew that. Before I'd decided how it could be managed I happened to see Hortense slip out of Ariadne's room the night she took that bracelet. When Ariadne said she'd mislaid it I suspected

what had happened, knowing Hortense. Then I
overheard Basil's conversation with Hogue over
an upstairs extension. So when Hortense brought
the bracelets home it was safe to take the genuine
one. Fortunately they were tagged so they could
be told apart. Once Roche had pawned the bracelet I wasn't worried about the copy; whether anyone ever discovered it was that or not.

Q. Had you and Roche settled things between
you before you left Bancross that summer?

A. Not definitely. We'd agreed that last morning that at least a year should elapse—

Q. Sure, to protect both of you. Did you write
each other?

A. Only twice and we were both very careful
what we said. Finally, about the eleventh or twelfth
of May, he came to the city. That's when we made
the final plans and I gave him the bracelet. I was
to make the ransom note and persuade Freddie to
play a joke on Smith by making a mound of his
pillows and then sneaking out to hide until I gave
the alarm.

Q. Then you killed him? How?

A. I—I didn't really mean . . . He became frightened and I had to choke him, and before I realized
it he was dead.

Q. [by Mr. Dundas] Had Roche specified he was
to carry dead cargo and not living?

A. Yes, but he would have killed him quickly enough himself. He was waiting at the back of the house to take him and the rest of it he did as you've guessed—

Q. And you'd doped Ted Smith to keep him quiet? What did Miss Parnell know about that?

A. I had to remove the decanter from his room, empty out the doctored whisky and put fresh in. She saw me coming out of his room—

Q. But how did you persuade her to keep quiet?

A. I told her I wondered if Freddie was all right; that I was afraid Smith slept too heavily to be a good guard.

Q. But good Lord! When he was gone the next morning—

A. She didn't want to make trouble for me. I told her that of course the police wouldn't believe I'd only had a premonition of evil and would undoubtedly suspect me. And that I wouldn't want to criticize Smith to them since they already suspected him. But that she must do what she thought right.

Q. Well, I reckon she might swallow that with you looking mournfully and nobly at her. Did she think you were fond of her?

A. I'm afraid she did. I was only polite—

Q. Oh, of course. Did you keep on being polite after she left?

A. I took her to lunch several times. No one knew that: we went to a very quiet place on Columbus Avenue—Morelli's. I was quite satisfied that she was—satisfied.

Q. Till Smith talked to her? Well, what was the situation between you and Roche during that year of waiting? Why did he come to the city again?

A. I heard Smith talking to Basil on the telephone and arranging to come to the house that Monday night. I slipped down and managed to hear what he said to Basil. Roche had been living in Sacramento—

Q. Where?

A. The Riverside Hotel. A small, rather cheap place, I think. I thought I had better telephone him Tuesday morning. He came down at once and we met that afternoon in Lafayette Park again. I told Roche what Smith had said. Roche said I must not see him again. And that for his own safety he must—see Miss Parnell. I gave him her address—

Q. But how did he get her to open the door to him? You must have told him what to say to her.

A. He said if he whispered she wouldn't be certain it wasn't my voice. I—suggested he tell her he'd—I'd just learned something about the kidnaping that was very upsetting. That I wanted her advice and help.

Q. I'll admit you knew the people you had to deal with. Did a letter from her to you happen to be among the things you burned in Roche's cabin?

A. Yes. There were his letters to me I'd kept and took there with me. I no longer needed them for protection then—

Q. Didn't you know you dropped a Pluma Blanca match folder in the stove?

A. I don't remember. Yes, I did use my last match. And I suppose I dropped the folder into the fire if you found one. I would have supposed it would burn. But I was rushed for time: I had to get back to the inn. I burned Roche's letters to me and mine to him. He'd kept those. He told me he'd destroyed the pawn ticket for the bracelet and I didn't find it. Then he also had this letter Miss Parnell wrote me the night she was killed. That I hadn't known existed—

Q. What did it say?

A. She told me in detail what Smith had told her. Said she was beginning to wonder if I'd told her the truth about—everything. That I had "neglected her lately." Then she said she knew Roche was in the city just before the kidnaping. That she had seen him. That was as far as she got with the letter.

Q. Lucky for Phil she didn't have time to mention that snapshot. And that you were the last person he'd be apt to show any of his pictures to. You didn't see Roche again until you went to Bancross? And not to talk to them?

A. No. He said he was going to try to find Smith. I had the address of the place where he was living when Basil had gone to see him. Roche said if he couldn't find Smith, at least there would be no one to verify his story if he dared tell it—

Q. Did Roche tell you he was going to Bancross?

A. Yes, to get the ransom money he'd hidden there. And he said he would stay there for a few days until he was certain no one was looking for him. I never saw anyone as cautious and—and willing to wait as he was. And he was going to shave off his mustache—

Q. We know about that. And why did you kill him?

A. He wouldn't tell me where he had buried Freddie. I was too old to wait for things to be settled. If Roche was found dead in Bancross with the ransom money you'd begin looking for Freddie. Roche said he was going to leave the country and never come back. But he might have changed his mind and hounded me for years.

Q. And where did you get your gun?

A. It was among the belongings an old actor friend of mine left me. No one knew I had it and

I knew he'd gotten it from a pawnshop years ago so it couldn't be easily traced. . . .

Valerie put down the typescript. She wasn't interested in the details of Daniel Holaday's trip to Bancross or in any of the other facts in the rest of his statement.

"Of course he'll repudiate that," Rocky said. "They always do."

"Then why did he make it and sign it?" Eleanor said.

"Somehow he got the notion he was dying," Rocky said casually. "He'd lost a lot of blood and was pretty weak. He got the notion he needed a blood transfusion too."

"And no one," Michael drawled, "was volunteering his life's blood until Mr. Holaday had made a statement. Odd, isn't it, how a man clings to life?"

"You can always figure a guy like Holaday will. But what he told us is going to be useful. We can check up at this Morelli's where he took Miss Parnell to lunch and at the hotel where Roche stayed an' where Holaday telephoned him. And the park where he and Roche met—"

"'We'? As Sullivan said pathetically, they'll do all the work and you'll take the glory. And he doesn't believe that my 'friend' from Los Angeles is unreasonably allergic to police in any form and wouldn't care to stay to talk to Sullivan. Or even that I ever mailed said friend a key to the apartment with an invitation to use it when he was in San Francisco."

"Hell, he knows you well enough to catch on you were laughin' at him when you said that. I heard you when you talked to him on the phone."

"It's time we were in bed," Eleanor remarked.

Smith looked his approval of this suggestion. It was nearly three o'clock but none of them seemed to care if they ever slept again, he thought. He yawned, covered his mouth very politely and ostentatiously and threw in another yawn for good measure. But no one paid any attention to him. Eleanor curled up more comfortably in her chair and went on:

"You're riding high—if you can just evade a number of very embarrassing questions quite a few people might ask. In any case you are not going to be popular with the F.B.I., my love. Your own constituents will probably come pretty close to knowing the truth, in time. But I'm afraid their local pride is going to lead them to approve of your methods—since they succeeded."

"And did Mr. Holaday get his blood transfusion?" Valerie asked.

"Oh, Dumont was standin' by, ready to oblige. But Doc Bradley decided he'd pull through without it. Hell, I'm sorry for all of 'em. But sympathy's about all you can give 'em. You can't convict Holaday without tellin' the truth about all the rest of them. Maybe we can stand by and help Ariadne pull out of it when it's all over—"

"I don't know," Valerie said. "She has a certain kind of courage but it's the kind that causes her just to endure things instead of doing something about them. I'm not certain she wouldn't be just as happy married to Basil Dumont as she will be if we try to force her to cut loose all her old ties."

"You don't know that Dumont would want to marry her. And if he did, it probably would take him a year or two to make up his mind whether or not he should," Michael said.

"He wouldn't," Valerie said sweetly, "be the first man who took some time to make up his mind on that subject."

Rocky chuckled. "Now will you lie down an' be good? We might as well leave Ariadne to the women along with any matchmaking that's to be done."

Smith considered saying, "And don't count me out." But whatever Ariadne did, there wasn't any place for him in either scheme of things Mrs. Dundas had suggested. Still, she shouldn't marry Dumont. And she might not. Dundas and Allan had both promised to help him get into some sort

of work that would have some future to it. And
you couldn't tell how Ariadne might feel several
years from now. . . .

"Just the same, you were lucky," Eleanor said.
"We'll believe you did think you'd find not just
a picture of Roche but one of him with someone
else. But you hadn't gone to the city with that in
mind. So when you did become inspired wasn't
it luck you were in striking distance of the Armstrong house?"

"Luck? I can think of other words for their
decision to break into the house," Valerie said.
"That was—"

"That wasn't luck or even exactly a decision,"
Smith broke in, grinning. "The way they were
feeling, they'd have tried to rob the mint if they
thought they needed to. You see—"

Michael and Rocky looked at each other, rose
with one impulse and hoisted Smith from his chair.

"S'pose we three go in the kitchen and mix up
a flock of drinks," Rocky said hospitably.

"Do you think you ought to encourage me
in bad habits?" said Mr. Smith innocently. "I'm
pretty young, you know."

"'We have children, we have wives, And the
Lord hath spared our lives.' That being the case,
Mr. Smith, I'm sure you understand our natural
desire to let matters rest there?"

"And if we ever hurt your feelings any way at all, we would like to apologize," Rocky said generously. "Wouldn't we, Michael?"

"Oh, certainly! That goes without saying. We consider Mr. Smith a third musketeer to end all third musketeers—"

"An' would you rather have rye or bourbon?"

"We-ell . . ." Mr. Smith allowed himself to be assisted tenderly toward the kitchen. "Only I'm not so sure you shutting me off did any good," he remarked. "Of course I'm not married but—"

"But that very astute observation would lead one to suspect you were," Michael said.

"You took the words right out of my mouth." Rocky opened the refrigerator. "I saw 'em lookin' at each other and I'll bet they've got their heads together right now."

"Then suppose I tell Valerie I was perfectly sober and only went along to look after you?"

"Why, you— Hell, you were tighter 'n I was!"

"I was able to turn a back somersault. That requires perfect co-ordination, *amigo*."

"Yeah? And I just wasn't tight enough even to try it. Also, you were first to admit you'd had enough—"

"Which only proves I had full possession of my faculties—"

"Oh, Lord!" said Mr. Smith. "Here we go again!"

COACHWHIP PUBLICATIONS
CoachwhipBooks.com

VIRGINIA RATH

DEATH AT
DAYTON'S FOLLY

COACHWHIP PUBLICATIONS

CoachwhipBooks.com

MURDER ON
THE DAY OF
JUDGMENT

VIRGINIA RATH

COACHWHIP PUBLICATIONS
CoachwhipBooks.com

VIRGINIA RATH

AN EXCELLENT
NIGHT FOR
MURDER

COACHWHIP PUBLICATIONS
CoachwhipBooks.com

THE DARK
CAVALIER

VIRGINIA RATH

COACHWHIP PUBLICATIONS
CoachwhipBooks.com

DEATH OF A
LUCKY LADY

VIRGINIA RATH

COACHWHIP PUBLICATIONS

CoachwhipBooks.com

COACHWHIP PUBLICATIONS
CoachwhipBooks.com

MARIAN
GALLAGHER
SCOTT

DEAD HANDS REACHING
———
DEATH'S LONG SHADOW

COACHWHIP PUBLICATIONS
COACHWHIPBOOKS.COM

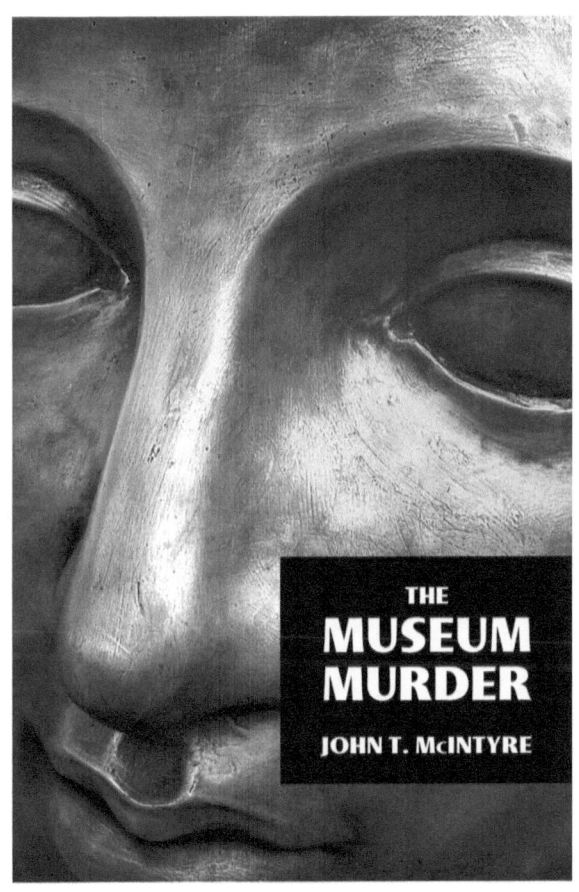

THE
MUSEUM
MURDER

JOHN T. McINTYRE